About the

Tim Thornton is a musician and writer from London. His previous novels are 2009's *The Alternative Hero*, described by the *Guardian* as 'the indiest book of all time', and 2010's *Death of an Unsigned Band*. Since 2005 Tim has been the drummer and guitarist for Fink, with whom he has recorded six albums for Ninja Tune.

FELIX ROMSEY'S AFTERPARTY

FELIX ROMSEY'S AFTERPARTY

TIM THORNTON

Unbound

This edition first published in 2018

Unbound

6th Floor Mutual House, 70 Conduit Street, London W1S 2GF

www.unbound.com

ISBN (eBook): 978-1-912618-53-8

ISBN (Paperback): 978-1-912618-52-1

Design by Mecob

Cover image:

© Shutterstock.com
©iStockphoto.com

Printed and bound in Great Britain by Clays Ltd, Elcograf S.p.A.

To my parents

Dear Reader,

The book you are holding came about in a rather different way to most others. It was funded directly by readers through a new website: Unbound.

Unbound is the creation of three writers. We started the company because we believed there had to be a better deal for both writers and readers. On the Unbound website, authors share the ideas for the books they want to write directly with readers. If enough of you support the book by pledging for it in advance, we produce a beautifully bound special subscribers' edition and distribute a regular edition and e-book wherever books are sold, in shops and online.

This new way of publishing is actually a very old idea (Samuel Johnson funded his dictionary this way). We're just using the internet to build each writer a network of patrons. Here, at the back of this book, you'll find the names of all the people who made it happen.

Publishing in this way means readers are no longer just passive consumers of the books they buy, and authors are free to write the books they really want. They get a much fairer return too – half the profits their books generate, rather than a tiny percentage of the cover price.

If you're not yet a subscriber, we hope that you'll want to join our publishing revolution and have your name listed in one of our books in the future. To get you started, here is a £5 discount on your first pledge. Just visit unbound.com, make your pledge and type FELIX18 in the promo code box when you check out.

Thank you for your support,

Dan, Justin and John
Founders, Unbound

Super Patrons

Guillaume Ferrand
Giovanni Forcina
Josefa Forcina
Erika Forsberg
Howard Fox
Paula Francisco
Max Gilkes
Anita Gohil
Jonathan Goldstein
Mike Green
Fin Greenall
Zhara Gregory
Adrian Griffith
Mat Hanson
Andy Harrower
Ruben Hein
Jan Hewitt
Simon Hollway
Matthias Hombauer
Rob Hopkins
Kaj-khan Hrynczenko
Miles Hunt
Nicky Hustinx
Maria Jansson
Paul Jones
Lewis Jones
Rob Kamer
Candice Karenin
Rebecca Karenin
Carmen Karuse
Kimitaka Kato
Dawn Kelly
Rich-Tea Kennedy
Dan Kieran
Karima Kingsley
Nina Kurth

Liva Lacaisse
Morgan Lacaisse
Katarina Lans
Håkan Larson
Catherine Lavender
Jimmy & Sue Lawrence-Jones
Tim Layton
Casey Leigh Martin
Sean Mackay
Jack Mangan
Michael Matthews
Katherine Mengardon
Elodie Mesgouez
Colin Midson
Dave Mitchell
John Mitchinson
Siân Monaghan
Jannik Tai Mosholt
Salome Müller
Paul Nash
Chris Nicholls
Annelien Noorman
Alex Nussbaumer
Michael Ogden
Leela Otremba
Catherine Peters
Bo Plantin
Justin Pollard
Mandy Price
Fabian Prynn
Samar Rad
Justine Randle
The Reeders
Sean Reilly
Kelly Robinson
Joni Rokotnitz

Chad Rushing
Damian Samuels
Jon Seabrook
Chris Sheldon
David Slaughter
Dillan Sondervan
Eline Soumeru
Helena Spencer
Hauke Steinhof
Robert Stokes
Olly Stoneman
Ruth Sullivan
Sian Sullivan
Mike Sweetman
Eden Teo Marosa
Nigel Thomas
Adrienne Thornton
Paul Turley
Crestina Velia Forcina
Marion Venema
Ian Ware
Robert Weatherley
Dimitri Weideli
Guy Whittaker
Clare Wickens
Heledd Williams

With grateful thanks to Sean Reilly, who helped to make this book happen.

Day

52

Felix texts me at 8.30am to say John Lennon will be early.

I wasn't asleep. I'd been awake since about five, going over a few things in my head, ruminating, worrying. I poured myself some coffee at six, gazed over the lake, watched the sun come up. As usual, a pretty underwhelming experience. It hovers near the horizon for a while and then just plops itself into the sky, like someone's flicking a switch somewhere. Perhaps they are. Then I turned some music on, did a bit of pacing. I've become very good at pacing. I finally lay back down at about ten to seven, but no sleep came. I've only had four hours, but of course that doesn't matter. We don't need sleep, but people do it anyway.

So Lennon was supposed to arrive at eleven, but now Felix says half nine. Everyone's always early around here. Drives me nuts. I'd better get my shit together. I sigh and swing my feet out of the bed onto the perpetually fluffy white carpet. It always amuses me, this carpet. Actually, that goes for the interior of my whole house, it's like some display home for a Floridian housing development. Yellow walls and pastel sofa covers. Too many cushions. Nondescript art in rubbishy gold frames. Glass coffee tables with those horrible curvy metal legs that I always bash my ankle on. Felix says this is the kind of stuff they give you when they don't know what you really want. Fair point, I suppose, I never did have a particularly strong sense of home style.

But my wardrobe, they got right. Decent jeans and some combats, Doc Martens, a couple of jackets: a reasonable denim, a bashed up leather and a geeky blue blazer with a few badges. Then an acceptable selection of rock T-shirts, including – coincidentally or not – one from a festival Saffron and I actually went to. So I don't have to fake anything there, at least.

I dive into the shower. We don't need to wash, but people do it anyway. For me it's one of the few things I actually enjoy; it feels real, calming, and it's free, obviously. I've been known to shower for many hours. Today I allow myself a diplomatic fifteen minutes and then jump out, marvelling, not for the first time, at the absence of that slight chill I used to feel between leaving the shower and wrapping myself in a towel. But no towels needed here. The water does its slightly creepy vanishing-into-the-skin thing and I'm ready to throw some clothes on, but I stop for a moment to glance in the mirror.

This glance reveals a curious crossbreed. The hair is from that brief moment in my late teens when it had both texture and gravity on its side; dark brown with the slightest hint of sun-bleached red, it flops in the right places and stays back if I ask it nicely. But I haven't the faintest idea what's going on with the body. It's relatively tanned and the shoulders are broad, but there's back hair, which is *totally* wrong, and an unbelievably horrible beer paunch that nothing will shift – and believe me, I've tried. To make matters worse, whichever dipshit selected the T-shirts didn't account for this bulge, and they're all size medium. Everything but the festival shirt makes me look like an out-of-shape A&R man. Just as well nothing needs to be laundered.

I sling on some jeans, light a cigarette and call Felix. He picks up on the first ring.

'Podge,' he says.

'Morning boss.'

'Nervous?'

'Yup.'

'Bollocks,' he replies. 'You're gonna charm the little round spectacles off him.'

'Why's he so early?'

'Who cares? Everyone's bloody early. But listen. I need you to bring him round to the West Gate instead of the East.'

'The West Gate?'

'Yup. Robert Palmer's meant to arrive at ten and I don't want one of those bloody awful clashes like when Barry White arrived at the same time as Luther Vandross.'

'Ah,' I respond distractedly, searching around for my sunglasses.

'Is that gonna be a problem for ya, Podge?'

'No, not at all. Got it.'

'I don't want any nasty surprises today, yeah? Things being the way they are.'

'Sure.'

'It's better anyhow, 'cos you can bring Lennon straight to my office before taking him through security, okay? I wanna say hi.'

'Will do.'

'Good luck. Oh… and don't ask him loads of Beatle questions.'

'Yes, yes. Of course not.'

'All right. Later.'

He hangs up. Bloody Felix. I wasn't even considering asking Lennon any Beatle questions. Now I have hundreds, and I'm more nervous than ever. Thank goodness it's Lennon and not Macca, is all I can say. I glance over at the drinks cabinet – I mean, a drinks cabinet, a mahogany drinks cabinet, who on earth did they think I was? – and I wonder whether I should have a quick shot of something before leaving, although I know this is certain to be completely pointless. I eye the rather dispiriting selection, if you'll pardon the pun: blended whisky, nondescript gin, random vodka and a bottle of dark something I've never investigated. I settle for the vodka, of which I pour a generous measure into one of the fussy cut glass tumblers neatly arranged on the little shelf. I knock it back. A slight tingle, a minor burn in my throat, a brief feeling in my head like I'm floating along… then nothing. Straight back to how I was before.

It's impossible to get even remotely fucked up around here.

I finish my cigarette, locate my shades in the kitchen then return to the wardrobe to grab the geeky blazer – I'm thinking the record-shop nerd look might soften a few of Lennon's famous edges – and stride to my front door. As usual, I stop at the picture I've stuck to the wall. A girl's face, hand-drawn, using some old coloured pencils I found in one of the bedroom cupboards. I was never any good at drawing, and the general rule is: everything I used to be crap at, I'm still crap at. But drawing is the one area where I'd have welcomed an exception. To say my drawings are childlike would be of considerable insult to most children I ever knew. This sketch hanging next to my front door is supposed to be a portrait of Saff: a pretty girl, but for some reason I've made her look like she's recovering from major facial surgery. But I got the eyes right. Every day I stare into her dreamy hazelnut eyes for a few moments before I leave the house. I kid myself that she's aware of me doing this, and that maybe she's doing something similar, and that it's keeping us connected somehow. Sad, isn't it? And we're not supposed to feel sad. But I do anyway.

'Have a good day, Saffy,' I mutter, then wander outside.

Despite my slightly gloomy tone, there are lots of things to admire about this place. The air is fresh, the bushes look neat and the grass always smells newly cut. Each house has chalky-white paving stones leading to a little gate, a low stone wall and, if you're lucky, a tree of some sort. The lakes are crystal blue and free from any pond life, which means wherever you are, you can always go for a swim in the perfectly clean, lukewarm water. We're generally never cold, although they've craftily ensured we're never too hot either. The sun is bright but doesn't burn and you don't need sun lotion, or even sunglasses, although plenty of people wear them – especially Felix, who has about fifty pairs. I'm not sure how many he arrived with, but most of his Memory Swapshop missions are part of one long search for shades. 'It's for the bands,' he says. 'I never want them to see me in the same pair twice.'

But the thing they've really nailed around here is the transport system, or the Trav, as we call it. There's the Local, and the main Trav. The Locals are just small, metallic tram-like vehicles which trundle along every street in your zone, ours being zone T109. The Local rolls up automatically as soon as someone starts waiting, it runs almost silently and appears to require nothing to fuel it and no one to steer it. Then when you reach the Trav station, the main Travs look like giant versions of the Locals, but they run underground and just go everywhere. You jump on, punch the number of your destination zone into the keypad, and off you zoom. No one needs to drive a car or ride a bike, although some people do anyway. But not many, because there isn't anywhere to go. No one minds. No one minds very much at all.

Felix, of course, insists that all his acts are picked up from the main Trav station in a fancy car. Smart move. It makes them feel special, it gives the Artist Liaison a little time alone with their charge to build up some rapport, and – the main reason, I suspect – it's great PR. Hardly anything's going to advertise the festival better than a silver Bentley, or a massive black Cadillac, driving through T109's central streets,

Afterparty flags fluttering from the front of the car like a presidential limousine, with an enormously famous rock star chilling in the back. And it's not the size of the car that's crucial; it just has to be *right*. I looked after Janis Joplin once and Felix laid on this amazing reproduction of her psychedelic Porsche. I even got to drive it. Sometimes it's not a car at all: last year we transferred Lou Reed and Nico on a fleet of Kawasaki motorbikes, and the time Freddie Mercury headlined, Felix managed to get an immaculate copy of Queen's *A Kind Of Magic* helicopter to fly him across downtown to the festival site. I have no idea where Felix gets this stuff. But Felix can get hold of virtually anything.

So I'm waiting for the Local at the end of my little pathway, taking in the view. The hills undulate for miles in every direction, all of them packed with identical houses: white, single-storey cuboids, flat grey roofs, largely featureless, although once you get up close you spot the minute differences reflecting whoever dwells inside. The occasional tree – usually a palm, but a pine or a birch here and there – breaks the monotony, as do the various lakes and swimming pools. Up behind one of these residential bumps poke the skyscrapers of downtown. Skyscrapers would be exaggerating; sky-botherers, perhaps. I guess some folk wanted to be in a high-rise apartment. I might have wanted to be in a high-rise apartment. Then again, perhaps I didn't. Felix is right: mine must have been a tricky brain to read. I glance over at his house, next door to mine. It's the standard setup, but typically Felix has managed to get himself a different door: a smart wooden affair in British racing green. It doesn't match the house at all, but I guess that isn't the point. It's also equipped with a lock. 'I'm not having any bastard just wander in,' I've heard him saying. 'Numbness or no Numbness.'

I'll explain that one later, because the Local is approaching and my phone is ringing.

'Walter,' I say, picking up.

'Hey, Mr Podge,' comes an excited American accent at the other end. 'Are you on your way?'

'Yep, should be there in roughly, ooh' – the doors open and I step lightly onto the vehicle – 'ten minutes thirty-five seconds.'

'Groovy! I've been here twenty minutes already. Oh boy. I am buzzed, I tell ya.'

Walter was a lawnmower salesman in Cincinnati in the 1960s, so his speech is frozen in a world of 'oh boy' and 'buzzed'.

'I can't believe little ol' me is gonna be driving *John freakin' Lennon*!'

'Shhh,' I reply, glancing cautiously around the Local. A sporty-looking girl is sitting on the opposite side with some sort of surfboard. She's staring vacantly out the window as the Local weaves us gently down the hill. 'Try to calm down a bit, Walter. You've gotta be cool... Remember what Felix said, that we've gotta be cool?'

'Sure, Mr Podge, I promise. I'm gonna be cool.'

'So you're parked outside bay 13?'

'Yep, sure thing, 13, absolutely Mr Podge.'

'And please... Walter. For the fifty-seventh time. It's not "Mr" Podge. It's just Podge.'

'Ha, right! I'm sorry Mis... um... Podge... sir.'

'See you there.'

I hang up and realise sporty girl is looking at me.

'Sorry,' she blushes. 'I couldn't help overhearing... Do you work at Felix Romsey's Afterparty?'

'Uh... yeah, that's right!'

'Wow,' she smiles. I wait for her to say something else but she looks away and plays with her hair. Odd. Must be my jacket.

The Local glides down the last half-mile of hill and things start getting a little busier. A privately driven car or two, a clutch of other Locals whizzing this way and that, immaculately dressed people wandering along past the coffee places, a Social or two, a few Memory Swap-shops, some more apartment blocks. At the other end of the street the concrete hulk of the T109 Trav station looms. Despite being the height of a cathedral and the length of three football pitches, it takes an amazingly short time for the Local to whisk you to your bay of choice. We drop sporty girl off at bay 59 first – there's a beach in zone S116 so she'll be off to ride some waves there, no doubt – and I'm heading to meet Walter right at the far end, but both drop-offs are performed within the same minute. The other Locals swarm about, zipping along the concrete plain between the bays, veering close to each other but never colliding. Some form of magnetism is assumed to be the powering force here, but no one's really given it much thought. Thinking's not awfully popular.

As my Local whisks me up towards bay 13 I can see a large, shiny purple car parked in the middle of the large platform, with a large smiling man in a chauffer's uniform standing next to it, giving the bonnet a polish. Looks like Felix has excelled himself. Which is just as well, things being the way they are.

'Well, good morning!' Walter grins, waddling over to the Local as I disembark.

'Morning Walter,' I reply, donning my sunglasses.

'You like her?' he beams, nodding towards the vehicle. 'Rolls-Royce Silver Wraith.'

'In black and burgundy,' I note approvingly.

'From the late 40s. The perfect era!'

'Beautiful, Walter. Your shoelace is untied,' I point out.

'Whoops! Will ya look at that,' he chuckles, bending down.

'Cigarette?'

'Oh, no sir, not for me.'

I watch the Local as it zips away on some other mission. It trundles along in a straight line and then turns sharply left, veering back the way we came.

'Do you think the same Locals go up and down the same routes all the time?' I ponder. 'Or do they just go wherever they're needed?'

'Err… well! I'm not too sure about that.'

'It's one of those things, isn't it? Like when you used to try to see if the light stayed on inside the fridge when the door was closed. Did you ever do that, Walter?'

'Heh–heh! I can't say I ever…'

'One day I'm going to leave a little red sticker on the inside of a Local and see if it comes back to me again.'

Walter reacts as if I'd just announced an intention to leave a bomb in the Main Central Restaurant.

'Mr Podge!'

'For the last time, Walter, it's not *Mr* Podge.'

'Sorry, sir. I really don't think it would be a good idea to put a… to put a… err…'

He trails off, then shakes his head and starts to fidget. I know I shouldn't say that kind of thing to people like Walter. It's a bit traumatic for the poor man. But sometimes I just can't resist. Hanging out with Felix tends to magnify one's cruelty streak. Never mind – Walter will have forgotten in a few minutes. In fact he's already giggling excitedly at his phone. I raise my eyebrows inquisitively.

'A little ol' message from my wife,' Walter gushes. 'We've just won thirteen Memory Swapshop credits on Gene Wilder.'

'Gene Wilder? Wow. Didn't have you down as a death-betting man, though, Walter.'

'Ha! You got me.'

'Well,' I shrug, 'it's been a busy year.'

'It sure has that. We won twelve on Nancy Reagan just a few months back… We've become a little…'

'Addicted?'

'Oh, no… I wouldn't say addicted, sir. All the same…' he lowers his voice conspiratorially, 'one of my friends predicted David Bowie and won themselves *two hundred*.'

'Right,' I reply, wincing slightly.

'Oh yeah,' enthuses Walter. 'I reckon that–'

But he breaks off, thank goodness, and turns to the automatic doors buried in the immense concrete wall of the Trav station: a thunderous whirring sound can be heard inside, and the orange light above the doors begins to flash. I glance at my watch, which has just clicked to 9.30am.

John Lennon is arriving.

The hardest moment is always just before they emerge through the sliding doors. With a complex superstar like John Lennon, the questions that rack up in the mental outbox can be endless. How do I greet him? Will he be alone? Will I even recognise him? What era Lennon did they pick? Classic moptop? Long hippy hair and round glasses? Or angular New York City? Will he be talkative, debonair, amusing, or tricky? Felix has prepared me, to a degree. Lennon is apparently pretty much as you'd imagine: straightforward, friendly, funny, but quick to dismiss bullshit. It's the bullshit part I'm worried about. I tend to blather when I get nervous.

So here we go.

But someone nearby is chattering softly under his breath.

'Oh boy, oh boy, oh boy…'

'Walter.'

'Sorry Mr Podge.'

And the whirring stops behind the doors.

And the buzzer sounds.

And the doors slide open.

And there he is.

He is standing in the doorway, alone, bashed up guitar case in hand. He lifts up his Ray Bans to reveal brown eyes.

'Fellas,' he mutters, then strolls forward.

Okay, he looks *wonderful*. Unexpectedly, it's the Hamburg era. Slicked hair at the sides, messy quiff on top, the aforementioned Ray Bans, black leather jacket with the collar turned up. After handing his guitar to Walter, who dutifully scuttles round to place it in the trunk, he leans back against the car door and produces a pack of Stuyvesants.

'Smoke?' he asks.

'Sure,' I reply.

'Filthy habit,' he says, giving me a light.

'I know. Never smoked at all until I got here.'

'Ain't that the truth. What did you say your name was?'

'Podge.'

'Podge?'

'Yeah, it's, um… Felix's nickname for me. On account of my, um…' I point apologetically to my protruding stomach. Lennon sniggers.

'Bloody Felix. Everyone has to have a nickname. Big beer drinker, then, were ya?'

'Not this big.'

'So what's your real name?'

'Adrian. Adrian Jones.'

Lennon takes a long drag of his cigarette and then raises his eyebrows craftily.

'Think I'll stick to Podge.'

He leaps into the back of the car. I hover for a second, then he gestures for me to join him. Walter starts the engine.

'You like the car?' I ask.

'S'all right. Never that much into cars, though.'

'Me neither.'

'Hold on to your hats, folks!' hoots Walter, and off we go.

Walter spins us around then drives slowly and regally towards the main square. It's a five-minute ride to the festival site, but Walter has been instructed to take the long way round. Consequently we're soon parading down one of T109's busiest streets, packed with Socials and Memory Swapshops. Lennon winds the window down and seems unconcerned about anyone recognising him as we pass. In fact, any stares we receive are probably more for the car than the passenger. Then we're into the main square and, on the left, a flat building with the size and charm of a ring-road supermarket: the T109 Main Central Restaurant. The place is jammed already, people wolfing full Englishes and stacks of pancakes. A vast outdoor space along the side provides the *al fresco* version, with the usual brightly-dressed hordes hammering their orders into tableside Infonet terminals, all smiling their overwide smiles and laughing their overloud laughs.

'Ah, zone T109,' Lennon sighs. 'How I've missed it.'

'Really?' I reply, then wish I hadn't. He glances at me, shakes his head and looks back out the window. Damn. I always find these exchanges a little tricky when they're wearing sunglasses.

'So,' I begin, 'now might be a good moment for me to tell you a bit about the festival... It'll have changed since you played here the first time, was it seventeen years ago?'

'Something like that.'

'Right. So I guess it was just a stage and a bar back then, but we've been expanding every year, there are four stages now, six bars and a whole range of food stalls if you, um...'

'I don't eat,' he states, flatly.

'Oh, that's okay, me neither.'

I pause briefly, wanting to give this snatch of personal information he's just divulged a moment of respect. He stares back and for a second I think he's going to high-five me or something, but instead he flicks his cigarette butt out the window and asks, 'So who's playing?'

'Ah! Well, we've got the Cliff Richard stage...'

He gives a little scoff of laughter.

'Yep,' I continue, 'with Bill Haley headlining, plus Eddie Cochran, Phil Everly...'

'Right. Next?'

Hmm. I was expecting a touch more enthusiasm.

'... then the Aretha stage with Minnie Riperton, Dusty Springfield, Tammy Wynette, The Temptations...'

'Okay.'

'... then the Mel Brooks comedy stage, and we're particularly proud of the line-up this year, Richard Pryor, John Candy, Peter Cook and Dudley Moore, even The Goons who... er... I've heard you might be rather fond of...'

Blank face.

'And, of course, you're headlining the main stage, which this year we're calling the Stevie Wonder stage.'

'Wonderful.'

'Uh-huh. And tons of great stuff playing before you, Donna Summer, acoustic set from Kurt Cobain, Michael Hutchence–'

'Hutch what?'

'Michael Hutchence, Australian singer... used to be the frontman of INXS, who were...'

Shit! Is it appropriate to say...

'Pretty big after I died?' Lennon suggests.

'That's right!' I exclaim, with a relieved giggle. Lennon manages a mildly amused grunt and stares back out the window.

The first famous person I saw here was Ian Curtis. Actually he wasn't just the first famous person I saw here; he was the first person I saw here who I'd previously been aware of in any capacity whatsoever. Via some curious twist of fate, nobody ever died that I knew personally. My parents are both still alive, as are my aunts, uncles, brother and all my friends. My grandparents had all died by the time I was a toddler, so I've never bothered to look them up. The only funeral I ever attended was my own, and whether I even went to that is open to metaphysical debate. I spent my whole life thinking I was so lucky that everyone I loved was still around, and now I spend much of my time thinking the precise opposite.

So, consequently, of all people: Ian Curtis.

It was the first time Felix had invited me to the Afterparty – out of pity, probably, for I was still moping around like a wounded donkey although I'd been here a good eighteen months. 'Come and have some fun backstage, you miserable git,' I remember him saying, but I didn't feel like socialising so I just showed up out front at 4pm when I knew Curtis was scheduled to play. He'd assembled quite a good little band for himself – Hole's Kristen Pfaff on bass and the guy from Lush on drums – and as you can imagine there was a pretty big crowd for an afternoon slot. But shit, it was weird. So many weird things about it, I didn't even know where or how to begin. I had about three panic attacks just getting onto the festival site. We're not supposed to get panic attacks, but of course I get them anyway. I'd stopped off at a Social on the way there and downed a whole bottle of wine to calm my nerves, but I was practically sober again by the time Curtis started. I got a brief grip on myself and managed to weave my way to the front, but then he came on – and I just lost it. I suppose I was expecting him to look like the dude who played him in the Anton Corbijn film, but, well, he didn't. He didn't even look like Ian Curtis. He looked like Ian Curtis after living in Los Angeles for ten years. Tanned, vivacious, prosperous, muscular... healthy, albeit with a cigarette in his mouth. He sported that odd pentagonal guitar from the

'Love Will Tear Us Apart' video and greeted the audience with an exuberant 'Good afternoon, zone T109!' All wrong. Then he started to play, and when I realised it was 'Dead Souls' I felt like I was going to be instantly sick, although as I've found out many times, there's never anything to be sick with. I had to leave. I turned and started to push my way out again before he'd even started singing. And when he did, everyone around me – smiling, pretty, blemishless young faces with their unfeasibly perfect indie uniforms – shouted out the ominous lyrics with him as if he were playing a Bon Jovi song. I had a harder time getting out than in, but people were so enthralled by what they were watching that no one noticed the desperate, heavy-breathing twat trying to make a run for it. Halfway out I started yelling at people. 'Why's everyone so bloody cheerful?' 'This is so screwed up, does no one realise?' 'This is *not* a happy song! Why is everyone roaring it out like a football chant?' – that kind of thing. And then, as if things hadn't become weird enough, I thought I saw Saffy standing far away in another part of the crowd. I froze... for what felt like half an hour. Then I screamed out her name and lurched over towards her. Saff was always fairly unmistakable in crowds: her bright red hair and her height – only an inch or so shorter than me – meaning I usually had no trouble returning with our drinks at a gig, or whatever. But here, I just couldn't reach her. I was so deranged, I kept losing my sense of direction and finding the stage in the opposite place to where I'd expected. Then I'd spot Saff again, seemingly further away than she was before. I carried on charging through the oblivious masses as they bleated out the sickeningly appropriate words, until I finally got there – and of course it wasn't fucking Saff at all, just someone who looked vaguely like her from a distance if you happened to be completely losing your shit. Poor woman, whoever she was, she had to endure me collapsing into a heap of tears in front of her before I finally broke free from the mob, ran all the way back to my house and lay on my lounge floor sobbing my face off for about a week.

And that was me having some fun at my first Afterparty.

But I got over it. Sort of. Especially since I started actually working for Felix. It certainly sorted out the 'meeting dead famous people' bit, and as for Saffy… well. The good days are when I'm working so hard I almost don't have time to feel anything, or to remember.

Felix kicked things off by suggesting I look after a couple of names that never registered too strongly on my radar: Eva Cassidy, who turned out to be charming, and Gene Vincent, who headlined the Cliff Richard stage the following day and barely said two words to me, so that was fine. But when it's people I really do care very deeply about, it can still be something of a headfuck. I was totally on edge for Nick Drake last year: I was worried he'd also be a victim of the Ian Curtis Californian affliction, so I nearly bailed that one. In the end Nick was exactly as I'd always imagined him. Felix always favours me for this kind of artist, which he explained with one of his typical backhanded compliments: 'You're an awkward, over-analytical bastard so I'd always choose you over the sort of numbed-out, grinning knobhead I'd get to look after Sid Vicious.'

But this apparently intriguing personality of mine has yet to cast a spell over John Lennon. Walter steers us imperially along one of the residential streets leading away from downtown, then left into another road where the houses abruptly end after half a mile and the trees start. I don't know what trees they are, but they're long and thin and always make me think of Italy. It's like driving into a forest, except the trees are all uniformly spaced apart with no undergrowth in between. The road is perfectly straight, the asphalt without a single pebble or bump, and at the far end we can see a clearing; or at least, it would usually be a clearing, but right now it's filled with a merry torrent of temporary structures which materialise at this time each year: blue, red and yellow marquees, an enormous silvery-grey bubble, a pile of white prefab cabins and, in the foreground, a beige concrete hut, the only permanent structure in the whole setup and by some distance the least alluring, suggesting a public toilet on a British seafront rather than the HQ of a celestial rock festival. But this is the constantly bubbling nerve-centre of the Afterparty, where the deals are made, plans are hatched, and much of the ship is steered from. As Walter rolls us along the smooth avenue, the muffled sound of loud music can already be heard. I glance at my watch: 9.50am.

'We always like to get rocking early around here,' I comment cheerfully in Lennon's direction. 'That'll be the Small Faces, kicking things off.'

Lennon glances over at me, but doesn't display much interest. Perhaps he isn't a morning person.

There are several differences between our backstage area and those at our earthly equivalents, and the first one you notice is there is no security. No security passes, no security guards. Actually, there is one security guard, but he's for a rather different purpose, which we'll see in a moment. So this lack of security, regular festival-backstagers will appreciate, cuts out half the crap. You park up, you get out, you wander in. That's it. There are no hi-vis vest-wearing chaps with walkie-talkies standing by the security fence, because there is no security fence. There isn't a Portakabin for handing out backstage wristbands, because there are no wristbands. The differences don't stop there. There are no record company people wandering around talking loudly on their phones with laminates around their necks, because there are no record companies and there are no laminates. There are also no vast fields packed with tour buses, nor roadies unloading equipment out of lorries, because there are no tours, and all the equipment is already here. There are, of course, pockets of frantic activity: the various stages run like clockwork and, particularly today, various Infonet crews bustle about, capturing reportage and positioning cameras. But in general, almost a hundred percent of our team's efforts are focused on the happiness and well-being of that most precious of commodities: the artists.

'They're a bunch of lazy fuckers,' I recall Felix delicately putting it. 'They don't need to do this. Oh, I mean... a couple of them have a burning desire to get off their arses and play some gigs, but most of 'em would rather be playing golf or sitting at home watching whatever nostalgic bollocks is dribbling out of the Infonet.'

If I remember rightly we were riding a Local at the time, next to one of the lakes on our way back from a Death Mission. Can't remember who it was now… Andy Williams, perhaps, as Felix was wearing his turquoise '70s shirt with the massive collar. I think we'd stopped somewhere so Felix could get an ice cream, and he was holding forth while waving his cone at the sparkly-blue water.

'But the one thing we can offer them… which they don't get anywhere else… is star treatment. Just for the day. You've gotta understand, right? For the likes of you and me… we're used to living in crappy London flats and squats and all that, so our existence here seems pretty luxurious. Not these guys. Someone like Michael Jackson spent his last twenty years living in a fuck-off Disney castle, and now he finds himself in a two-bedroomed shed on the outskirts of a city so boring it makes Swindon look like Manhattan. But the worst thing of all is… and I know this is true, because Freddie once told me… suddenly they're back to being on the same level as everyone else, and there ain't nothing they can do about it. That's where we come in.'

Felix's emphasis on this part of our operation has always been pretty intense. This year, with things being the way they are, it has bordered on the maniacal.

Not that the untrained eye would notice anything amiss on a morning such as this. Walter slides the Rolls up to the drop-off area and the atmosphere seems very much its usual jolly self. Sarah, our Artist Village manager, a flurry of curly-blonde hair and nondescript orange T-shirt, steps out of the HQ doorway, sees us arriving, waves at me and skips back inside. In the background some chilled-out looking characters wander past: a clutch of trippily dressed girls, some guys with dreadlocks, an elegant man in a suit swigging not quite so elegantly from a bottle of Champagne, a couple of long-haired chaps with flowery-shirts – a typical selection of Afterparty backstage folk. I can also see Frank, our one security guard, sipping coffee while chatting amiably with a very familiar-looking brown-haired, moustached bloke in a zigzag cardigan. The general rule backstage at the Afterparty is: if you see someone who looks like a famous person, it probably *is* that famous person. I glance over to see if Lennon's noticed his old bandmate standing there, but he's paying more attention to the tall, flamboyant figure striding out of the office hut.

'Blimey,' Lennon mutters, opening the car door. 'Where does Felix get his bloody clothes?'

Today Felix is wearing an immaculate black pinstripe suit, crocodile-skin brogues and a jauntily angled trilby hat. I'm not quite sure if it's Sinatra circa 1948 or Kid Creole 1981. Probably both, with a bit of East End spiv thrown in for added zip. He has an open-necked yellow shirt with an orange kipper tie loosely slung around. His pencil moustache is sharper than ever, and when he takes off his hat for an elaborate welcome bow, his straight black hair has been slicked back mercilessly enough to withstand any drama. He rises from his bended gesture and stretches his arms out, even going so far as to shake his hands like a cartoon evangelist. When he speaks, his usual Camden Town twang has been embellished with a layer of mock-poshness that no one is particularly fooled by, least of all himself.

'Mr Lennon!' he exclaims, trotting across the pavement. 'Good morning, my friend. As Madness once sang, "welcome to the house of fun".'

'Filo,' Lennon smiles, receiving a hearty bearhug. 'You must introduce me to your tailor.'

'The Memory Swapshops of S751, baby.'

'Bleedin' hipster.'

'Won't find any schmutter like this in T109, that's for damn sure.'

Approaching us now is the aforementioned moustached, cardigan-clad chap, grinning toothily and putting a familiar hand on Lennon's shoulder. There are many strange and great things about doing what I do: seeing two youthful Beatles greet each other is certainly among the strangest and greatest. Or so you'd imagine.

'Morning, Johnny boy,' George Harrison says.

'Hi,' Lennon replies curtly, turning straight back to Felix.

Ever the effortless host, Felix cackles with laughter and whacks Harrison on the back.

'I'm sure he's pleased to see you, George, perhaps it's still a bit early for him.'

'George!' Lennon exclaims, taking off his Ray Bans and putting an arm around the slightly affronted lead guitarist. 'Great to see you, my brother. These shades are too damn dark.'

'Who did you think I was?'

'Oh, I dunno, one of the roadies,' Lennon deadpans, then flashes a cheeky grin in mine and Felix's direction. On cue we both laugh, a touch nervously.

'Huh,' grunts Harrison. 'Nothing much changes.'

'Come on, then,' Felix commands, putting his arms around both Beatles. 'Let's go and have a fucking drink…'

He leads the pair of them past a few starstruck members of staff, and into the Artist Village proper we go. I keep a deferential five or so metres behind, enabling Sarah – the usual slightly nervous smile on her face – to ply me with a dozen questions and a dozen updates as we stroll along. We're heading down the main street of the compound: a decked walkway in the middle, manicured hedges, seated areas and little trees, with maisonette dressing rooms on either side. Elliott Smith hovers by his dressing room door pretending not to watch Lennon go by, while Donna Summer runs out of her own to greet John like a long-lost friend. Then we reach a wider area – the town square, if you like – which includes sofas, deckchairs, two full bars, a massage station and a medium-sized swimming pool. The booming noise of the Small Faces on the Stevie Wonder stage is complemented by the direct feed of their live sound pumping through the various loudspeakers dotted around, the visuals of the show also beamed onto the numerous plasma screens. It might be early but the place is buzzing, either with those playing later, or those just here to hang out. There's a frisson as our party enters the vicinity – Lennon isn't someone you tend to see around very often, unlike the more visible Harrison – but otherwise it's business as usual. I wave at Kirsty MacColl who's sitting having some breakfast with Phil Lynott, while John Peel is parked on one of the sofas enjoying a morning pint with Bill Hicks. Sitting at the cocktail bar, and deep in conversation, are Serge Gainsbourg and Marvin Gaye, and a nearby covered area features Heath Ledger playing table tennis with someone I initially can't place, but realise a few moments later is Syd Barrett. Also under the awning is a fiercely animated game of table football fought by Rik Mayall, Michael Hutchence, Paula Yates and Linda McCartney.

McCartney breaks off as we approach, enthusiastically greeting both Harrison and Lennon.

Finally we've reached the headliner's private lair: a white wooden fence, a little white wooden gate, behind which is a neatly trimmed lawn, a smaller swimming pool, a private bar with some funky red 1970s seating and a few sun-loungers. Relaxing here and there are some groovy-looking chaps who I soon recognise to be John Lennon's stellar backing band (his regular keyboardist Nicky Hopkins, Elton John's longtime bassist Dee Murray and ABBA's drummer Ola Brunkert). A little further along there's a private food station with a barbeque currently being lit by our head cook Matthias, who's rocking a full chef's outfit. Behind this area lies the copious, two-storey dressing room complex itself, where Lennon, Harrison and Felix repair after greetings and back-slappings for the backing band. Sarah is already inside, skipping around opening windows and checking the contents of fridges, while Lennon and Harrison wander around inspecting the facilities. Felix corners me by the stairs.

'Holy shit,' he whispers. 'Beatle on Beatle.'

'Surreal,' I murmur.

'Even by our standards,' he nods. 'So, Podge – have you got this?'

'I think so.'

'Don't think so. Know so.'

'Absolutely.'

'Let him chill for a bit, then take him through security.'

'Of course.'

'And get Matthias to make him something to eat, yeah?'

'Oh… but he's a non-eater.'

'You what?'

'He's a non-eater. Like me. He told me just now, in the car.'

'What are you chatting about? Of course he eats. I've had the man over for dinner.'

Sarah rushes up to Felix with a phone call for him to take.

'You must have misheard him,' Felix frowns, then mooches off with the phone pressed to his ear.

Of the four rooms in Lennon's domain, John and George have gravitated upstairs to a library-type affair with a pool table, yet another bar (this one specialising in Champagne and single-malt whiskies), four large leather armchairs and a stout bookcase harbouring a crop of rock'n'roll classics (Nick Kent's *Apathy For The Devil*, Luke Haines' *Bad Vibes* and Sammy Davis Jr's *Yes I Can*, to name but a very few). There's even a real fireplace with a heap of firewood ready to be lit, should the mood strike, and a marble mantelpiece on which sits a gold carriage clock.

'Civilisation,' Lennon sighs, flopping down on one of the chairs.

Felix returns, flicking on a vintage Sanyo tape deck from which Joe Jackson's 'Steppin' Out' starts to play. Harrison chuckles.

'A cassette player.'

'Just for you, dear boy,' smiles Felix, pouring some drinks.

I'm not sure what I ought to be doing at this point, so for lack of any better ideas I light a cigarette and offer one to Lennon.

'Good lad you've got here, Filo,' he says.

'Podge? He's a hero. He's my crutch. He's my knight-in-shining. He's the only one who knows what's really going on around here.'

'Nonsense,' I respond, failing to suppress a proud grin. I give George Harrison a light while Felix hands round the drinks.

'So,' Harrison begins, 'I heard a rumour.'

'Oh, yeah?' Felix comments, sipping his drink and leaning against the mantelpiece. 'You know I love a rumour.'

'Yeah… well… Rumour has it, we've recently been joined by a certain royal… purple-wearing someone?'

Felix's smile vanishes like someone's slapped it off his face. He does his best to hold it together, but ultimately fails.

'Uh… Prince? Um… yeah. Shocker.'

'You knew?'

'Yeah. We knew.'

Too bloody right we knew.

'Prince,' recites Lennon, a blank look on his face.

'Yeah, that's the feller,' George says. 'American superstar. After your time, John boy.'

'Who told you?' Felix asks. 'If you don't mind.'

'Malcolm,' George replies.

Felix glares over at me, grinding his teeth together.

'Why,' George frowns, 'who did you hear it from?'

Felix exhales, knocks back his whisky, then claps his hands together.

'Right, so... if you guys have everything you need, I just need to go and... uh... attend to something. Podge? Let's give these gents some space.'

He claps his hands again, marches down the stairs and out the door.

I shrug a little apologetically at the pair, then hurry out after him.

Felix strides straight across the decked chill-out area and heads down a little alleyway between two dressing room blocks. We emerge in the quiet little gap between the Main Stage and the entrance to the public arena, where he turns to me and lets rip.

'Fucking Malcolm!' he shouts. 'What an utter cunt!'

'Calm down,' I tell him. 'You'd show off too if you got Prince.'

'He hasn't *got* Prince! Has he done a Death Mission yet?'

'Um… I don't–'

'No, he fucking well hasn't. It's been months, Podge! Months! Sarah spoke to him last week. He still hasn't a clue what to do.'

'Look, it's–'

'And Malcolm's shows are always shit. Crap sound, crap venues, and the support acts are always bloody Renderings. It's a disgrace. What a way to treat a legend like Prince.'

'Felix, we don't yet know–'

'I mean, what's the bloody point? Why are they giving Malcolm the information when he has absolutely no idea how to handle it?'

'I dunno, maybe they're just–'

'No, they're not *just* anything, Podge. Open your eyes. First Bowie's gone to that Mancunian wanker, and now this. Get it into your head. *They… are… fucking* with us!'

He turns and stomps back up the alley.

'Not necessarily,' I reply, but he's gone.

Felix quite often talks about 'them' fucking with us, to a greater or lesser extent. It's one of his favourite topics. Most people around here haven't had much experience with 'them', so their reactions to Felix's ramblings can range from mildly-entertained bemusement to evening-finishing outrage. Usually the latter. The first time I heard one of his lectures on the subject, I'd been here about two years and I'd only recently started to calm down and socialise a bit. It was at Felix's house, late in the evening, with the usual assortment of people lounging around on his various squashy sofas and giant beanbags: Kurt, Amy, Sarah, a few others. The lights were low and the drink was flowing, as was the music: Lamb, Orbital, Massive Attack, Felix's Infonet radio responding to the post-club comedown mood in the air that night. Felix wore a karate suit he'd found in a Memory Swapshop earlier that day and had tied a long chequered scarf around his head, which he quite often does when he's missing having long hair. Then he called for a bit of quiet and announced that his girlfriend Suzi – a St Lucian former *Playboy* model, by the way – had something to show us. She came in from the kitchen with one of those cute little French biscuit tins, in which was, fairly obviously, a hunk of decent looking hash.

'Felix, what the fuck?' laughed Kurt.

Amy practically screamed. 'Where in fuck's name did you get that?'

Like I said, Felix can get hold of anything.

So we nailed the whole lot; to feel any sort of hit you need to smoke triple, quadruple the amount you would have done in the old days. Kurt had been absent-mindedly strumming along with 'Unfinished Sympathy' on Felix's bashed-up acoustic, but after a few tokes – during which he'd continued to do his guitar-face, staring blankly into the middle distance – his playing shifted to something more abrasive. As first I thought he was approximating the dramatic orchestral chords towards the end of the Massive Attack tune, but this was different: a couple of bright major sevenths up near B and C, followed by some discordant, partial shapes down near to F and E. Something Kurt might well have played… well, back in the early '90s. Felix practically leapt out of his beanbag with excitement.

'All *right*! That's wicked, man! What was that?'

'Nothing,' Kurt replied gruffly, putting the guitar down with a clunk and standing up.

'Oh, come on!' Felix beamed. 'That sounded like something *new*!'

The effect these words had on the room was nothing short of seismic. 'New', in this environment, came across like the most unutterably offensive of swearwords. No, worse than that. It was as if Felix had just opined what a jolly good chap Hitler was. There was a universal sharp intake of breath and everyone worriedly shifted in their seats.

'Oh, what?' Felix snapped. 'What have I said now?'

'Man,' Kurt mumbled, 'I knew there was a reason I didn't like coming round here. Nine o'clock and you turn into an asshole.'

He shuffled out of the room towards Felix's lakeside patio.

Felix took a large swig from a bottle of Bacardi. I've never seen Bacardi in a Memory Swapshop, but then Felix knows some rather quirky ones over in S751.

'Judas Priest,' he growled. 'The bloody Numbness.'

'What,' I asked, 'is the Numbness?'

'Felix, baby,' came a note of warning from Suzi.

'Nah, it's all right, sweetheart. Podge can handle it. Look. This is how I see it, right? Eternity's a long fucking time. Can you imagine how totally shit everything would be in forty, fifty years, if we were all just… normal?'

I shook my head. Felix hopped over to the recently vacated beanbag next to me.

'So they *do* something to keep people in check. Fuck with 'em a bit. Know what I mean?'

'Such utter bollocks,' commented Amy, who was sitting on the arm of the sofa, fixing her eyeliner as if getting ready to leave.

'Think about it,' Felix said, holding his outstretched index finger like a pistol to the side of my head. He was so close I could smell the booze and smoke on his breath, his piercing green eyes gazing straight into mine. Nervously, I looked down, settling on the small round scar just above Felix's right nipple, visible tonight on account of his karate suit. It's a dark purple scar about the size of a penny, but dry and self-contained. He has a very small tattoo directly underneath: a Banksy-style Cupid, pointing his arrow directly at the scar. No one's supposed to have scars around here, but of course Felix has one anyway.

'Enough, honey,' Suzi was saying, trying to pull him back.

'Think about it,' Felix repeated, this time in a whisper.

That was that. The guitar was never touched again, and everyone left for home within twenty minutes.

And I certainly did think about it. It's not as if I haven't had the time. How happy and unconcerned everyone seems, even the new arrivals. But with that happiness comes the... blankness. Flatness. Numbness, indeed. People really do seem to have something missing from upstairs. They lack... curiosity. Bite. Edge. Even their memories – not their earthly ones but those of their current existence – seem to dissolve into a sort of vague stew. You only have to quiz a member of the Afterparty team about, say, something that happened at the festival last year, to realise that whether it's last year, two years ago, five years ago, or last month, last week, sometimes even yesterday – it's all faded into a general timeless mulch. And creativity? Forget it.

Then I think about how I felt myself when I arrived here. Those first few, terrible years. I spent most of them wishing I could just be like everyone else. But at least right now, I feel awake; present. As for Felix himself, he claims to feel no different from when he was alive: 'angry and horny'.

Anyway, things being the way they are, it's high time I stopped all this thinking and took John Lennon through security.

To cheer myself up after Felix's rant I take the long way round, via the Stevie Wonder stage. The staging and equipment are all housed in a huge plastic blob that looks like a cross between an alien mothership and a giant, elaborate balloon animal. I trot up the ramp towards where Maggie our Monitor Tech presides over the sound desk and glance at my watch as the deafening din increases: it's half ten so the Small Faces will be building up to their finale. The already three-quarters full crowd are hollering out the words to 'All Or Nothing' while a nice gaggle of swinging-60s backstagers – Oliver Reed, Peter Cook, Cilla Black, among half a dozen others – frug about at the side, happily witnessing the thunderous spectacle of Keith Moon on drums, performing hummingbird-like drum fills that would shame his earthly self. Maggie turns from the sound desk and waves: all is as it should be. I hurry back down the ramp, across the grass, around the corner and back along the main drag, noticing a bit of a kerfuffle around one of the dressing rooms – I think Lux Interior and his band are arriving, I'll probably have to go and deal with that later – then continue straight on towards Lennon's private region. His band are still hanging out, sunning themselves and drinking in the outdoor area, but I can see a concerned-looking George Harrison hovering by the maisonette door. I give him a friendly smile as I arrive.

'Podge, isn't it?' he says.

'That's right. Help you with anything?'

'You're in charge of John for the whole day, right?'

'In theory,' I laugh. 'Gonna take him through security right now.'

'I'll come along,' Harrison says, lighting a cigarette. 'For the ride.'

I pop inside and find Lennon still parked in one of the armchairs, shades on, the same drink in his hand, which he doesn't appear to have touched. I invite him to come with me, he rises without a word, and the three of us begin the walk back down the main street. Again, I keep a few paces behind the two Beatles as they amble along, mumbling quietly to each other, stopping occasionally to shake hands with someone. As we pass Robert Palmer's dressing room, drummer

Tony Thompson, in a perfectly pleated leather jacket and huge round glasses, bounds out and gives them both a hearty, backslapping hug. They chat for a couple of minutes, and then with promises to hook up later, we continue walking.

And that's when everything goes still.

No, I mean *really* still. You know those nightmares when you can see and hear the world around you, but you can't move? That.

It's really quite weird. I can't move any part of my body, but I'm still standing up. Every single person nearby – the Beatle pair, plus a few passers-by coming the other way – has also completely stopped, as has all the music. Even the flags on top of the marquees have paused in mid-air, ditto the blades of grass on the ground, and the folds on the dress of the girl coming down the steps of one of the dressing rooms. Remarkable how they've achieved it. Then I suddenly hear a calm, English-accented voice coming from somewhere behind my left ear.

'The security check will be missed.'

'Jesus!' I exclaim.

I can still speak, then.

Two men appear, walking around the side of me and coming to a halt in my direct field of vision. Which is just as well, because I can't move my eyeballs. They are both of medium height and wearing white lab coats. One is bald and wears glasses, the other has scruffy black hair containing, if I'm not mistaken, quite a lot of dandruff. An almost absurd amount of dandruff. Flakes of various sizes seem to flutter down whenever he speaks or moves. The bald guy carries a clipboard that he rarely looks up from, and seems to be the one in charge.

'The security check,' he repeats calmly, flicking between two pages and jotting something down in one of the margins, 'will be missed.'

'Who are you?' I croak.

'Who we are is irrelevant.'

'How have you stopped everything?'

'We've stopped nothing, buddy,' says the dandruff guy. American accent. 'The only thing stopped is *you*.'

I think for a few seconds. I can't really breathe, but nor am I struggling for breath. Bizarre. If this had happened back in the old days

I'd be screaming blue murder. But right now, frankly, it's just another odd suburb of the whole Weird City in which I dwell.

'So,' I begin slowly, 'You want me to…'

'Come on, Adrian,' says the American. 'Do we really need to say it three times?'

He called me Adrian. If this has been calculated to get my attention, it works.

'I'm not allowed to miss the security check,' I offer, finally.

'Not allowed? Says who?'

'My boss.'

Bald bloke looks up from his clipboard for the first time, his grey eyes peering at me through little gold-rimmed spectacles.

'Er… your "boss"? I assume you're referring to Mr Romsey?'

'Of course I am.'

'Do you describe what you do as a "job", then?'

'Of course I do.'

'But there is no money here, Mr Jones. How can it be a job when you receive nothing in return?'

'I receive plenty in return.'

'Oh?'

'Friendship. Guidance. Fun. Music.'

'Peace and love, man,' comments the American. He's leaning against one of the dressing rooms, closing his eyes, pretending to sunbathe.

'That's right,' I retort. 'And it gives me something to do. Anyway, why do you want Lennon to skip security so badly?'

'We have our reasons, Mr Jones. None of which I am afraid either of us has time to elaborate upon.'

'Well, then,' I reply. 'I can't do it.'

'Oh, but you will.'

'No, I bloody well won't.'

'You will. Believe us… we know *all* about you.'

I say nothing to this. After a moment the bald one sighs, then consults his clipboard.

'Adrian Jones, born 1973… Bedford, England. Local school, university in… Plymouth…'

If a shiver were capable of running down my spine, it would do.

'... became a... disc... jockey...'

'A *DJ*, for goodness' sake.'

He looks up.

'Very well... a DJ-for-goodness'-sake.'

He pauses, as if expecting a laugh. He doesn't get one.

'Worked for... a marketing company in Wandsworth... lived with a Miss... sorry, a *Ms* Saffron Bailey...'

Another imaginary shiver darts spinewards, then a pretend flurry of adrenaline boils in my digestive system at the very mention of her name. Exactly how it was when we first got together: saying 'Saffron' out loud, reading her handwriting on a note, seeing her jacket hanging on my bedroom chair. Shit, these guys mean business.

'Okay, you've made your point,' I manage to mutter.

'... never married...'

'I said you've made your point!'

'Died of... ooh, renal cancer. Nasty. In 2008.'

'All right! Enough!'

'Hit a nerve, Adrian?' drawls the American, as another light dusting of snow escapes his scalp.

Baldy continues.

'If you agree to help us, Mr Jones, we are able to offer you certain... rewards.'

'What rewards?'

He consults another page of his clipboard.

'Well... let's see... we could have a look at certain problems you might be experiencing... certain deficiencies... certain, as your friend Mr Romsey would doubtless put it, *death defects*...'

'Like what?'

'Ah... feelings of anxiety... depression... loss of appetite...'

'Loss of appetite? I don't eat.'

'Exactly, Mr Jones, loss of appetite... overactive mind... and... '

'A protruding belly,' concludes the American, fixing me with a smirk and prodding me in the stomach with his pencil.

'Get stuffed,' I respond. 'I don't want any of those things fixed.'

Baldy sighs again and turns away, scribbling something on his clipboard. American takes over.

'I'll say it another way, Adrian. If you *don't* help us, maybe we can talk to our friends from the Minus zones... see whether they can accommodate you.'

The Minus zones. Luckily, Felix has briefed me about these. He didn't tell me much, only to dismiss any mention of them as total bollocks.

'Total bollocks,' I dutifully counter.

'Oh, yeah?' leers American bloke. 'We'll see about that when you're strapped to an electric fence for all eternity.'

'Bullshit,' I leer back. 'Which bloody comic book have you been reading?'

'Let's calm it down a little,' Baldy instructs. 'It's really very simple, Mr Jones. The gentleman you're escorting is a Mr John... er... Lennon, who I'm given to understand is a trusted, beloved and most prestigious entertainer. No one would think it at all strange if you waived the security check on this occasion. And nothing calamitous is going to happen as a result. Why would we want to cause an outbreak of panic? So... please. If you have any value for your current existence whatsoever. The security check. It will be missed.'

I say nothing.

'And nor will you mention this to any of your... ah...'

'Work colleagues,' sarcastically concludes the American.

Baldy wanders off, still studying his clipboard, as if already reading up on his next assignment. American gives me another poke in the belly.

'So long... Podge.'

I struggle to formulate a corresponding insult as I watch them go. I'm just drawing breath to shout 'Up yours, dandruff man' – or something similarly sophisticated – when Baldy stops walking and suddenly points at a strange-looking diminutive figure, paused in mid-stride near the shortcut to the Main Stage. I don't remember seeing anything like it before. It's facing away from me, but I can tell it has a vaguely human form. It's short – around five feet, I suppose – has dirty black hair in a kind of knotted ponytail and is wearing some rather old-fashioned, cumbersome, dusty boots. The whole figure is wrapped in a torn, greasy-looking brown sheet. In my sphere of (for the most part) absolute perfection, this sight is most unusual.

'What,' pronounces Baldy, 'is *that* doing here?'

'Ah, heck,' exhales the American. 'Would you believe that? Those guys at border control are asleep on the job.'

'See that it is captured and returned.'

'Sure thing.'

Then they disappear round the corner and everything unstills itself again. Apart from me. I'm standing there, rooted to the spot, trying to process what has just happened. The strange sheet-wrapped being hobbles away quickly and darts down an alleyway before I can study it further. Lennon and Harrison walk on for a bit, then Lennon realises he has no idea where we're supposed to be going. He turns around.

'You okay, man?'

I stare at him for a few seconds, then shake myself out of it.

'Yeah, sorry. I just thought I might have forgotten something. We'll, er… we'll go round to security.'

John waves George off, and we troop round the corner towards the security hut. I'm studying Lennon closely now; I can't help it. The newness of his jeans, the spotless black suede shoes, the immaculate hair and skin. None of which is remotely unusual round here, of course. Even my pot belly is immaculate. No... there's no way of telling. Apart from taking him through security, just as I'm bloody well supposed to. I can see Frank the security guard, an enormous German man with a huge moustache made even huger by his giant smile, loitering next to the hut in the distance. Not an easy man to sidestep. Then I think about the stillness. It was pretty alarming. I'm not sure I'd want to be stuck like that for very long. Shit, this is ridiculous. I turn and touch Lennon lightly on the arm.

'Um, sorry... Mr Lennon.'

'John.'

'Um, John. Sorry. Would you mind waiting here for just one moment?'

He takes out a cigarette and flicks it into his mouth.

'No problem.'

Gingerly, I approach Frank.

'Morning Frank.'

'Ah, good morning, Mr Podge!' he booms.

'Just Podge.'

'Ja, Podge! Party time today, or? And you have Herr Lennon over there, yes?'

'Yes, Frank. About that...'

'And I think he is wearing the Hamburg Beatles costume!'

'Well, yes, not really a costume...'

'Ah, ha-ha! Yes, not really a costume! So please, you will bring him over here and we make the process short and sweet.'

'Well, actually Frank, since he is... um... such a prestigious guest, Felix has requested that we... *not*... take him through security.'

The big man's big smile vanishes and is replaced with an even bigger frown. His eyebrows form a small brown forest above his eyes and he stoops slightly, putting his hands on his knees as if speaking to a six-year-old. His whisper is louder than most people's shout.

'Mr Felix has requested this?'

'He has.'

'He has not forgotten the number one selling point of the After-party that he is always reminding me?'

'I'm sure he hasn't forgotten, Frank, but I guess he knows Mr Lennon pretty well and doesn't feel he needs to—'

'Ja, ja… but this is very bad for me, you see, Mr Podge, because I have promised my wife…'

Frank looks around again and lowers his whisper to the lowest he can possibly manage.

'… an autograph,' he squeaks. 'I have the *Abbey Road* in the hut waiting for him when he emerges from the security scanner and I was so hoping that he might…'

'Fine,' I reply, 'fine. I'll bring him over for the autograph, but just tell him the machine's broken, okay?'

'Broken?'

'Yeah.'

'I cannot tell him this.'

'What? Yes, you can.'

'I cannot, because it is not true.'

Ugh. The bloody Numbness.

'Oh, fuck it, look… *I'll* tell him the machine's broken, okay? You just get your album.'

And so it is that a slightly reluctant John Lennon is frogmarched over to an enormous German security guard who smilingly proffers a well-thumbed copy of the famous album for Lennon to scribble on. Taciturn as Lennon is, Frank is still absolutely thrilled. After this, we head back to the dressing room. Lennon by this point has abandoned even the vaguest attempts at conversation, so after giving him a few half-hearted bits of info – what time The Goons are playing, and that Lonnie Donegan is hitting the Cliff Richard Stage mid-afternoon – I too decide that it'd be okay to remain silent. Which is just as well, because things being what they are, I can't think of anything else to say. I have simply no idea what to do. I should, of course, tell Felix what has just happened. But what then? We take him back through security, discover the truth? Even if everything turns out to be normal, I still have the wrath of the lab-coat men to worry about. But what if it *isn't* normal? We abandon the whole show? Have you any idea how much is riding on this?

Probably not.

When John Lennon last played Felix Romsey's Afterparty, I was still alive. No one's particularly hot on timekeeping around here, but most agree it was seventeen years ago, and I'm pretty sure I've been here eight years, so that would make it 1999. It was only the second time Felix had put the festival on, so he hadn't quite mastered the art of convincing dead rock stars to come out of eternal retirement. To be fair, hardly any of the really big names were here by this point; they only started to pop off in earnest after about 2000: Joe Strummer, Johnny Cash, James Brown, Jackson... indeed, George Harrison. The Afterparty's first year was really just a gig: a single outdoor headline performance by Jeff Buckley, which Felix had convinced Buckley to do after a night's drinking. The second year was headlined by some strange supergroup featuring Harry Nilsson, John Bonham and, of all people, Frank Zappa. Originally John Lennon was supposed to join them, but he and Zappa had apparently differed on the song selection during rehearsals (oh, to have been a fly on the wall during those debates) so instead Lennon just showed up with an acoustic guitar and did a short set on his own at about teatime. It was, reportedly, bloody marvellous. Felix told me he played 'Instant Karma', 'Norwegian Wood', 'Mind Games', 'I'm Only Sleeping', 'Gimme Some Truth', 'You've Got To Hide Your Love Away', closing with a massive singalong version of 'Help!' – and succeeded in completely upstaging the headliner. Only a handful of audience even lingered. 'I learned an important lesson that year,' Felix told me. 'Never put anyone on after a Beatle.' Despite promises to come back soon with a full band, Lennon has been hard to convince.

Anticipation for his slot this year, then, is high. The main arena has been completely redesigned to allow an extra ten thousand punters, bringing the total up near the seventy-thousand mark. Wisely, Felix has scheduled the top-billers on the other two stages to finish twenty minutes before Lennon is due to start, so nothing will distract from, or be distracted by, his set. The big screens will beam the action across the field as usual, but this year, for the first time, the show will be broadcast live on the Infonet to everyone in our local zone group. In addition to an hour's worth of awesomeness from Lennon and his killer band, he's also going to be joined for about twenty minutes by George Harrison, although no one knows that yet.

All of which would be quite enough to send Felix's anxious-and-hyper-ometer into the red. But in the last six months he's also been paranoid, neurotic, occasionally violent, quite unbearable. And it all started, as these things often do, with an evening in one of zone S751's rather funky Socials.

It was Felix and me, plus Kurt, who'd brought along Malcolm. Hanging out with rival promoters isn't usually our thing, but Kurt seems to like Malcolm so out of respect we've always tolerated him. So anyway: there we all were, sitting in this mock-Caribbean Social, Eddy Grant cannoning out of the Infonet radio, Felix rather inappropriately wearing khaki Empire-builder shorts and a pith helmet. We were gazing through the window at the girls walking along the sunset-washed lakefront, periodically pouring ourselves more drinks from the tap in the centre of the table (a nice touch: much more entertaining than the boring rising-up-from-the-hatch thing the Socials have in T109). So far I'd had a very nice mojito with an ice-cold lager chaser. Felix, necking his usual Guinness, had started to hold forth on his outlandish ambitions.

'I swear,' he spouted, 'in twenty years' time, the Afterparty is gonna be *massive*.'

'It's pretty massive right now, dude,' Kurt muttered.

'Nah. You ain't seen nothing yet. Just think about who's gonna die in the next twenty years.'

'That ain't nice, man,' Kurt frowned.

'What do we care?' Felix replied. 'The sooner the better, as far as I'm concerned. Macca. Jagger and Richards. Wonder. Bowie. Dylan. Brian Wilson. Chuck Berry. Get 'em all up here. All the greats. All the stars, and in their prime too. Entire bands'll be able to reform. Zeppelin. The Clash. Queen. It'll be the biggest party any of us has ever seen.'

'If they wanna reform,' Kurt grunted.

'Fuck all else to do, isn't there?'

'Plenty to do here, man,' Kurt huffed, rising and mooching off in the direction of the pool table.

'Numbed-out space cadet,' Felix snarled. 'Where's all his fire gone?'

'Take it easy, man,' I muttered, to which Felix responded with a belch.

Eddy Grant gave way to the thumping rhythms of 'Our Lips Are Sealed' by the Fun Boy Three. Malcolm shook his curls and leaned forward with a cunning smile.

'Well,' he began. 'Funny you should say all that, Felix. I notice that... on your list of names... was a certain Mr... Bowie?'

'Yesss...?'

'Well. I was recently speaking to my old friend Tony Wilson... and interestingly enough, he received a message the other day which you might find... interesting?'

'Interestingly enough I might find it interesting?' Felix growled. 'What's your point, Malcolm?'

'Mr Bowie,' he pronounces theatrically, 'is apparently already among us.'

Felix and I both gaped at him for a few seconds. Perhaps even five. Felix, predictably, broke the silence, with expletives screamed at such a volume that a few people hurried straight out of the Social. Before Felix started to get physical I managed to drag him outside too, down to a quiet spot near the lake so he could simmer down. We didn't know Tony Wilson well, but all the signs suggested he and Felix would not hit it off: educated where Felix was not, Manchester where Felix was London, achiever of mainstream, if inconsistent, earthly success where Felix – aside from a few tours and all-dayers – had failed. Plus, there was the basic fact of his being a threat to the Afterparty, although as yet a minor one: I'd heard Felix acidly describing Tony's own festival, Factory of the Firmament, as 'a great festival... in about twenty years time.'

Felix glared out over the lake. A steamboat chuffed past, a deckful of happy people looking in our direction, some of them waving. Felix stuck two fingers up at them and they all turned away.

'I'm gonna rip his arms off,' Felix seethed.

'No, you're not,' I replied. 'You don't wanna be enemies with a guy like Tony. We may not like him, but he's popular. People will just think you're a dick. And anyway – sorry, but what's to stop him getting Bowie? What makes you think you've got a monopoly on all this?'

He glared up at me.

'You don't get it.'

'No, I don't,' I replied, sitting down on a little wall next to the water. 'Really, I don't. Please explain.'

'Okay,' he sighed. 'I'll tell you why this is so fucked up. The only people who could have sent Wilson a message like that… are The Men. I've mentioned them to you before.'

'Yes,' I frowned. 'The ones who interrogate you?'

'Yup.'

'The ones who put you on pause when you're in the middle of shagging Suzi?'

'The very same. Anyway, they're the ones who tell me when people die.'

'Sorry… they do what?'

'They tell me when people die! When they arrive. Where they are. How did you think I knew?'

'Um… you just looked it up on the Infonet, I guess.'

'Judas Priest, Podge. Sometimes I wonder whether you haven't got a bit of Numbness yourself. New arrivals don't appear on the Infonet for weeks… months sometimes. But these dudes let me know as soon as a new one appears. Here,' he said, showing me his phone. 'I got this only a few days ago. Look.'

A text message was displayed on his screen, from someone or something called 'SP'. The message was short, but its meaning profound.

'Lemmy' has arrived. Zone S502/House 475265.

'Lemmy? No way.'

'Yup,' Felix nodded, slipping his phone back in his pocket. 'Took the old bastard a while. Surprised he hasn't been here since the '80s, know what I mean?'

'We'd better call the hard rock stage something else next year, then.'

'Whatever.'

'Have you done the Death Mission yet?'

'Course not, how busy have we been? Anyhow. I've been getting these messages from The Men since the start.'

'Who are they?'

'I don't know.'

I gave Felix a dubious look. He never, ever claims to not know something.

'Don't look at me like that, you little shit. I really, really don't know. They're on the inside. Who or what that is, I do not know. Seriously. I might be well connected, but I'm not *that* bloody well connected.'

'Okay, got it.'

'And I've spoken to every other promoter, and no one' – he inhaled dramatically, his choking-back-the-tears act, I've seen it before – '*no one* I've ever spoken to has ever received a message like this.'

He lit another cigarette.

'Until now.'

Of course I attempted my usual policy of smoothing things over, showering him with optimism, suggesting there'd been some mistake, maybe they texted Tony by accident. But I was wrong. Some weeks later we were informed – via a phone call to the Afterparty HQ, the smugness of which I could feel from ten feet away – that Malcolm himself had been similarly notified of the death and whereabouts of one Prince Rogers Nelson.

'It's an absolute bastard,' Felix muttered darkly, once his hurricane of a tantrum had subsided, 'but I'm afraid the party might be finally over.'

Any screw-ups on the Lennon front, then, will take on a cataclysmic significance, and my goodness, don't the team and I know it. In the last few days Felix has yelled at every single one of us for a variety of minor offences, and everyone has been on edge. He screamed at poor Sarah for positioning chairs a few millimetres in the wrong place, displaying chocolate bars in the slightly incorrect order and making ice cubes that were 'too icy'. He threatened to slice Matthias's hands off with his own carving knife after he served Felix with a burger that was a touch light on the salt, then was heard to complain loudly, 'that Austrian tit always over-seasons everything'. I can see him right now, next to the Main Stage where Elliott Smith is due to play, barking at Maggie the monitor engineer over some inconsequential shortcoming. I myself have managed to escape the sharp end of Felix's ire, but only just. So why, you might ask, does anyone bother? We're not getting paid – why don't we just sod off home? Well, some people do. But Felix has a knack of inspiring loyalty even after the fiercest of remonstrations. A well-timed compliment here, a rare gift from some exotic Memory Swapshop there. And also, an existence without the Afterparty stretches forward like a gaping eternal yawn, with – speaking personally – all accompanying emotional turmoil. No: we just need to stay on top of it, today and tomorrow, ride this tricky period out, and with any luck Felix will be back to the more regular, manageable level of exasperating pretty soon. In the meantime, there are plenty of other things to busy ourselves with.

Example? Robert Palmer. Now, don't get me wrong. The idea of Palmer playing the classic *Riptide* album in full this afternoon with the original drummer and bassist, Chic's Tony Thompson and Bernard Edwards, is awesome, and something I definitely don't want to miss. But just when I'm settling into a few precious minutes of Elliott Smith (he starts with 'Sweet Adeline' exactly as I'd hoped he would) I get a call from Sarah, who's in a right flap, asking me to come and help immediately. I grudgingly kiss the sound of Smith goodbye and hurry away to see what all the arse is about.

I come haring around the corner and present myself at the door of Palmer's maisonette dressing room, where Sarah stands awkwardly in the centre of the spacious ground floor. The room has been nicely themed with brushed white floorboards, white muslin, candelabra and some intriguing *chaises longues*. At one end of the room, Tony Thompson and a few other band members recline, sip cocktails, tinker with instruments and look perfectly content. In between, near the stairs, is Robert Palmer himself, open-necked linen shirt and chinos, tapping his feet restlessly, one hand on the wall, the other massaging his brow as if suffering from some sort of migraine, which I'm certain can't be the case. And at the far end of the room is… well. Perhaps I ought to explain. You'll recall what I said about making the star feel special, how this is a crucial part of our operation? When our stars' managers send over their backstage requests we're used to seeing some fairly unusual things, however when Palmer's contract arrived it had but one demand.

> Mr Palmer and band will be provided with one (1) private sushi bar, restocked with fresh produce throughout the day; the sushi bar will be staffed by one (1) character of 'Nick-Nack' from the James Bond film *The Man With The Golden Gun*.

So, as contractually requested, Palmer's dressing room contains a large varnished wooden counter with an appropriately Japanese-looking canopy, under which sits a generous array of sushi: handrolls, maki rolls, ngiri, sashimi, even an abundant pile of tempura, plus assorted condiments. Behind the counter, resplendent in an oversized white uniform and small accompanying hat, is Nick-Nack off of James Bond, with the eyebrows and bum-fluff moustache to prove it. After I've taken in the scene, and perhaps a touch undiplomatically, the first words to emerge from my mouth are, 'And the problem is?'

'He's a bloody Rendering!' Palmer barks, in an unexpectedly strong West Yorkshire accent, flinging a hand out in Nick-Nack's direction. Then he resumes his brow-rubbing.

I glance over at Nick-Nack, who shrugs. Sarah also shrugs. I mean, really. It's not even midday yet, and frankly I don't have time for this shit.

'Of course he's a Rendering,' I reply.

'He's not supposed to be a Rendering.'

'Where does it say that?' I ask.

'The contract.'

'The contract,' I insist, 'specifies the character of "Nick-Nack" from the James Bond film. That's all. Nowhere does it say it has to be the actual actor who played Nick-Nack.'

'Hervé Villechaize,' mutters Palmer.

'That's the chap,' I nod. 'I met him last month.'

'So why isn't he here?'

'He's an actor,' I reply, 'not a sushi chef.'

Palmer looks over at his band for some support. None of them looks remotely interested.

'Look,' I say, striding over to Nick-Nack and grabbing a maki roll. 'Have you actually tried the sushi?'

I dip it into some soy sauce and hand it to Sarah. She munches away for a few seconds, then nods enthusiastically.

'You see?'

'Right,' Palmer says, getting out his phone. 'I want to see Felix.'

'Er, hang on.'

'I'm calling him now.'

'Er, he'll be in the middle of something.'

'Well he can bloody talk to me instead.'

Curses – my blustering tactic hasn't worked. Palmer paces around the room while the phone rings, but thank goodness Felix doesn't seem to be answering. There's nothing for it; time for a bit of pleading.

'Look, Mr Palmer. We spent a long, long time on this… trying to track down Hervé Villechaize, going all the way out to his house… in zone S398…'

One of the band grunts in a suitably impressed manner.

'That's right,' I concur, 'all the way to the French zones… We asked for his permission, did the deed, then we had our own chef

Matthias train up Nick-Nack here to make the sushi, which took at least two weeks... Surely you can see that we've gone to enough trouble to try to meet your needs?'

Palmer plonks his phone down on a table and then gets even more of his West Yorkshire out.

'Well, I'm still not bloody happy. I mean, the least you can damn well do is...'

But thankfully, we don't get to hear what the least we can damn well do is. For that very second, on schedule at 11.30am precisely, all the women from the 'Addicted To Love' video march through the door, and Robert Palmer forgets Sarah and I exist. Uniform with tied-back black hair, white make-up, blood-red lipstick and short black dresses – elegant and dazzling, if you like that kind of thing – they spread around the room, draping themselves over the various seats, immediately mingling more or less seductively with Palmer and band. After hanging around making small-talk with Nick-Nack for a few minutes, Sarah and I sidle out of the door. The irony is, of course: all five video girls are also Renderings. But who cares when you look as good as that?

I spend most of the afternoon trying to keep myself busy and not think about any Lennon-related forebodings, which for the most part isn't much of a challenge. There are dozens of things to sort out, and Felix is too busy welcoming new acts and hobnobbing to attend to any of the nitty-gritty. Quite common for a festival day like today, he doesn't communicate with me beyond the occasional phone call and, if in person, a nod and a low-whispered command ('Podge, go and get a tape-measure and find out how wide Tammy Wynette's dressing room is, will you? She thinks it's smaller than Dusty Springfield's and she threw a shit-fit just now') – so I've really no idea whether or not he's still fuming about the Prince thing and quite frankly I don't hover near him long enough to find out. There is, of course, some fine music, which I try to grab a few minutes of here and there. The Stevie Wonder stage hosts a pretty kick-ass supergroup in the early afternoon – supergroups, for the frequent lack of a given band's full original membership, being something of an Afterparty tradition – this one featuring Gerry Rafferty, who gives a rapturous crowd 'Baker Street' and 'Stuck In The Middle With You', Kirsty MacColl, who trills her way through 'A New England' and 'Walking Down Madison', and Rory Gallagher, who joins the pair for a completely bonkers extended version of 'Fairytale Of New York'. I'm out in the arena for most of this; giant Christmas baubles are released into the audience, Guinness flowing like the Powerscourt waterfall. A while later I'm helping Sarah locate the ingredients of a mint julep for Serge Gainsbourg on the Shirley Bassey stage, fortuitously at the exact moment Lee Hazlewood invites Dusty Springfield up for a spellbinding rendition of 'Some Velvet Morning'. I also manage decent pitstops in front of Palmer's *Riptide* set – Nick-Nack's sushi skills don't seem to have done the show any harm – and, in front of an audience so immense it could possibly rival Lennon's later, Kurt's acoustic set. Dressed in his classic beige cardigan and faded jeans, the dear chap's on fine form: 'Been A Son' and 'Sliver' roar outwards across the field, and on

'Lithium' the crowd are singing so loudly Kurt actually stops halfway through to jokingly berate them ('I can't hear myself fuckin' think, man'). These are the moments that make me feel like collaring the lab-coat men and shouting, 'Look! This! This is what I earn from the job!'

But then I see George Harrison.

He's having a cigarette and chatting quietly to Gerry Rafferty by the ramp to the side-of-stage, then he spots me, frowns, excuses himself and wanders in my direction. I'm just about to check Michael Hutchence and band are in place to play next, but Harrison corners me. He seems bothered and slightly out-of-breath.

'Seen John?'

'Um... not for a while, no.'

'Do me a favour, will you?'

'Sure.'

'If you notice anything... unusual about him. Let me know?'

'Um... yeah, will do! Anything you have in mind?'

'Just anything, man. He doesn't seem... right.'

I glance at my watch. It's a little before 5pm; the sky is just beginning to darken before its rather abrupt sunset at around six.

'Man, are you listening to me?'

'Of course!' I reply.

'Where's Felix?'

'Um... I'm not sure.'

'I'm gonna call him,' says Harrison, whipping out his phone.

'No–no, *I'll* call him.'

I'm not having someone call Felix on me twice in one day. I let Harrison see me press the Felix button, but of course I do nothing of the sort. I wait a convincing amount of time and then leave what I hope is a convincing fake-voicemail.

'Ah, yeah, Felix, it's Podge... Can you call me back please, I'm here with George Harrison, he has one or two concerns. I'll try to find you over in the office.'

George watches me closely as I hang up, then narrows his eyes, flares his nostrils and flounces back towards Rafferty, leaving me to flounce off to HQ. The benefit of having worked here as long as me is that I know, with 99.9 percent accuracy, Felix will not be there. Right now Felix will be happily watching Bob Monkhouse on the Mel Brooks stage, but Harrison need never know that.

Instead I find Amy and Sarah sitting on the little wall outside the office, enjoying a cigarette and a few Camden Town reminiscences. We all hung out in Camden over roughly the same period, but never met. I join in for a few minutes, until the conversation mindlessly drifts (as it often does around here) to death betting.

'Aw, mate,' begins Amy, 'I lost a ton the other day. Dick van Dyke versus Alan Rickman.'

'Ouch,' Sarah winces.

'I mean, Alan Rickman. Seriously? Who'd have thought it?'

I can't *stand* death betting. Can't believe it exists. It's the sort of cheap scratchcard garbage I thought we'd left on Earth. Felix of course is banned from doing it, what with his unfair advantage, and I've only tried it once: in a rare moment of intuition I picked Caroline Aherne over Delia Smith, but the experience left me so depressed I've actually never bothered to claim the winning Memory Swapshop tokens.

'I had a tricky one before,' Sarah continues. 'Fidel Castro versus Jacques Chirac.'

'Hmm,' Amy thinks. 'Castro, I'd say.'

'Huh,' Sarah replies. 'I went for Chirac.'

'Actually, fuckin'ell, speaking of politics… I was chatting to Chris Penn last week, he heard a shocking rumour about America from a newbie…'

'Ooh, go on, I think I heard this one too…'

But I don't get to hear this juicy piece of Earth gossip, for right then, Felix calls. My heart sinks when I answer and hear the deafening chatter and laughter on the other end of the line, which can only mean one thing.

'Podge mate! I'm in the hospitality tent! Go into my office! There's a fuck-off case of vintage tequila I need you to bring!'

The hospitality tent is right next to the Mel Brooks stage but with views over the main arena. Around this time of day it's stuffed with wankers and I tend to steer massively clear of it, but Felix spends an unfortunate amount of time there; in theory, he says, because 'that's where next year's headliners are usually decided.' After a few minutes' ferreting about in the depths of Felix's den I find a box containing four bottles of AsomBroso Añejo tequila, which apparently Felix had to trek out to a Memory Swapshop in the Mexican zones to locate. Meanwhile, the sun has done its dropping-straight-out-of-the-sky thing, and suddenly the nightlife is awakening. Little lanterns switch on in every part of the site, strewn along all the walkways and surrounding every tent and prefab cabin. The whole Artist Village is engulfed by the sound of Hutchence and crowd yelling out the various INXS choruses, and the drink begins to flow fractionally quicker; not that drunkenness is, of course, a big problem.

Unless you're in the hospitality tent.

I don't know what it is about the place. For one thing, it's full of men; women avoid it like the plague, and I don't blame them. Here people drink faster, favour stronger liquors, and ingest the alcohol almost without cease. Consequently, it's the only place where one can encounter people who seem to be properly arseholed. Working the bar in the hospitality tent is considered by far the worst job at the festival, so much that it's the only role for which Felix arranges some sort of payment: gifts, of course, but with Felix's knowledge of the local zone group's Memory Swapshops, you can be sure to walk away with an Armani suit, a Chanel dress or a flashy set of golf clubs. A couple of years ago I even saw a bartender drive off in one of the vintage cars used for ferrying the stars around.

I show up and ease my way through the crowded tent with my precious box. A few guys try to grab it off me; one of them looks a lot like Richard Nixon but I could be wrong. The conversations are far louder in here, more animated; I get elbowed in the ribs and the crotch a good couple of times on my way through the mob. Felix, still instantly spottable in his trilby, can be seen in the far corner, towering over everyone, chatting with a few guys including a small, energetic figure with curly hair. Today's bartender, a tattooed, tough-enough-for-the-job dude known to all as Nashy, is presently being harangued by Eric Morecambe about something or other – at least that's what I imagine, until Nashy roars with laughter, obviously having been told some sort of joke. On the opposite side of the bar is the open view to the main stage, where Donna Summer, amid much dry ice and ethereal lighting, has just floated on in a floaty costume while the majestic opening beats to 'State Of Independence' float out across the vast crowd. There are plenty of nodding heads and tapping feet among the hospitality punters, and actually the vibe is not quite as hideous as I was anticipating.

Until I get to Felix.

Felix and his three chums are smoking large cigars and gabbling away. The curly-haired man turns out to be Michael Winner, next to him a stocky, hard-faced chap I don't recognise but who seems to exude menace, and finally a guy who looks quite alarmingly like Johnny Cash. Like I said earlier, if someone looks alarmingly like someone in the Artist Village, it probably *is* that someone. The four of them cheer drunkenly at the arrival of my box, then the hard-faced chap glowers at me and says, with a slight Manchester accent, 'So, are you just going to stand there like a prick? Open the box and fill us up.'

I'm not used to being spoken to like this, but Felix has warned me many times not to argue back with the hospitality guests. I dump the box on the floor and extract one of the bottles, a fussily-shaped curvy thing, which I crack open. I'm about to pour the first glass when Manchester bloke leans forward and wrenches it out of my hand, managing to splash it all over Johnny Cash's trousers.

'Hey fucker,' slurs Cash in my direction, 'you wanna watch what you're doing there.' I draw breath to protest but out of the corner of my eye I see Felix giving me a warning look. Winner, meanwhile, hoots with laughter.

'You impatient man, Donny, you should let the poor boy do his job.'

Donny, whoever he is, seems to have commandeered that particular bottle all for himself, so I bend down to pick up another. Unfortunately Johnny Cash has the same idea and we clash heads. More hooting with laughter from Winner.

'Romsey,' Cash growls, 'where d'you get this klutz from?'

It's classic school playground stuff – if you happened to go to school with Michael Winner and Johnny Cash and whoever this Donny charm-merchant is. Reckoning that I've fulfilled all my obligations, I decide to bugger off again.

'You be mother, Felix.'

Felix gets the message and bends down to pick up one of the wretched bottles, but just then his bloody phone rings. He fishes it out of his pocket and squints at it. Please don't be George Harrison. Please don't be George Harrison.

He answers.

'George! What can I do you for?'

There's nothing for it. I've earned the reputation as a clumsy arse in the last two minutes so I might as well put it to some use. I squat to pick up the two remaining tequila bottles but then pretend to trip over the box, or my shoelaces, or something, and tumble forward into Felix, who goes flying backwards into Peter Sellers waiting to get served at the bar. As I fall, I also manage to kick my legs out sideways in my struggle to regain balance, and land one right in Johnny Cash's crotch. He, too, stumbles backwards, right into Bob Monkhouse and Bernard Manning. Amid the hoo-hah, Felix drops his phone, and as he's apologising profusely to Peter Sellers I make a dive for it and disconnect the call.

Michael Winner is roaring with laughter, Johnny Cash is yelling drunkenly at me and Felix seethes 'Podge, what the fuck?' in my ear, but thankfully, the Numbness being what it is, no fists are brandished. I scoop up the tequila box and hand it to barman Nashy, then make my excuses and bustle out of there as quickly as I can. As I depart, I hear Felix wondering loudly where his phone is.

And that's why I never go into the hospitality tent.

39

George Harrison calls Felix another couple of times as I hurry back towards HQ. I haven't quite figured out how I'm going to return Felix's phone to him, but never mind; nothing's more important than keeping any Lennon-drama well away from him right now. I know I'm probably coming across as something of a chicken-shit. I know I should bite the bullet, talk to Felix and nail this Lennon mystery once and for all. But as I see the film crews wheeling themselves into their final places for tonight's headline show and think about the millions of people, all over the local zone group, waiting at home to watch Lennon do his thing… I can't. If the worst comes to the worst, the show will be a little disappointing and it won't quite blow the sky off the place like it ought to. Maybe there'll be a few clunking errors. But a bad John Lennon is still ten times better than anyone else. Right? And – as that lab-coated moron said himself earlier today… what was it…? 'Nothing calamitous will happen… Why would we want to cause a panic?'

After this I just hide in the office for a while. Most of the team are congregating in various places to watch the headline show, but a few are still beavering away in HQ, including Sarah who's still trying to satisfy some of the more outlandish backstage requirements (Kurt Cobain's endless requests for Kraft-brand macaroni cheese, for example). I waste about twenty minutes dithering on the Infonet and then my own phone rings. I blink at the screen. Harrison, of course.

'Where's Felix?' he begins, without overture.

'Oh, ah, um, I think he's, um, having a terribly important meeting in the hospitality tent…'

'He hasn't answered his phone in bloody hours…'

'Ah yes, sorry, I think that…'

'… and something is definitely wrong with John, and no one, not the band, not you, not Felix, *no one* is bloody listening to me.'

'Okay, sure. I'll come and, um, listen to you right now.'

'I'll believe that when I see it.'

The man is becoming a right pain in the neck and I keep having to remind myself that he's a Beatle. I kill a few more minutes and then amble back towards the action; Donna Summer is done, and the Lennon anticipation is mounting. The VIP viewing platforms to the left and right of the stage are overflowing, and I can see Felix's girlfriend Suzi standing with Maggie behind the monitors desk, but there's still no sign of Felix. Harrison of course is waiting for me at the foot of the ramp, with the ever-present Gerry Rafferty nursing his latest pint of Guinness. Harrison gives an exasperated sigh and puts his hands on his hips. I make an attempt at a relaxed smile.

'Everything all right?'

'You know it bloody well isn't.'

'Where is John now?'

Harrison jerks his head in the direction of the side-of-stage area.

'Up there. He's forgotten... *everything*.'

'Ah.'

'You were supposed to be in charge of him today.'

'Um, yeah, I was. I am, still.'

'Haven't done much of a job of it, have you?'

Now I can see Felix turning the corner in the distance and striding down the path from the Artist Village. Harrison currently has his back to the ramp. If I'm lucky, Felix will just march straight past us.

'Um, George,' I mutter, trying to move him away from the ramp, 'perhaps you can come over here a bit, so we can speak with a bit more privacy?'

'Jesus, man, have we got time for that? John's about to go on.'

'No, but... please, this way...' I manage to encourage him about five metres forward. Better than nothing. 'So... what sort of things is he forgetting?'

'Very important things. How to play the bloody guitar being one.'

'Well... you know what people's memories are like... around here.'

'No! Not John.'

He's getting more and more exasperated. I sneak another glance at my watch. 7.28pm. Just... stretch... it... out... It'll be over soon...

'You took him through that security machine before, didn't you?'

'Yeah, of course.'

'And there were no problems?'

'No, none at all!'

I hate lying. Really. Hardly anyone is capable of doing it around here and it makes me feel like a child murderer.

'Impossible,' George hisses.

'What are you suggesting?' I ask.

'You *know* what I'm suggesting.'

Felix has made it to the ramp, Harrison spots me glancing upwards and whirls around, just in time to see Felix reaching the top and striding forth into the side-of-stage area.

'Oy!' George shouts. 'Hey! Felix!'

He races to the ramp and dashes up after him. Luckily I know the place better than Harrison does: I sprint around to the other side and up the steps that lead to the monitors desk, where I suspect Felix is heading. I have no idea what I'm actually going to do; manhandling George Harrison is a little above my paygrade. It's pretty crowded at this side of the stage and I can see Felix shuffling through to join Suzi; meanwhile, Lennon and his band are walking onstage from the opposite side, to a roar so loud it's rattling my teeth. It's quite dark in here and I blink around to try to see where Harrison is. After a moment I spot him. He's emerged from the throng on the opposite side, and now he's standing still, white-of-face, glaring outwards. For one horrible second I think he's going to follow the band onstage and collar Lennon. Thankfully he doesn't, but he still looks pretty frantic. Then he flashes a look over to the monitor side, where he spots Felix, who is directly behind Maggie, drink in one hand, his other arm around Suzi. Harrison races over, almost crashes into me, gives me a vicious scowl and runs to the other side. In the gloom I soon see him reappear next to Felix, but now the slow piano chords of the first song are striking up, and after an initial shriek of recognition, a dramatic hush falls over the whole place. I can see Harrison whispering something in Felix's ear, but good old Felix waves George away with gestures to the majesty of the musical moment about to occur. Harrison persists. I can see Felix squinting, his lips forming the incredulous question: 'You think he's a *what*?!'

Meanwhile, Nicky Hopkins is playing the song's two opening

63

chords back and forth, and Lennon pauses a little way away from his mic. Everyone – the band on the stage, the techies and inner circle at the side, the fans at the front, the audience further afield viewing most of the show on the giant video screens, the Infonet viewers at home – they're all transfixed by the singer, about to utter the immortal opening line. The pianist repeats the chords one more time, then Lennon finally steps forward and takes a breath. In that split second I glance over at Felix, who is now staring forward with something approaching pure terror.

And that's when the figure hitherto known as John Lennon flickers once, then vanishes. *Completely* vanishes. His clothes – leather jacket, black jeans, black shirt, even the Ray Bans that were perched atop his head – all drop and crumple into a lifeless heap upon the floor.

Okay, seven shades of shit. You may unleash now.

Night

It's quite something when a Rendering vanishes. There they were: a totally credible, tangible, complete human form, with all the infinite facial expressions, postures and moveable, shifting surfaces you'd expect; and then, there they went: flickering like a pirate VHS movie and instantly disappearing from your, and indeed everyone's, field of vision. Absolutely nothing remains in their place, no puff of smoke, no strange wisp of plasma like when a kid's bubble bursts, not even a thin hazy guff of dust. I've only seen it happen a handful of times, and most of these were at Felix's place during a rather strange and fleetingly drunken evening with his girlfriend Suzi – who, while charming, hospitable and eye-poppingly beautiful, is herself a Rendering. Felix convinced Suzi to strip, then kept turning her off and on just for a laugh. I'm not sure what I was more weirded-out by: my friend's girlfriend standing nude in front of me, or her bloke making her appear and disappear by flicking a red switch on the side of a machine. On balance, I think the latter.

So, officially, I guess Renderings are supposed to be naked when they vanish and rematerialise, but it's arguably even more impressive when a fully-clothed Rendering is switched off because there's a spooky sort of *Wizard Of Oz* vibe to it: the clothes suddenly fall to the ground in an untidy pile, particularly entertaining when they're wearing a hat. It would be tempting to say the clothes retain their shape for one suspense-filled second before giving up the – if you'll pardon the expression – ghost, but they don't. And if we're searching for a whiff of comedy about the whole thing, I'd suggest that it's also somehow *funnier* watching a Rendering power down when they're fully dressed. But believe me, there were very few people laughing half an hour ago when 'The Rendering Formerly Known As John Lennon' disappeared.

There are thousands of completely unsolved puzzles about this strange existence of ours, but the question 'Why do Renderings exist?' (along with its more complicated sibling '*How* do Renderings exist?') remains one of the more mysterious. The story goes that the first Rendering machine was discovered about forty years ago in a disused building in downtown zone S287. Whoever found it was intrigued by the Han-Solo-esque humanoid imprint in the plasticky surface on the inside, and just climbed in. Must have been a dull afternoon. Then they became even more curious and pressed the blue button, remained inside for the duration of the vibrations (around eight hours for most people, depending on their size), climbed out when the machine fell finally silent, and pressed the red button. I guess all of this must have taken place over several attempts, possibly by a couple of different people, but eventually a woman by the name of Beatrice Luckham wound up staring (horrified, no doubt) at a life-sized, and life-filled, perfect duplicate of herself. She managed to resist the impulse to instantly attack the Rendering, and instead turned it back off again and carted the machine over to some inventor dude who toiled for a couple of months to discover how it worked. He failed, but he did manage to document a few key facts, which remain vital to the whole Rendering thing to this day:

1. The machine can only render one person at a time. You want to render someone else? You need to erase Rendering #1, and start again with the new person. You want two Renderings of the same person? You need two rendering machines and, with respect, there's something slightly deranged about you.

2. The machine has total on/off control of the Rendering, regardless of how far away the Rendering is. It's been tested between zones, and it works fine. (No transmitter has been found on the Rendering machine, so it's still a mystery how this happens: the phrase 'quantum entan-

glement' has been bandied about by some of the smarter, less numb people in town). So anyone with access to the machine has absolute power over the Rendering.

3. The Rendering does not eat, or drink, or sleep.

4. The Rendering is just a copy. It's not as smart as the original, and suffers from a few significant flaws. Sometimes these flaws remain undiscovered until it's too late.

5. The Rendering has less than a tenth the magnetic field of regular people, so – with an appropriate device – it's possible to screen a person to check whether they are a Rendering or not. Take a bow, Frank, our security guard.

At this point, like all the cheesiest science fiction stories, Bea Luckham's inventor refused to continue with his investigations because he considered the machine dangerous, particularly in the wrong hands. So Luckham flounced off, taking the machine and all the inventor's notes with her. And where did she go? To the place where everyone goes if they want to do something slightly unscrupulous: zone S751.

Goodness knows what happened next, but I suspect it was a bit like when someone can't open a jam jar, and they pass it round the whole family to have a go. The upshot was, eventually one of S751's boffins unlocked the machine's fabulous secret, and not only that, managed to build another one. Word spread among our local zone group's chattering classes that a woman called Bea Luckham in S751 had started flogging machines that created these jaw-droppingly real, three-dimensional, fully-operational copies of people, known forever more as Renderings.

Now, a good question might very reasonably have flopped into your mental out-tray. Namely: why would anyone want to create a copy of themselves? It's not like anyone needs robots to do the housework, like in Woody Allen's *Sleeper*, because there is no housework. And even if they did, it'd be rather creepy having someone who looked exactly like you hanging around, doing the hoovering. But, people being people, some very appealing uses were soon hit upon. You can probably use your imagination here, but let's look at Mr Felix Romsey as the ideal example. Back on Earth, Felix was never married, but had a string – a very long string – of rather attractive girlfriends, predominantly working in the, ahem, fashion industry. So he arrives here, and in the absence of any life-partner to either wait for, or reunite with, he simply swaps himself a second-hand Rendering machine and makes a copy of someone who fits his requirements. Renderings aren't terribly choosy in the romantic line, nor are they particularly taxing opponents when it comes to stuff like domestic arguments. And if he does occasionally get sick of the sight of her, he can just switch her off. Felix's ideal girlfriend, then.

More of a challenge is convincing a real person to let themselves be rendered. Aside from the inconvenience of having to spend eight uncomfortable, vibrating hours in what looks like a combination of a chest freezer and a sunbed, most people would have a few moral issues with allowing a copy of themselves to roam the streets, not to mention shack up with – and much more besides – a stranger. Talk about cheapening your own brand. But, as with most things around here, an appropriate price can usually be reached. In Felix's case he was lucky: the lady he found was in fact unspeakably vain, and quite liked the idea of being recreated and then carnally worshipped by someone. Felix of course had plenty of other things to offer too, and I believe this lady was treated to a private acoustic concert by Jimi Hendrix before she was packed off to whichever zone she came from.

So, back to Bea Luckham. She turned out to be quite the entrepreneur, and soon her little racket grew into an impressive cottage industry, producing as many as ten rendering machines per week and netting an outrageous haul of bartered items: rare and valuable bits and pieces that people had arrived with, like paintings, cars, musical instruments, book collections, jewellery, extravagant items of clothing – some of which Luckham distributed among her 'workers', while keeping the cream for herself. Rich people from T136 would throw their most expensive stuff at her, then bugger off with their machines to copy their favourite film stars, or whoever tickled their fancy. Within a few months Luckham had completely filled her house with other people's random shit. She acquired so much she had to stop taking it in – a two-bedroomed bungalow quickly reaches luxury-good capacity – and instead gave most of it away, which is one of the main reasons the Memory Swapshops are so brilliant in S751. She carried on making the machines but her prices went up. Well, not up, but maybe sideways: she started to trade for experiences rather than material goods. A private performance of Shakespeare's soliloquies by Olivier; dinner with JFK; even, if rumour is to be believed, a day or so in bed with River Phoenix.

Another question might have occurred to you, as it certainly did to me. Why, by this stage, had she not received a warning visit from our friends in the white lab coats? Apparently, for whatever curious reason, this didn't happen. There are several theories. One is that The Men were quite content with all this rendering business, as it was just another way of keeping people occupied; indeed, some maintain the first machine was left deliberately in zone S287 for this precise reason. In any case, the inbuilt limitations of the rendering process prohibit anything really bad from happening; it's not like someone's going to make an army of undefeatable Renderings and stage a coup. Some of our more spiritual colleagues suggest it's a kind of divine gift, as Renderings can bring comfort and companionship to those who never ended up with a spouse. There are, however, a pack of melodramatic souls who think it's all been a giant, sin-ridden mistake, and who expect fire, brimstone and other comparable substances to be visited upon those who use the wicked process, in the fullness of time.

In the end, it was probably the good old Numbness that prevented things from getting truly out of hand: after about five years, Bea Luckham got bored and simply stopped making the rendering machines. I guess there are only so many cars, jewels, furs, Van Goghs and nights out with a peak-condition Marlon Brando one can have. More odd is that she disposed of all the paperwork showing the inventor's findings, and the instructions for how to make new machines. Perhaps this was the lab-coated chaps' doing after all. So that's it. Unless someone's making them in a distant zone somewhere, no more rendering machines. It's estimated that there are only about three thousand of them knocking around our zone group. But it often seems like most of these belong to pop stars.

'It suits the idle bastards down to the ground,' Felix said to me, that very first proper festival day I worked for him. 'Oh, sometimes it's because they're busy and need to be in two places at once, but usually it's because they can't be arsed. So what do they do?'

'Send a Rendering along.'

'Bingo. Spend a few hours making sure the Rendering has the moves, and then send it off.'

I remember us having this conversation in the middle of the main stage arena; it was called the Dr Dre stage right then because it was hip-hop year and 2Pac was doing the rap supergroup thing with Notorious B.I.G. and Ol' Dirty Bastard. It was around lunchtime and the place was already heaving: girls and boys of all shapes, sizes and clothing styles, sunning themselves, slurping drinks, scoffing burgers, the usual. Felix was dressed in an enormous pair of metallic-blue shorts, a Public Enemy T-shirt, an L.A. Lakers baseball cap (on backwards, naturally) and some wraparound shades. He got away with it, although I remember thinking he was trying a little too hard. He was smoking as usual and drinking some kind of tropical cocktail, neither of which was improving his mood. It had been a tough morning: a Rendering of Karen Carpenter had been caught in the security machine and booted out, leaving the Shirley Bassey stage with no headliner.

'I saw some fuckin' awful Rock'n'roll all-dayer gig about fifteen years ago in S183, and I swear all the acts were Renderings. They played like shit... whoever'd done the preparation was a complete nonce. And these weren't even particularly famous people, so fuck knows what the real ones were up to. Watersports, probably. But it was woeful. One of the drummers got turned off by mistake halfway through a song.'

I made the mistake of laughing.

'You think it's funny?'

'Sorry, no,' I replied, pulling myself up.

'It ain't. After that, I drew the line for good. No more Renderings. Our entire reputation as a festival depends on that unique, unbreakable guarantee' – he hopped over to one of our festival posters tacked to a fence and tapped at the line written underneath the main heading – "*NO RENDERINGS*". These, my friend, are the most important two words in our whole operation. This is what puts us head and shoulders above the rest. All sorts of charlatans are putting on festivals now, and it's gonna get worse. But they all use Renderings from time to time. Not us. Nothing particularly wrong with Renderings – my own missus is a Rendering, after all – but people wanna know for sure that they're seeing the real thing, even if they've no way of telling. And of course… there are some of us who can *always* tell. I'm one of them. It's not the way they look, or the way they play. It's more the unpredictable stuff, like audience interaction, communication with the other musicians, all of that. Renderings… well, they're colder, aren't they, and often they're a little bit dim. They get easily frazzled if something weird happens and they dunno what to do.'

'Example?'

'Yeah, I'll give you a fucking good example,' he sneered. 'I saw Elvis Presley last year in T134. Now, he was also booked for a show in S289 on the same day, so anyone who bothered to check would know one of them had to be a Rendering. I had a little bet with Suzi that I'd be able to say by the end of the gig whether ours was or not.'

'Did she mind?'

'Eh?'

'Did Suzi mind… you know. You wondering whether he was a Rendering.'

'Course not,' he frowned, 'she's a fucking Rendering, isn't she? She doesn't care. Anyway, the show starts, and it's all good, and he gets to the encore, which is "Love Me Tender". Just him and a guitar. So he's on the final verse, and he does this really long pause before the very last line, like he always does, but the crowd go barging on, roaring out the final line straight away like it goes on the record. And this *totally* throws him. You can see on the screens, he's got literally no idea what to do. Does he think… okay, the audience are already halfway through singing the line, so just smile and fuck it, join them for the last few words? Or, does he stick to his guns and sing the whole line, in his own time? He hasn't a clue. So in the end he does neither. He waits for a good ten seconds, stony-faced, then hits the final guitar chord and walks off really awkward. No *way* would the real Presley have done that. And of course everyone's had a few drinks and no one really gives a shit, but I turned to Suzi straight away and said, "Rendering". Next day I get on the phone to the promoter, a mate of mine, and I ask him.'

'And?'

'Renderings played both the shows. Presley's such a lazy fucker.'

Lecture over, he blew a lungful of smoke in the direction of two passing girls, wandering along arm-in-arm singing the chorus to 'Mo Money Mo Problems'. He turned back to me.

'Right, if you'll excuse me, mate... Now I've gotta go ask Bobby Darin whether he'll move up to headline the Bassey stage. Bloody Renderings. Bane of my fucking death.'

And off he went. I remember watching him go, and wondering whether Felix's zero tolerance of Renderings didn't have more to do with his natural hatred of any 'lazy fuckers' than not wanting to disappoint his public. He carries with him a perpetual frustration with anyone he feels hasn't worked hard enough, which must have also accompanied him through his life. We're not supposed to feel frustration, but Felix does anyway. This must be why we're friends. It's not like we've got many other similarities, music aside. My parents are reasonably well-off and terribly middle class; his mother was a council estate alcoholic and he didn't even know who his father was. I went to a private school in Buckinghamshire, he went to some dead-end secondary modern in Camden. We both have a death defect, of course, me my beer belly, Felix his chest scar; which, incidentally, he claims has nothing to do with his actual death, although no one's really sure *how* he died – apart from some vague thing he once said to me about 'overdosing on fun'. We're not even the same virtual age: Felix for some reason has been cast permanently in his late-thirties, giving him the unlikely vibe of an elder statesman, while I seem to be forever twenty-three. No, the main things we have in common are our most prized possessions: our feelings. I have my sadness, Felix his anger.

And this evening at the Afterparty, make absolutely no mistake. Felix is probably angrier than I've ever seen him before.

The thing about anger around here is that no one expects it. It's as if people have forgotten what it's like, what it can do. So when Felix is going as mental as he has been for the last thirty minutes, people seriously don't know where to put themselves. He started by trashing all the drums. Then the amps. Then all the sound gear. Then he pinned each and every one of John Lennon's band to the floor, demanding to know whether they knew anything, and where the real Lennon was. The answer to both of these questions was of course a categorical and terrified 'No', but not before Felix had inflicted some good old North London violence. He whacked poor Dee Murray the bass player in the bollocks a few times, and threw Nicky Hopkins' electric piano at him. Gerry Rafferty tried to calm Felix down, and received a cymbal in the face. Frank the security guard was completely useless at being, y'know, an actual security guard. Suzi went into full Rendering meltdown mode, which is basically sitting in a corner, shielding her ears and eyes, gently rocking.

The audience reaction was mixed, but largely, and predictably, subdued. A massive, collective gasp, a few nutters starting to chant 'Rendering! Rendering!' and then giving up after about twenty seconds, a little sobbing here and there, some angry faces, and then seventy percent of them just shuffled off home. Those that remained just stood there, transfixed by this altogether different kind of entertainment taking place in front of them.

I mean: wondering what someone hopes to achieve by going this nuts is pretty futile, but nonetheless, I wonder what Felix is hoping to achieve by going this nuts. I've only seen him like this once before, and that was when John Martyn hit on Suzi after headlining the Bassey stage last year. Back then I remember thinking that, for Felix, a big part of it is showing people that he *can*. I know from experience that it takes a while to boil off the most hysterical bit of his temper, and then he calms down to most people's idea of furious. Consequently, and also because I don't fancy being impaled by a percussion instrument, I make no attempt to intervene tonight. A couple of times people have said, 'Podge, *do* something!' – as if I alone possess some magical Felix-calming properties – but I've sidestepped them.

More worrying has been the continuing, suspicious presence of George Harrison. In the immediate aftermath he muttered to me under his breath, 'I told you', and then again looked confounded when I failed to take any action. I pass him just now as he's comforting Rafferty; wounds heal very quickly around here so Gerry's facial injuries have pretty much gone already, but he's still quite shaken up. 'I can't believe you didn't listen to me,' Harrison hisses, followed by, incriminatingly, 'it's almost as if you *knew*.'

I glance over at Felix, whose fire of rage has died down fractionally, inasmuch as he's stopped hurling bits of equipment about. He's pacing the stage back and forth like a jilted female tiger, his phone pressed to his ear. Now he's speaking, or barking really: apparently leaving a voicemail.

'Brian? It's Felix. Call me back, right now, and explain to me what the *fuck* you're doing sending a Rendering to my fucking festival.'

He hangs up and dials another number.

'Malcolm? I want an explanation, you little twat. You seem to be flavour of the fucking month right now, so if you don't call me back within five minutes I'm gonna assume this is *your* doing, and I'll be round to dismember you quicker than you can say "Purple Rain".'

More pacing. I look back at Harrison, who is helping Rafferty up. He catches my eye and glowers again. I do wish he'd piss off. The thing is: what *did* I know, really? That the lab-coated men were up to something? Big deal. And they never mentioned the word 'Rendering'. I know nothing else. Who started it? Who turned the Rendering off? And where's the machine?

Meanwhile, Felix is leaving yet another vitriolic voicemail.

'Wilson, you flappy Mancunian cocksucker. Pull your head out of Bowie's arse, call me back and tell me where the blue Monday my fucking headliner has gone. And don't even *think* about saying you don't know anything. Romsey, out.'

Instead of hanging up he just hurls his phone across the stage and unleashes an almighty roar. I hear another, softer voice behind me, and I turn to see Harrison, still propping up Rafferty, but now also on the phone, leaving his own much calmer message.

'Johnny boy. It's me. Dunno where you are, but call me back and let me know you're all right. Peace.'

Felix squints over at Harrison, with a look of unbridled contempt.

'Peace? *Peace?* What the fuck has this got to do with peace?'

George worriedly slips his phone into his pocket.

'Just a turn of phrase, man.'

'And what,' Felix spits, stomping over to our side of the stage, 'are you doing worrying about how *John* is? I'll tell you how he is! He's dead! He's a fucking dead man!'

'We're all fucking dead men,' Gerry Rafferty points out.

'Do you want another piece of metal in your face, tithead?'

George Harrison holds up both his hands.

'Felix… look, man… we know you're fuming. But you've gotta try seeing some sense. John wouldn't do this.'

'Oh, yeah?'

'He wouldn't. And you know it.'

'Do I? I don't know anything. Apart from he's another fat rock star who wouldn't let anything get in the way of another night lounging around on his arse cramming genetically-engineered smoked salmon into his gob.'

'John's not like that.'

'Isn't he?'

'No! And… and let's say it *was* him… why would he turn the Rendering off? Eh? Why would he do that?'

'Oh, I don't fucking know, maybe one of his bloody girlfriends kicked the switch or something! Maybe the machine went wrong! They do go wrong sometimes, you know. Things do sometimes go wrong in this stupid shithole, believe it or not. Anyway, we'll soon find out, won't we?'

'How?'

'Because I'm gonna go round there, right now, and pull his bony arse out of his swimming pool…'

'No!'

'... and kick his fucking head in. And if he isn't there, I'm gonna go straight round to Brian's house and kick *his* fucking head in. Podge?'

'Um, yeah?'

'Get me a car. Now.'

I know what you're thinking. Now would be a good time to mention my little episode with the lab-coated men. Well, it would, wouldn't it? At least then we'd have some direction. Felix might think of a better use of his time, and spare himself a long Trav journey. But I keep schtum. And why? Because I'm a coward and I don't want to tell Felix right now. Especially not in front of George bloody Harrison.

So I streak off to find Felix a car. HQ is in a right state when I get there: the abrupt end to Lennon's set means every musician in the whole Afterparty wants a car to the Trav instantly. Three or four assistants are on the phone, frantically trying to coordinate, while a few jaded-looking performers smoke and loiter: Phil Everly, Tony Thompson, even tomorrow night's headliner Whitney Houston who seems to have formed an unlikely bond with a rather bedraggled-looking Serge Gainsbourg. I signal to one of the assistants that I need transport, *quick*, but she shakes her head at me. Impossible. Then I remember I have a secret weapon. The sudden, car-less departure of our headline act means there's a certain black and burgundy Rolls-Royce at our disposal. I whip out my phone and hit Walter.

'Hey, boss! How are ya? Is he done already?'

'Meet me at the East Gate in two minutes.'

'Sure thing, Mr Podge! Boy, I can't wait to drive Mr–'

I hang up and run back towards the main stage. People are drifting in the other direction, everyone looking a bit dazed and down-in-the-mouth. I pass a swaying Michael Hutchence, with a smiling Paula Yates on his arm. At least someone's happy. Then I see Felix stomping down the ramp and I'm back in anger-ville. He's still ranting at George Harrison.

'Well, I'd fucking ask him, wouldn't I? But he's not answering his fucking phone! Where's the car, Podge?'

'East Gate, one minute.'

'And you're coming with me.'

80

'Um… really? Me?'

'Why,' he sneers, 'have you got loads of other more pressing things to do?'

'Um… no, of course not.'

And so – despite continuing protestations of Harrison and Rafferty – Felix and I hotfoot it round to the East Gate and leap into the back of the Rolls-Royce Silver Wraith, an extremely confused and disheartened Walter slamming the doors and conveying us along the back road towards downtown. We turn right into the residential road, past a steady trickle of backstagers who couldn't be bothered to wait for transport, then we're joined by a fleet of Locals, all full to the brim with punters on their way back from their foreshortened day of music.

'There they are,' Felix notes. 'Bunch of grinning sheep. Sometimes just looking at them makes me feel ill.'

'Better not bite the hand that feeds the eternal boredom,' I comment quietly.

'Fuck all that, man. Constant hassle. Never-ending work. No pay. Hardly any decent birds.'

'Suzi?' I suggest.

'Dude,' he frowns at me, as if that's all the explanation needed. 'Hobnobbing with boring, arrogant celebs. Loads of booze, no fucking effect. Can't get hold of any drugs, and even if I do – as the bloody Verve once sang – the drugs don't work.'

I snigger. He looks up at me dolefully.

'Sometimes, Podge,' he mutters, 'I don't know why I bother.'

It's an interesting question. Why *does* he bother? There's the prestige, the feeling of importance, that he's in with the in-crowd. He practically *is* the in-crowd. But there must be more to it than that. I gaze at the Local next to us, gliding along, the blindly cheerful masses within. It's a strange sight, seeing so many people in such a closed-up space. It's not something you see very often around here. In this concentrated context, I always find the mix of clothing and hairstyles absurd. People are dressed in about five decades' worth of summer fashions: polo shirts, white vests, tie-dyed dresses, granddad shirts, flowery frocks, Ben Sherman collared shirts, '90s indie T-shirts, smart jeans, baggy jeans, cut-off jeans, denim skirts, mini-skirts, ra-ra skirts, everything under the sun. It's like some elaborate advert campaign for a chain of vintage shops. I'm assailed by that familiar pang of sorrow: it's exactly the sort of madcap sight I'd like to share with Saffy. What I wouldn't give to send her just one letter, somehow, with all of this stuff described for her. Everything, every last detail, from the great stuff to the boring stuff to the depressing stuff... and the weird stuff, such as... well, this next bit I still find endlessly creepy, despite my having been here seven years now: after a whole day standing around at the Afterparty, sweating in the sun, the features of every last person on the Local are quite swiftly morphing back to pre-festival flawlessness, the clammy complexions disappearing, the hairstyles returning to the slick perfection of the morning, the clothes uncreasing and sweat-patches vanishing. It's the same story with the festival site. Although I'm usually enjoying the Afterparty's actual after-party when it happens, over the course of the night hours, the litter will evaporate and the stages will tidy themselves. If only we could bottle this secret and sell it back to Earth, Michael Eavis would snap it up in a Pilton second.

I glance over at Felix – his shirt half-unbuttoned, his jacket and trilby hat fallen by the wayside somewhere – as he stares out of the window, goodness knows what deranged plans of revenge and retribution fizzing about in his brain. By rights, we should still be watching a scintillating set from possibly the biggest rock star ever. And the crazy thing is, neither of us need to do what we're doing right now. We could both go home, kick back, with absolutely no responsibilities and nothing threatening an eternity of chilling. Yet, here we are, stone-cold sober, about to jump on a Trav in the middle of an Afterparty Friday night. Why? Because we have no choice. It's the only thing that makes us who we are. And it's right now I realise what we're going to have to discuss on the Trav journey to T136, all on our own. There's nothing inside the Trav for Felix to throw, and nowhere for him to stomp off to. The definitive captive audience.

Can't wait.

Felix remains uncharacteristically silent until after we reach the Trav. There's a glut of festivalgoers leaping off the Locals and swarming towards the bays, but luckily we have Walter to whisk us far beyond anything that could be described as a queue, to the furthest bay of the entire station, where Felix wordlessly disembarks and strides off. Nervously I move to follow him, but Walter spins around from the driving seat.

'Is he okay, boss?'

'Not really, Walter. What does it look like?'

Walter makes a funny sighing noise: possibly the first note of exasperation I've ever heard from him.

'I didn't mean is Mr Felix okay, Mr Podge... I meant, is Mr Lennon okay.'

'Oh. Right. Sorry. Um... well, he's...'

'*Podge!*' Felix hollers from the bay.

'Gotta go. Sorry Walter.'

I run across the little stretch of concrete and join Felix. Unusually, I'm suddenly aware of some rustling in a nearby hedge, like a little gust of wind, and I suddenly have the strangest notion that I might feel a little chilly.

'Are you cold?' I ask, feeling that Felix might possibly respond to small talk. He winces.

'Cold? Of course I'm not fucking cold.'

'There was a little gust of wind just then.'

'No, there wasn't, you tit.'

'I'm sure there was. I think I might be cold.'

The yellow lights start flashing, accompanied by the familiar whirring sound of an arriving Trav.

'Podge, sometimes I think you're weirder than I am,' Felix responds, as the doors open. He pushes past a well-dressed disembarking couple, punches 'T136' into the keypad, the doors slam shut and the Trav lurches off.

You've got to admire the efficiency of these things. Inside, they're like a cross between a state-of-the-art cable car and a futuristic boutique hotel room: black padded seats on either side, metal walls, big glass windows (not that there's ever anything to look at, although apparently the Trav briefly comes up from its tunnel if you're travelling between S158 and S148, the mountainous region where people go skiing). All very slick, but of course they're totally lacking any kind of romance or ceremony. Sometimes I miss having a little wait, a scheduled departure time, a bit of hanging around in the station or even at an airport, buying a coffee and a sandwich, that kind of thing. Silly really. I attempt to engage Felix in my Trav musings, I guess to provide something of a buffer to what I really need to talk about.

'How did you discover how this thing worked when you first got here?'

Felix frowns again.

'What is this, Podge, some sort of philosophical evening you're having?'

'I dunno, it's just... I guess all this stuff has made me think a bit.'

'How did *you* find out how it worked?'

'You showed me,' I replied.

'Well, aren't I the nice big brotherly figure,' he smirks. 'I've no idea how I knew. I guess I just... knew.'

'They put it in there. The knowledge.'

'I s'pose. But to be fair, Podge, it's hardly rocket science. You punch in the code. Off you go.'

'Sure. But you needed to know what the code was, and you needed to know what the zone was, and where the Trav station was, and what the Trav actually did.'

'Yeah, yeah... and they missed you out, Podge, and you arrived here with no knowledge, and you were miserable, and poor, poor you... We've heard this sob story before. Why are you mentioning all this shit again?'

'Oh, I was just... um... marvelling at what *They* were capable of doing.'

Felix narrows his eyes dangerously. A man of thin patience, even at the happiest of times.

'Podge. What are you on about?'

I give myself five seconds to decide how to tell the story. Hammer horror, or Camden council estate? Then I figure: what's the difference?

'They came for me. Earlier today.'

'You *what?*'

'I'm sorry. I wanted to tell you, but... I couldn't. For all sorts of reasons. They stopped everything.'

'The stopping,' Felix nods, through impossibly gritted teeth. 'Right.'

'The men in white lab coats.'

Felix jumps up and starts pacing angrily. Oh dear.

'The men in white fucking lab coats,' he growls.

'One bald, the other–'

'A pig-ugly Sherman with crap hair, tons of dandruff and shocking breath.'

I give a little shrug.

'I didn't notice the breath.'

'*Fuuuck!*'

Felix punches the side of the Trav, then screams out in pain, shaking his hand.

'I'm sorry,' I yelp.

'Why? *Why* didn't you fucking tell me?'

'Would it have made any difference?'

'Oh, *Podge!* After everything I've ever told you! Of *course* it would've bloody made a difference!'

He keeps doing this thing: storming over to me, appearing like he's going to punch me, then backing off and stomping to the other end of the Trav. All the veins in his face and neck are bulging and his eyes look like they've been drawn by some twisted graphic novelist.

'So what the fuck did they say?'

'Nothing much. They just ordered me to miss the security check. Told me nothing bad was going to happen.'

He laughs nastily, then whacks the wall again.

'What would you have done if I'd told you?' I ask.

'Oh, never mind what I would've done! Stop trying to wriggle out of it! I'd have done *something*, wouldn't I? Replaced the headliner, shifted up the bill, got George Harrison to fill in... something. I don't know! It's not like people would've asked for their bloody money back, is it? I've told you six million fucking times, it's all about the spotless reputation!'

'I'm sorry... I was scared. Confused.'

I swear I didn't deliberately calculate this to sound like a wounded flower.

'Oh, don't give me the fucking wounded flower,' he snarls. 'You fucked up. Accept it.'

He sits down again and puts his head in his hands. Then he lights a cigarette. I pat my jacket pocket for mine. I've run out. Ah, well, they'll probably reappear when we leave the Trav.

'I knew this was gonna happen,' Felix mutters, as if to himself. 'If I'm really honest, I knew.'

'How?'

He doesn't reply to this, but puts his head back in his hands for a little while longer. Like maybe the next forty-three minutes.

So the Trav goes screaming on towards our most prestigious of destinations. This isn't my first visit to T136. I've been before, on Death Missions with Felix. Most of the rock stars that interest us appear in T136 because for some reason it's ended up being one of the poshest zones. The houses are exactly the same boring shape and size as ours, but they've almost always squeezed a swimming pool into the garden. There are loads of golf courses. The Memory Swapshops are more luxurious because of all the luxurious junk people arrive with. Everything's just a bit... richer, is the only word I can think to use, as befits its formerly rich inhabitants.

But the funny thing is, a lot of its residents hate the place. The Socials and restaurants are really boring and the general levels of excitement plummet beyond even that of T109, and believe me, that's saying something. Lennon himself – the real one – referred to T136 as 'like Bel Air without any of the interesting parts.' Most of our T136 clients end up hanging out in other zones, probably wishing they could move house. It's yet another argument for not accumulating vast wealth back in the real world, because ironically, if you're practically penniless when you die you'll end up living somewhere much more interesting for the rest of eternity.

Anyway, the first time I came here was on a Death Mission for Bee Gee Robin Gibb, i.e. to 'welcome' him here, about two days after he died. That may sound monstrously insensitive, but as Felix says, 'who better to greet a musician upon their arrival in the afterlife than a pushy gig promoter.' Plus, like some twisted version of Happy Families, Felix needs to be on his toes when a second or third member of a band dies (we already had Maurice Gibb on our books) so he can be in with a chance of getting the full set. There are so few complete original bands here thus far, and those we've got – the Jimi Hendrix Experience being the jewel in Felix's crown – are pursued relentlessly by Felix's rivals. The memory of what happened with The Doors is still raw: Felix had befriended Jim Morrison, but when Ray Manzarek arrived, he coincidentally ended up living a few doors down from Bill

Graham in S501. Before we knew it, the pair were out playing shows for Bill as 'Two Doors', and Felix was too furious to speak for about a month.

So, for Robin Gibb's Death Mission we arrived in the early afternoon, jumped on the Local and rode through the gloomy streets. I was struck by how deserted even the shopping district was: a few boring-looking couples strolling along, the occasional car, sometimes a limousine, but the area seemed so lifeless it made T109 look like Notting Hill Carnival. I presumed everyone was at home, glugging Champagne and enjoying Rendering orgies. We passed what looked like a country club and a casino, then the street sloped steeply upwards, curving round a leafy hill. Finally it flattened out to a sunny plateau and the Local stopped outside a standard-issue house overlooking downtown. In the distance I could see some sort of beach-lined lake; quite a few zones have lakes at the end of them, or are they seas? No one seems to know, but reportedly, any attempts to sail to the other side tend to mysteriously wind up back in the same place again.

'Boring, eh?' Felix commented at the view. 'Come on, let's go inside. I'll do the talking.'

He marched off towards the house, a confident vision in a white suit, Hawaiian shirt and a pair of aviator shades. I sported my usual denim jacket, and not wishing to scare the pop star with something too indie-tastic, I wore a red 1970s Coca-Cola T-shirt that I'd picked up in a Swapshop that morning. I lingered nervously at the other end of the little pathway.

'Shouldn't we... um...'

'What?' Felix frowned.

'Be a little tactful?' I suggested.

'Trust me,' he smiled, and strode straight in through the front doorway, which – as usual with new arrivals – was wide open.

I followed Felix through into a plush corridor: stripped, varnished wooden floors, purple wall-coverings, black velvet furniture, platinum discs on the wall, paintings, antique books here and there. Soft music emerged from one of the rooms. Felix took off his shades and peered through a few doors until he came to the lounge. At this point he turned to me and put his finger to his lips. Here, clearly, he had located the Place of Arrival. I caught up with him and looked over his shoulder. This was a large room – via some strange, TARDIS-like distortion of space, it seemed larger than the whole house – with bright walls and one huge window running the entire length of the right-hand side. The soft music – a mixture of a harp and a synthesiser – was apparently emerging from a pair of nameless speakers near the window, and could have been a Brian Eno album entitled *Music for God's Waiting Room*, but as the piece developed I realised it was actually a very loose instrumental arrangement of the Bee Gees' floaty ballad 'I Started A Joke'. In one corner of the room sat a white grand piano and a blue acoustic guitar on a stand. In the opposite corner lurked a transparent screen and a white computer keyboard that appeared to be hovering in mid-air. Nothing at all like my Infonet terminal, I assure you. But most confusingly, the giant windows showed us a view, an apparently endless view of a spotless white beach and a calm sea. Like a dunce, I nearly said out loud, 'But… I thought we were up a hill!' – before Felix turned to me again, and said in a soft voice I'd never heard him use before:

'He's here.'

I must admit it took me a while to see him. I was just about to say – again, like the class thicko – 'Where?', when I realised that the large window was not a window at all, but a completely open, missing wall of the house, and that the beach was actually not a beach, but a bed. An epic, preposterous, eternally-proportioned white bed, with white silk sheets the size of tennis courts and pillows the size, and even the shape, of sand dunes. The calm sea continued to look like an actual calm sea, but there was a clever sort of hazy area where the bed ended and the sea began; it wasn't as if the sheets were getting soggy as the waves lapped against them, which definitely wouldn't have tallied with the soothing vibes. And lying right in the middle of this whole affair was a tanned man with long, lustrous dark hair and a familiar face. He wore… well, I wasn't quite sure what he was wearing. It looked like a long, flowing white gown, but then I couldn't really tell. I decided the bed sheets were part of his bedclothes, and vice versa. He was facing our direction, and his eyes were open, but with an endlessly dreamy expression on his face. He looked like he'd seen us, but he didn't seem worried or surprised by our presence.

'Hello, Robin.'

In any other circumstance I would have laughed. Felix had altered his harsh Camden Town accent to something akin to Hal the talking computer in *2001: A Space Odyssey*. It seemed to be doing the trick, though, so I bit my cheek and watched the whole thing unfold.

'How do you feel?'

Robin Gibb thought about this for a moment. He didn't lift his head from the incredible sand dune pillow, but his eyeballs surveyed the room, then returned to us. Finally he said:

'Good.'

Felix, leaning casually against the doorjamb, nodded slowly.

'I'm glad to hear it.'

It was a scene of endless tranquillity, patience and warmth, as if all the questions Robin Gibb had – and there surely must have been many of them – could be answered in due course. The harp and synth segued seamlessly into another of the band's trippier compositions, and continued in that vein for roughly the next three hours, during which Felix and I stayed with our new associate; talking little, but developing a sort of mutual trust and understanding, strangely similar to that which exists between a baby and its parents. At length Gibb surfaced from his beachy-bed-shoreliney thing, drifted inside, still wrapped in his robey-sheet-combo, and sat himself down on a sofa as soft, inviting and ample as a skyful of fluffy white clouds. Felix served him herbal tea – a drink I was surprised Felix knew existed – from an antique Chinese teapot.

Now contrast this with my own arrival. I woke up on a bare, regular-sized bed in a boring room with just a boring (admittedly quite fluffy) white carpet and a boring window, outside of which I could see a boring tree. There was no soft music, no lapping waves and no white robe, never mind any Earthly comforts or possessions (what I wouldn't have given to arrive with my record collection, for example). I was just wearing a pair of navy underpants. My first thought was that I was still in the hospital, and that someone had stolen all the equipment, all my belongings, all the hospital staff, the hospital bed, the chair Saff had been sitting on, and Saff herself. I gasped, leapt up, screamed, ran into the corridor and screamed again. Then I fainted. We're not supposed to faint, but I bloody well fainted anyway. I collapsed onto the floor and lay there a good long time, eventually coming sort of vaguely to, then carried on lying there, trying to figure out where all the nurses had gone, where Saffy was, why I felt... better, physically speaking, why I was once again capable of sudden, energetic movement, and where this ridiculous beer belly had appeared from. Aside from a brief trip to the bathroom, where I screamed again at the surreal sight of a twenty-something me in the mirror, I remained on the floor of the corridor, freaking out and shaking like a short-circuited Duracell bunny, until Felix, curious at the new house that had materialised next to his, poked his head through the door a couple of days later. I certainly did not get the Hal from *2001* voice, nor the soothing, carefully chosen words, and certainly not the herbal bloody tea. I just got Felix, cackling with laughter and asking, 'You all right down there, mate?'

As Felix and I departed back up Robin Gibb's little pathway to the street, I complained that the newly dead Bee Gee had shown absolutely no signs of panic, confusion or even much curiosity as to the nature of his new surroundings, and wondered aloud, as we jumped on the Local again, why the arse this might be the case.

'Simple,' Felix replied, without hesitation. 'Robin Gibb's been pumped up to his eyeballs with Numbness. You weren't.'

I looked back at him glumly.

'Hey,' he grinned broadly, lighting a cigarette and giving me a friendly whack on the shoulder. 'Fuck it, dude. I know which I'd prefer. Fancy a drink before we return to our proletariat paradise? I know the one decent Social in this thrillsville... They do a cracking margarita and you can sometimes see Princess Di hanging out with Dodi.'

I pondered my wealth of more attractive options.

'Let's do it,' I shrugged.

So now we're outside John Lennon's house and it feels like about midnight, although it's actually only a quarter to ten. Being an urban sort of chap, Lennon's house is right on the edge of downtown, overlooking a park and a small lake: a home from home when he first arrived, in theory, but unlike New York's perpetual bustle the streets of T136 are almost spookily empty. Lennon's managed to get himself an oversized black wrought-iron fence, but this slightly forbidding fortification is purely for appearance; the gate is unlocked. In every other respect the house's exterior is the regular affair. Felix is smoking, limbering up, both mentally and physically. He cracks his knuckles and even starts to stretch his calf muscles as if planning a brisk jog around the park. Even though I am still a one hundred and fifty percent paid-up resident of the Felix doghouse, I risk trying to chill him out a little.

'Take it easy, okay? Even if he's there, none of this might be his fault.'

'Fuck that,' Felix snarls. 'I'm going to tear the bastard apart.'

He flicks his cigarette away and nods curtly at me. It's about as close to 'Are you ready?' as I'm gonna get from him right now. He stomps off towards the door. Thank goodness they don't bother with locks around here, or he'd definitely have kicked his way in.

The interior of the house is strange: it looks like some rich person's urban pad in Shakespearean times, but with touches of 1950s chintz, as if Hyacinth Bucket has moved in with Black Adder: black-timber beams overhead and running along the white walls, some bearing antique china plates and ornaments. Crisscrossed windowpanes with stained-glass trim, patterned but slightly threadbare carpets, flimsy mahogany chairs, prints of old Liverpool city scenes hanging here and there, and a couple of grandfather clocks that tick out of time with each other. Out in the back I can see a swimming pool behind the patio, lit up with old street lanterns. A record is playing somewhere: Bowie's 'Fame', of all things, but the record's stuck at that bit near the end where they're sodding about with the pitch of the vocals; it's rather unsettling.

Felix is standing in the middle of the lounge, scowling at the furniture, the fireplace and then out at the pool.

'Lennon?' he shouts. No reply from anywhere. Just more stuck record. I reflect that if John Lennon were here, he might appreciate his first name being hollered instead.

'John?' I holler.

Nothing.

'Nah, fucking place is deserted,' Felix spits, whipping out his phone. 'Find that record and turn it off, will ya? It's giving me the creeps.'

He flounces back into the hallway and starts to leave another angry voicemail for Malcolm. I dive through a few doors to locate the turntable, soon finding myself in a very elaborately decorated bedroom: thick, ornate curtains, four-poster bed, and a 1970s wood-panelled record player balanced precariously on a round metal stand. I lift the needle off the Bowie vinyl and silence prevails. Apart from Felix.

'... I don't care what you know or don't know, just call me back right now, or I will dedicate the rest of eternity to fucking your poxy little gigs up the arse. Romsey, out.'

Ugh. I hate it when he says 'Romsey, out.' Who does he think he is, Captain Kirk?

I'm just about to leave the bedroom when something catches my eye. There's a guitar lurking nearby, a sunburst acoustic lying face down on the floor, and it's resting on something else. I look a little closer and realise it's another guitar: an electric, a black Rickenbacker. Neither guitar looks like it's been placed down with much care. Instinctively I pick up the acoustic to position it somewhere more sensible, and find a white piece of paper flapping underneath.

'Podge,' Felix shouts from somewhere, 'where you at? We gotta go...'

'Hang on.'

I can't help being a bit nosy. I grab the sheet and study it briefly. You don't tend to find pieces of paper hanging around people's houses like this. It's handwritten: some scribblings, some doodlings, some sentences that don't seem to make much sense. Some are crossed out and then written again underneath, with one or two words changed. It seems to be something about the mind, letting your mind soar, freeing your mind, saying 'No'... and then something else I can't quite read. Fighting, perhaps. Fighting for what is... yours? Ours? Dunno.

'Felix... you'd better come and have a look at this.'

The important bit isn't *what* is written, but that something is written at all. Something that didn't exist before. Something new. Something original.

Felix appears next to me, and blinks at the page I'm holding.

'Judas Priest,' he whispers after half a minute, a cautiously excited look in his eyes. 'He's done it. The old boy's only gone and done it.'

Felix is sitting on the edge of John Lennon's bed, smoking perhaps his one hundred and fortieth cigarette of the day. I can't see any ashtrays, so I assume Lennon himself smokes outside. I feel like pointing this out to Felix, but it's unlikely to go down well.

'This is huge,' Felix says at last, blowing smoke at the window with a little whistle.

I'm well aware of this. I suppose if anyone were going to start doing it, it would be Lennon. It isn't much: half a song, at the very most; assuming he hasn't got reams of other lyrics stashed in a drawer somewhere. But it's a significant development. No one, to our knowledge, has done this. And believe me, we've asked everyone: the most creative minds on our radar. We've asked Syd Barrett, Ian Curtis, Brian Jones and John Barry. We've asked Hendrix, Harrison, Strummer and Morrison. Felix has harangued Lou Reed, Nina Simone, Nick Drake and even Michael Jackson. We've hassled Elliott Smith, Layne Staley and Jeff Buckley. And no one, anywhere, has done this. Not only have they not done it, they've not even expressed an interest in doing it. Not only have they not expressed an interest in doing it, they've become actively hostile at the very proposal. Often when you slip it into a casual conversation, like I did a few years ago while escorting Sandy Denny and Bert Jansch back to the Trav after their excellent set on the Bassey stage, they react as if you've just advised they set fire to their neighbour's house. The suggestion has started arguments, stopped a couple of people from playing the Afterparty, broken up social gatherings. You remember the story of that evening round at Felix's with Amy and Kurt. It was all going perfectly well until Felix's trivial remark that the chords Kurt was jamming sounded good, and like 'something new'. Then suddenly everyone's straight out of there like Felix had dropped a stink bomb. Felix also says he's been warned about it by the lab-coat crew, which I find bloody weird. Typically, when I asked Felix about it, he downplayed it.

'Oh, some hare-brained theory of theirs about keeping things under control. I don't bloody care. If they want people to be bored

shitless until the end of time that's their own problem, I was only trying to help.'

But I often wonder whether their concerns were slightly more
defined. If Felix managed to convince someone – Lennon, just as an
out-of-the-blue example – to start writing new material, and then
figured out a way of actually recording it, even releasing it... well.
Felix would be the man. Even more of the man than he is already.
And I doubt the lab-coat men would be thrilled about that.

Anyway, now his phone's ringing. He whips it out of his pocket
and answers.

'At long fucking last.'

A sullen Scouse voice can be heard on the other end.

'He did *what*?' Felix spits. 'Did you call it back? ... Did you leave
a voicemail? ... Why not? ... There wasn't a *what*? ... Impossible ...
Must be something wrong with your phone ... Well, try it again in
a minute ... Yeah, we're going round there right now ... Nothing
much ... All right ... later ...'

He hangs up and gapes at me.

'Lennon tried to call Harrison. It rang once and then he hung up.'

We stare at each other for a perplexed moment.

'And when George tried to call back, it just went dead.'

'No voicemail?'

'No voicemail.'

We whirl this piece of intelligence around our heads for a moment.
No voicemail. The phone service, like the Trav, is admirably simple.
Everyone has a phone. No one has a number. Just their name. No
phone bill, obviously. But everyone has a voicemail. As with most
things in this place, something breaking, or just plain stopping, takes
on a somewhat deeper meaning.

'No voicemail,' Felix repeats. 'Can you remember the last time that
happened?'

I shake my head. 'Never.'

This is heavy, and baffling. If Lennon was locked in a room somewhere, or if he'd been stopped by our lab-coated chums, his voicemail
would still work. But it doesn't. This is some next-level, rip-in-the-

fabric-of-reality shit. Not that our fabric of reality feels particularly unripped at the best of times.

'Come on,' I tell him. 'To Brian's.'

Felix flicks his spent cigarette onto the carpet.

'Yup,' he nods, jumping up. 'To Brian's.'

He marches out the door. I wait until he's fully departed and pick the butt off the floor. This is John Lennon's bedroom, for goodness sake.

Around here, everyone appears to be the same age. Oh, there's a little bit of room for manoeuvre: Felix, as I mentioned before, looks at least ten years older than I do, but generally speaking everyone looks between their early twenties and early thirties. This makes it harder to read a person from their appearance. On Earth, a human in their eighties has all their years and experiences etched into their face; George Orwell's adage that 'at fifty, everyone has the face he deserves', largely rings true. You can tell a conniving, money-grabbing septuagenarian a mile off, while a kindly, wise old thing's warmheartedness shines out of them like a Ready-Brek glow.

But here, things aren't so straightforward. There's never a face more confusing than a 'full-termer' – our phrase for anyone who's lived life to a decent age, let's say anything over eighty – but who has the hair, eyes and skin of their early-twenties self. We have to rely on other things to decipher what their 'Earth age' is. A few clues come from clothes, cut of hair and so on, but as soon as you start talking to them, it's all about their vocabulary and behaviour. Throw into the mix the era in which they died, and you've got a proper hotchpotch of variables. If I had the time and inclination to study the subject in detail, I'd like to find out who we're statistically more likely to gravitate towards: those who lived as long as we did, or people who died during similar eras? Example: Felix and I were both in our thirties when we died, and he popped off in 1997 and me in 2008, so we're a fairly close match. But if someone died in 2010 aged, say, ninety, would I hit it off with them better than someone who died in 1960, but was my age when they died?

Weirdest of all, unquestionably, are people who died when they were very old, and a long time ago. You don't tend to bump into too many of these. Received wisdom holds that no one in our local zone group was born much earlier than 1930, and no one died much longer ago than 1965. Occasionally, though, you chance upon someone who really is uncommonly old, in both senses. It's a peculiar feeling. There was this guy a few years ago, a handsome-looking chap with Brylcreemed hair and khaki shorts, looking like he'd just stepped out of a British colonial club in Calcutta or somewhere. Why or how he'd ended up in our zones, I've no idea, but he came to the Afterparty and amused us by asking for the volume to be turned down. We politely ignored him, but later we saw him dancing to the Four Tops and he looked so unusual that I couldn't help bowling up for a chat. Fascinating dude: he had the appearance of a top-notch Cary Grant, but there was so much knowledge and so many memories knocking around in his skull, it was almost scary. I enjoyed the idea of this strange mixture: someone from a totally different era, finding themselves among people from a different age, and *of* a different age, but appearing to be the same age. I promised myself that if I ever met a slightly misplaced character like that again, I'd make an effort to hang out with them a bit more.

Be careful what you wish for.

Felix and I are stalking down the lit pathway from John Lennon's front door to his gate, when I hear rustling in the hedge next to the iron fence. We halt.

'What the fuck is that?' Felix muttered.

'Dunno. Like a squirrel or something?'

'A squirrel? Here?'

'All right. Not a squirrel.'

We stay still for a few moments longer, then Felix shrugs.

'Must've been the wind, man.'

I follow Felix onto the quiet street, but he stops in his tracks again. Parked ten or so metres from Lennon's gate is an old car. Actually, it's more of a van. It wasn't there when we arrived. I'm no car expert but it looks British, and maybe from the 1960s. Comfortable curved edges, light-brown wood around the windows. It's too dark to see the colour, but I'd guess it was sort of army green.

After a moment's pause, Felix and I both turn back to the place where we noticed the rustling.

'Oy,' Felix begins. 'Someone in there?'

Whoever or whatever it is doesn't reply.

'Nice car,' he continues to me, in a stage whisper. 'Shall we take it?'

He wanders up to the van and tries the driver's door, which is unlocked.

'Hey!' comes a loud female voice from the bushes. 'Hands off!'

'Ahh,' Felix chuckles. 'There she is. You all right, love?'

'We'll have none of the "love", thank you very much,' says the bush. The bush seems to have an Australian accent.

'Why are you skulking around in there?' Felix asks.

'That's none of your business.'

'Fair enough,' Felix replies, jumping into the driver seat. 'Let's go, Podge.'

'Hoy! Leave my motor alone, you lanky oaf!'

The bush erupts in a flurry of snapping twigs and scattering leaves, and a young woman emerges. She races out of the gate and up to the car, and before I can do much about it she's yanking Felix's arm behind his back and holding a sizeable pistol to his neck. Felix yelps in pain and bursts out laughing at the same time.

'Hey! Easy, easy!'

'Get your bony backside out of my car.'

'All right!' Felix chuckles, disembarking.

There isn't much for me to do but stand here and watch the scene play out. The woman has the gun pressed just below Felix's right ear, and while we know a gun can't do much lasting damage in this neck of the woods, a bullet in the head would certainly be enough to put you out of action for a few hours. So Felix, for now, complies with this strange newcomer. And what an unusual specimen she is: average age, maybe mid-twenties, but she's dressed like some sort of 1940s office worker – long checked skirt, white collared shirt with a sensible, dark wool cardigan and smart shoes. Pale face, scarlet lipstick. Pretty, if you like that kind of thing. Her shoulder-length curly brown hair has been clipped back, except a long strand has come loose, presumably during her exit from the hedge. The giveaway, however, is the pair of horn-rimmed glasses. No one needs to wear glasses, so those that do are either making a fashion statement or trying to appear intelligent.

'Why are you dressed like that?' I find myself saying out loud.

'Less of your cheek, schoolboy,' she snaps. I glance at my blazer. I hadn't clocked the school thing, but fair enough.

'Okay,' Felix says, 'now I'm out of your old banger, you can stop with the whole girl-secret-agent thing.'

She frowns quizzically, but keeps the pistol in place.

'By that,' Felix iterates, 'I mean stop pressing that museum relic into my neck.'

'Not until you tell me what you're doing here.'

'Not a chance, babe.'

'Don't "babe" me, clever-clogs.'

'Fuck's sake, what is this?' spits Felix. 'An episode of *The Famous Five*? And Podge, can you tell me why you're just standing there like a lemon?'

'What do you suggest?'

The woman glances over at me and Felix uses the slight crack in her attention to grab the gun with his left hand. With admirable speed, she knees him in the bollocks and pushes him onto the pavement. Then she stands on one of Felix's legs and keeps the gun pointed straight at his face.

'Make no mistake, drongo, I'm not afraid to use this little blighter. So come on, spill the beans. Why were you in John's house?'

'John?' Felix squints.

'Don't mess with me. You know exactly who I mean.'

'Felix,' I sigh, 'it might be easier if we just tell her.'

'Aha,' she exclaims. 'Felix. So that would be Felix Romsey, I presume.'

Felix glares at me. 'Well done, dick-brain.'

'Not very nice to each other, are you?' she comments, tucking the escaped lock of hair behind her ear. 'Now. First things first. What have you done with John?'

'We haven't done anything with John,' Felix groans.

'Why was he a Rendering?'

'If we knew that, we wouldn't be here.'

'Where is he?'

'Who are you?' Felix asks irritably.

'It's rude to answer a question with another question.'

'Look, are we gonna play this game all night? Who are you?'

She says nothing for a moment, then her gun arm wavers slightly and she takes her foot off Felix's leg.

'Jane,' she replies. 'I'm John's friend.'

'Jane and John,' Felix scoffs. 'Are you having a laugh? What's your real name?'

'Jane,' she insists, stepping back. 'So where is he?'

'Why do you want to know?'

'I'm John's friend,' she repeats, this time with a little break in her voice.

'His friend? Are you sure you don't mean his fan?'

'Has someone taken him?' she croaks, sitting down in her driver's seat doorway. Felix looks over at me and rolls his eyes. Blimey. I didn't know superfans existed around here. I didn't think people quite had the passion for it, or the self-discipline. She exhales sadly and tries to regain her composure, but it's clearly something of a struggle.

'Calm, Jane' she whispers, fanning herself with her non-gun hand. 'Calm.'

'Were you at the gig?' I ask.

'No, of course I wasn't at the gig. I don't go to gigs. I don't like gigs.'

Felix picks himself up from the floor and brushes himself off.

'Well, we'd love to stand around and chat, but we need to crack on. Podge?'

I nod, and we start to walk away.

'Where are you going?' Jane says.

'Never you mind,' Felix grunts. I can already hear the soft whir of a Local approaching from the end of the street.

'But, really!' she pleads, looking at me. 'Just tell me where you're going.'

'Um, just to see someone,' I mutter.

'Brian?'

I blink at her.

'I'm right, aren't I?' she squints. 'You're going to Brian's. Are you going on the Trav?'

'Podge!' yells Felix, one foot in the doorway of the Local.

'Come with me,' Jane says, starting her engine. 'It's quicker in the car.'

'Um... thanks, the Local will be fine...'

'No, I mean all the way to Brian's.'

'But it's not even in this zone!'

'I know it isn't,' she snaps. 'Get in. I'll show you.'

I get into Jane's car mostly out of curiosity. Travelling manually from zone to zone is not something I'm aware of anyone successfully achieving and I wouldn't mind seeing this strange girl have a go, even if it fails. Plus I'm rather tired of Felix being a moody old git and some different company would be welcome, even if she seems more than a little unhinged. Amid much moaning and gnashing of teeth, Felix jumps in the back – literally the back, through the rear van doors. Jane, doing a U-turn, laughs off his complaints.

'Take the Trav if you want. We'll race you. I bet we win.'

I can't remember the last time I rode in a car like this. It's the kind of car my dad had before I was born; he probably drove my mum in it on their first date. The engine sounds warm and reassuringly chunky and I feel like I'm being driven to school. Jane yanks the enormously long gear stick and gets to about fifty up the hill away from Lennon's abode, deftly weaving her way past the occasional Local. We drive on the same straight road, at the same level of incline, for what seems like twenty minutes. The stream of identical houses on each side give no clue as to our progress, the only landmarking features being the adjacent streets and an occasional tree.

'How do you know where you're going?' Felix asks.

'Trust me,' Jane replies.

'I'm gonna give this five minutes. At the very most.'

'Suit yourself, Scrooge.'

'This hill is so long,' I comment, gazing out the window. 'Doesn't it look really weird in daylight?'

'Seen the top of your own road before?' Jane enquires.

I think about this for a second. I've never had much reason to travel further upwards, so I've really no idea where our street goes.

'Um… no, I guess it just vanishes into… some haze.'

'There you go,' she nods. 'Why did you let a Rendering onstage?'

'We didn't,' I reply. 'We had no idea.'

'I thought you fellas had some kind of security device?'

'How do you know that?'

'Because I'm clever.'

'Well, we do, but...'

'Podge forgot to take Lennon through the fucking thing,' comes an irritable voice from behind us.

'Why does he call you Podge?' whispers Jane.

I point ruefully at my beer paunch.

'Charming,' she comments. 'So did the Rendering arrive just before the show?

'Um, no. I picked him up first thing this morning.'

Jane squints at me.

'You mean... you spent the whole day with that *thing*? And you didn't click that it was a Rendering?'

'Er, no. It was... um... a pretty good Rendering.'

'You pair of dimwits.'

'Like you'd have noticed,' Felix grunts, leaning forward and lighting a cigarette. 'Bloody superfans. Always think they know everything.'

'Call me a superfan once more, numbskull, and you get a thick ear. And that' – she turns, snatches the cigarette out of Felix's hand and flicks it out the window – 'isn't allowed.'

'Fuck's sake,' Felix hisses, retreating to the back of the van.

We continue upwards. It's a while now since we've passed a Local, let alone any other cars. But the houses continue. Jane's eyes stare rigidly through her glasses, her wool-clad arms gripping the steering wheel like a pair of clamps.

'Where did you get this van?'

She glances over at me, turns back to the road and waits about half a minute before replying.

'Nice big Memory Swapshop in S235. I had a couple of army uniforms the guy wanted.'

'Where are you from?'

'T116.'

'No, I mean, really.'

She silently keeps her eyes on the road for a moment, then sighs.

'Adelaide.'

'Been here long?'

'Nosy parker, aren't you?'

'Just making conversation.'

'Can I take a wild guess?' Felix asks.

Jane shrugs. 'Whatever makes you happy.'

'Two years. You arrived here two years ago, and you're still giddy with excitement. Hence the fancy dress costume and driving this pedal car around like you're playing a computer game.'

'Ha,' she laughs. 'You're about as wrong as a granny's moustache.'

We drive on for a few moments, then she grins over at me.

'Podgy?'

Felix snorts with laughter but I ignore him. I take a second to assess Jane's clothes, and general manner. It's the specs that throw me.

'Um... well. I'd say you've been here a little while, which is why you know a thing or two. But... not that long. And you're a bit retro, hence the glasses. So... I'd say... similar to Felix, about nineteen, twenty years.'

The hill suddenly gets fractionally steeper and she changes gear.

'Nope. Turns out you're no Holmes and Watson.'

She leans forward and switches on the radio. Crackly music emerges. It's old jazz band stuff, maybe Duke Ellington.

'An Infonet radio in the car?' Felix blinks. 'Who on earth has that?'

'Me,' Jane replies, and turns the volume up. Conversation over.

The houses have now come to an end, and the headlights are illuminating a fine mist. It's something we don't see a whole lot of, mist. The car has naturally slowed, but Jane's still managing to do around thirty-five. Then the slope steepens again, and the mist increases. For someone who's been gliding around flat cityscapes on Locals for the last seven years, I'm finding this moderately hair-raising. I can sense Felix's hair being raised a touch too. Jane changes down to second gear, then turns to us and beams.

'Isn't it lovely to have a nice little drive in the country?'

An even steeper gradient, then even more mist. We now can't see anything out of the front windscreen. Also the road has become as bumpy as a farm track and, what with the hill and the reckless speed at which Jane is still clattering along, it's just a little terrifying. It reminds me of being inside a car wash when I was a kid. Felix would usually be panicking by now, but I actually think he's too shocked to speak. Thankfully the car isn't making any life-threatening axle noises and Jane's grip on the steering wheel seems vice-like as ever, but quite where this is going to end is intriguing to say the least. I now notice that Jane has a strange smile on her face, bordering on the maniacal, and I'm reminded that we know absolutely nothing about this person. She could be bad. She could be *anything*. I'm gripping my seat so hard, my fingernails are almost bursting through the leather. After about half a minute – the point at which I'm just about to ask what sort of infernal amusement park she's really taken us to – we go zooming over a giant speed bump, seeing us properly airborne for a couple of seconds, then we come slamming back down to the ground. The road, at last, starts sloping in the opposite direction. The mist thins, the asphalt smoothens and everything – comparatively – is normal again.

'Gentlemen,' Jane smiles breathlessly, 'welcome to zone T134.'

I sneak a look round at Felix. He's lying flat on the floor of the van. He lifts his head and blinks at me.

'Think I'll take the Trav in future.'

'Nonsense,' Jane replies.

'Can I have a fucking cigarette now?'

'No.'

Once we've descended the hill into the usual identical stream of houses, Jane takes a couple of lefts and a couple of rights and soon we're trundling into T134's downtown, which looks pretty much the same as all the other downtowns. It's just gone 11pm so you could still expect a buzz of people, but the nightlife here in T134 clearly isn't much to shout about. With the accuracy of a satnav, Jane zooms straight up to one of the apartment blocks and parks right outside. She switches off the engine and yanks up the handbrake.

'Here we are, boys.'

We both sit in silence for a few seconds, temporarily too stunned to speak.

'You're welcome.'

I try to say something but it emerges from my mouth as a kind of strained grunt.

'So what now?' Jane asks.

Felix coughs and his voice reappears.

'What now,' he decides, opening the back door, 'is I'm going to finally have my cigarette, then we say thank you very much for the lift, and good night.'

He disembarks and slams the door. An empty Local goes by. I turn to Jane and I'm about to dredge up some sort of half-baked apology when she gives a little sarcastic laugh, jumps out of the car and marches straight through the glass doors of the tower block. I get out too, and watch her go. Felix, smoking and leaning on the car, exhales and shakes his head.

'So, Podge. Any more fuck-ups today? Gonna burn my house down, break my Infonet terminal, erase Suzi from my Rendering machine?'

'Did you know you could drive from zone to zone like that?'

'I wouldn't really call it driving, would you?' Felix counters, moving towards the entrance.

'But did you know you could get from one zone to another... you know... manually?'

'Oh, I heard something from someone once or twice… Look, who cares? Let's grab her before she buggers anything else up.'

'Who do you think she really is?'

He stops and turns to me, with a smirk.

'Podge. Have you got the hots for her?'

'No!'

'You have, you little perv. You're digging her crazy Vera Lynn styles. Wait 'til I tell Saff…'

'Fuck you, Felix.'

'… and the last thing I need is you wimping-out over some colonial sweetheart. We've got a Beatle to find, and we've got exactly' – he glances at his watch – 'ten hours to find him. Got it? Or the After-party becomes a distant, pleasant memory. When we're done, you're welcome to indulge in whatever Aussie-belle fantasies you want, but right now, she's gotta go.'

In truth, it looks like we have little control over this. Jane isn't even diplomatically lingering for a moment in the lobby, but has barged straight into one of the elevators. We dash inside and jump into an adjacent lift, but by the time we emerge on the twelfth floor she's nowhere to be seen. We hurry down the plain, carpeted corridor and up to Brian's door, which is ajar.

'Fuckin'ell,' growls Felix. 'No stopping this mad old bird.'

He goes inside.

'Brian?'

The apartments here are exactly the same layout as the houses: a couple of rooms on either side of the hallway, which then opens out into an open-plan lounge and kitchen. It's like they employed an architect for half an afternoon and then applied the same design to the next billion residences. Brian's been here since the late '60s and, unlike John's rather antiquated style, the interior of his place is all Austin Powers-futurama, coloured plastic fittings, Pop Art and beige leather, like he's bought the entire stock of a vintage home decor shop. An impressive array of black and white pictures adorn the walls of the hallway, some starring Brian's various acts: Gerry and the Pacemakers, Billy J. Kramer, Cilla Black *et al*, but rather a lot featuring Brian himself. His lounge has been reserved for the crown jewels: Beatles paraphernalia. Gold discs, original LP cover art, a poster advert for the band's final show in San Francisco, and umpteen photographs; a superficial scan suggests there are slightly more of Brian with John Lennon than with anyone else: backstage at a gala show, on a plane, by a swimming pool in some sun-drenched holiday resort. Speaking of which, through Brian's sliding glass doors we can see they've managed to squeeze a small pool into the wide balcony, a couple of empty Champagne glasses lingering at the side, and then beyond, a view of... well, not much really. Lots and lots of identical streetlights twinkling in the dark.

'Brian?' Felix shouts again.

'Save your breath, you twerp,' comes Jane's voice from the direction of the bathroom. 'He's here.'

With all the delicacy of a couple of bulldogs, we race back along the corridor to the large bathroom where we're greeted by a scene of almost Shakespearean tragedy: Jane kneeling on the floor, fiddling with a little syringe, while a well-dressed man lies motionless on the floor alongside a sunken, kidney-shaped bath, one of his arms stretched out in front of him, pointing at something. We follow the line of his index finger and realise what he's pointing at. No less than half a foot away from his finger sits the rectangular, black and chrome monstrosity that is a rendering machine. The various lights and dials are all off, and Brian's finger hovers in the region of the reset button. As I study this arrangement for a few seconds I realise that Brian is not, in fact, completely lifeless, but his finger is wavering a little and he emits the occasional quiet little moan.

'What have you done to him?' splutters Felix.

Jane looks up at him, and rolls her eyes.

'You really are thick, aren't you?'

I push past Felix and pull open the rendering machine's chest-freezer-like lid.

'Don't bother,' Jane murmurs. 'There's nothing in there.'

This is true. I slam the lid shut again, then turn to see Jane flicking the syringe a few times. Brian's eyes are open but they're drooping to one side. Jane lifts his head onto her lap, smooths down the skin on his neck, then prongs him with the needle and pushes the stopper. Immediately some proper movement returns to Brian's eyes and his breathing becomes audible. Jane remains on the floor, cradling his head.

'He's waking up,' I state.

'Clever old you.'

'What is that stuff?'

'Life juice,' she deadpans.

'No, really?'

'Even if I knew,' she says, withdrawing the needle, 'I wouldn't tell you.'

Brian coughs a little and sniffs. Jane helps him up to a seated position, leaning him against the machine.

'It's just something I happen to know brings a little life back to these funny old bodies they've got us all trapped in.'

'Where d'you get it?'

'Hang around here for as long as I have, you discover a thing or two. That is,' she sighs, 'if your brain isn't swimming in sludge.'

Brian blinks around him, taking in the room and its new occupants. He looks at Jane, squinting, as if trying to place her.

'Ah... uh...'

'Hello, Brian,' she says quietly.

'Oh... you're... uh...'

'Jane.'

'Oh... yes... Jane...'

'Just relax.'

Brian glances around. He's never seen me before, but he clearly knows Felix.

'Felix... I... I'm sorry...'

Felix just gapes at him.

'I tried... I tried... to...'

'Shhh,' Jane utters, soothingly. 'Take it slowly. No one needs to know anything yet.'

Felix clears his throat.

'I said,' Jane snaps, 'no one needs to know anything yet.'

I whisper to Felix, 'Cigarette?', at which he nods sullenly.

We shuffle out of the bathroom and pad wordlessly into the lounge, then smoke for half a minute, Felix apparently deep in thought. Normally when Felix appears to be deep in thought, he's really smoulder-ing with anger about something. This time it's different.

'Where are we?' he asks, suddenly.

'What do you mean?'

'Seriously. Where are we?'

'Um... Brian Epstein's apartment?'

'No, you berk. I mean, really. Where the fuck are we?'

I consider this for a second.

'Rather a strange time to be asking this.'

'Oh, I'm sorry,' he sneers. 'Could you suggest a better time to be asking this?'

'I... I guess I'm just not used to you asking existential questions.'

'I'm not asking you an existential question. I'm asking a bloody simple, physical question.' He takes a massive drag and fires a plume of smoke at a painted portrait of our host hanging on the wall. 'Lennon's disappeared. We've bumped into some crazy old cow who injects people and knows how to travel from zone to zone in a car. And she mentioned the Numbness.'

'She did?'

'That "brain swimming in sludge" comment?' He mooches across the room and plonks himself down on one of Brian's giant sofas. 'So, all in all, after the evening we've had, I reckon now's the *perfect* time to be asking where we really are.'

'And you mean you've never thought about it before?'

'No, Podge, I don't mean I've never thought about it before. Just... not very much. I try to keep myself busy. How about you?'

'All the time,' I reply. 'From the moment I wake up to the moment I fall asleep. I think about where exactly I am, where exactly Saffy is, how far apart we are, and so on. That's why I sleep, because I'm so bored of thinking about it. And it's definitely the main reason I work for you.'

'Really?'

'Yeah. Fun though it is to hang out with a bunch of dead rock stars.'

Felix nods, pondering this.

'Figured anything out?'

I sigh. 'Not really.'

'Brilliant,' Felix grunts, rolling his eyes.

'Well, no one really knows, do they? Scientists can't be arsed. It's almost impossible without the stars, anyway.'

'The stars?'

'You remember... all the astronomers on Earth did everything in relation to the stars. But there are no stars here, so it's impossible for anyone to calculate. The moon looks and behaves like the moon... although I don't think the lakes have any tide. Do they?'

'You're asking me?'

'Yeah, all right... then there's the sun, which is kind of weird and artificial and there are no seasons. Right?'

Felix nods, his mouth slightly open.

'So,' I continue, 'we're here in all these zones, and the only way we can make sense of those... unless you're some strange Australian with an old car... is with the Travs. They only go up to a certain number, but a load of numbers are missing in the middle, I've no idea why. We've got S zones and T zones, and that's our local zone group. I guess the non-local zones are the other letters, and that's where people from other... eras end up? Other ages? Possibly? Which is a good thing, otherwise people would be swarming off to find da Vinci and Isaac Newton and so on. And I guess some of those old guys would be coming here, strolling around our downtown areas, gaping at the skyscrapers and wondering how the phones worked. Right?'

More nodding.

'So, consequently, no one's got any idea about this... *thing* we're on. How big is it? Is it a planet? Is it a huge disc? Maybe we're inside some giant greenhouse thing? We could be in another dimension, a parallel universe, on the inside a planet with a shitload of air-conditioning... or just a very long way away in a kind of non-galaxy thing.'

Felix remains silent; quite usual for when he's totally confused.

'Then there are the Minus zones.'

'Ah... now, come on, Podge. I've warned you about all that shit.'

'Actually I just said that to wake you up.'

'Don't joke,' he instructs.

'Fair enough. So that's my view, really. Not much of a revelation, I know… but hardly anyone seems bothered. Things might get slightly more interesting when Stephen Hawking shows up, but then again, he might be so happy to get his working body back, he'll probably spend his whole time playing tennis and shagging.'

This was intended to get a laugh, but Felix is plainly not in the mood.

'How about you?' I enquire.

He finishes his cigarette and wipes his mouth with the back of his hand. He stands up and stares out of the window for about a minute with a rarely seen far off look in his eyes.

'I think,' he begins, 'all of this… is just…'

But, maddeningly, that's as far as we get with Felix's theory. Edging around the corner of the corridor with a shell-shocked, broken expression on his face, comes Brian. He shuffles over to the sofa and sits uneasily on the arm, blinking at us, smoothing down his tweed jacket and straightening his dark tie. Lurking behind him is Jane, who cautiously tiptoes over to Brian's dining table and seats herself stiffly on one of the moulded plastic chairs, pulling awkwardly at her skirt.

'So,' Felix says, a little too loudly. 'Feeling a bit better, are you, Brian?'

'Somewhat… thank you,' he replies.

'Have a cigarette,' Felix commands, offering his pack to Brian. Jane winces, but doesn't intervene.

'No, thank you.'

'So,' repeats Felix. 'Can I have some answers now, please Brian?'

'Of course… but first… I should like some coffee.'

'Coffee,' Felix repeats, looking automatically over at me. 'Podge, coffee?'

I get up and plod over in the direction of the kitchen.

'No, no,' Brian says. 'We need to go and… get coffee from downstairs.'

'Downstairs?' Felix says, incredulously.

'Yes,' Brian nods delicately. 'Downstairs. The coffee place.'

Felix widens his eyes and looks frantically around the room for support. Jane and I stare back vacantly at him.

'All right,' he seethes. 'The fucking coffee place it is, then.'

The four of us are sitting in the coffee place. Along with a canoodling couple at an adjacent table and a fidgety man at the Infonet station dressed in construction site overalls (people do end up with the oddest clothing), we're the only customers. I don't know what it is about coffee places around here. The coffee tastes good – which I suppose is the main thing – but it's like they've designed them all to look like old European laundrettes: massive windows, plain, dark, plastic canteen-style benches and tables, all fixed to the tiled floor. Even the coffee machines, dotted all the way along the back wall, are over-sized and seem, incongruously, to make noises like washers and dry-ers. No music plays – which, given most people's appalling Infonet radio selections is perhaps a good thing – and no pictures adorn the walls. Consequently, coffee places are among the least relaxing joints imaginable, although obviously none of us has come here to relax.

I feel like I'm at some really awkward tea party with a bunch of rel-atives who all hate each other. Brian is holding his coffee cup with both hands, taking very small sips, staring down at the table. Jane is rather obsessively stirring an over-frothy mug of hot chocolate. Felix has no drink at all, but is, of course, smoking. I've nailed an espresso and now I'm on my second, and to be honest I'm beginning to feel a little frustrated. Despite my concern for the fate of Mr John Lennon, my mind can't help wandering back to all the stuff I need to do for tomorrow, which is – although it seems strange to think of it right now – another full-length, fully functioning day at the Afterparty. Whitney Houston is headlining so we're having to convert about four dressing rooms into a vast complex for herself, her wardrobe and her entourage. She's got a team of Renderings, mostly male underwear models, with whom she spends much of the afternoon 'reclining' on several four-poster beds, so the whole place needs to be decorated in white silk, with giant candelabra, chandeliers, white mink blankets, the works. Earlier in the day we've got Ian Dury, a last-minute addi-tion after Bon Scott from AC/DC went AWOL.

But none of this comes together on its own. Felix employs – or whatever you want to call it – a large team, but the team has to be constantly motivated, watered, bribed, cajoled and complimented into continuous action. There are only two people who can really do that, and we're both here. I glance at the time. Almost midnight. I wonder how long all this nonsense is going to last. At some point I'll definitely have to raise with Felix the question of me sodding off back to T109, but as I see the fury returning to Felix's eyes while he waits for Brian's great explanation to start, I can tell now is not the moment.

'Ready?' Felix asks.

'Be patient,' Jane says, glaring.

'It's all right,' Brian says delicately. 'It's… it's fine. Felix has a right to know.'

'Thank you,' Felix says, giving Jane a wide, sarcastic smile. We're only a few steps away from them sticking tongues out at each other.

'Could I first have another cup of coffee?'

I can feel Felix desperately fighting the urge to scream and slam his fist into Brian's face. He wins, only just.

'Podge?' Felix whispers, teeth clenched. 'Would you…?'

I traipse over to fetch another coffee, not bothering to offer one to anyone else. While I'm waiting for the drink to pour, I absent-mindedly glance over at the Infonet terminal. Construction-overall man is looking at the betting site, of course. He's trying to decide between Jimmy Carter and Carrie Fisher. He plumps for Carter. This death porn is getting out of hand. That said, I often find myself day-dreaming of the haul I could walk away with if I slapped a large bet on Prince. Not that the contents of Memory Swapshops interest me much.

I take the cup, plonk it in front of Brian and stir in some sugar.

'Oh, thank you… er…'

'Podge,' I shrug.

'Oh. Why do they call you Podge?'

'Because he's a fat bastard,' blares Felix. 'Can we get on with it, now, please?'

Brian takes a fortifying sip and sighs.

'They came… they came yesterday evening, just before mid-night… I had John and Julia round in the afternoon, and we had a swim… and a drink, and… then Julia went home, but John and I sat inside talking until late… quite, quite late… and then he…'

Brian breaks off, sips his coffee, starts sobbing softly. Jane shifts up the bench, putting a comforting arm around him. Felix rubs his hands together tetchily. After a minute, Brian continues.

'He told me that he'd started to make… to make…'

A long pause; longer than Felix can handle.

'New songs?'

Jane looks up, surprised. Brian, horrified. That look. That 'new song' look. Seen it before.

'How did you know?' blurts Brian.

'We just went round his house, saw some song sheets in his bedroom. Continue.'

'He told me he was,' Brian sniffles, 'you know… doing *that*… and I couldn't say what I wanted to say…'

'Which was?'

'That I didn't think it was a good idea, of course… but he was so very enthusiastic and proud of what he'd done… proud that he'd finally done it… after all these years thinking about it, trying to do it, and so on… so I had to go…'

'Go?'

'I just had to get out… out of that room… so I lied and said I needed to fetch something from my bedroom… and… and…'

Tears overcome him once more.

'And then they just arrived, after that?'

'No, no… of course not… but they'd given me the name of someone to call…'

'Sorry,' Felix asks, a dangerous tone in his voice. '*Who* gave you a name?'

'They,' Brian replies. 'They did. But this was years ago. Oh, decades ago. Not long after John arrived.'

Felix stamps his foot and stands up.

'Felix, please… I know this will seem hard to understand, but back then they were different. They were pleasant in those days. They were softer, warmer, more angelic… if you'll forgive the expression… They told me John might need help because of… you know.'

121

'Because of what?'

'Because of how violently he died. That it might fill him with certain... feelings.'

'Dicks,' Felix spits.

'No, really. They seemed to have the best... you know. Intentions. Said if I'm ever concerned about him, I should call them. And... and... I never thought for one moment that I ever would... I suppose I've had my suspicions from time to time that John might have been up to something... when George arrived, for example... but it always came to nothing, thank goodness... so I forgot all about it. But then last night... I just panicked...'

'So you actually *called* those idiots?' Felix shouts.

Brian's voice is practically obliterated by sobs now.

'I... I... I only did it for John's own good... I thought he needed help... and I couldn't... I wouldn't let him...'

'Gimme the name,' Felix snaps, pulling his phone out.

'Chill out, Felix,' I tell him, as firmly as I can manage. 'You wanted Brian to give you some answers? Well, shut up and let him talk.'

Felix hesitates, but then growls loudly and plonks himself back down on the bench. The other occupants of the coffee place have all left in rather a hurry. Brian takes another sip of his drink and somehow pulls himself together.

'Well,' he begins, 'I dialled the name and someone answered but I couldn't hear who it was... I just said, "Please come, please help"... and someone whispered "Yes"... and that was it. So I went back, back to John, and he was sitting with my guitar in his hands and he was... oh, God... he was playing... he was playing one of his new songs... oh, God, please help me...'

'Was it any good?' Felix asks.

Brian gasps.

'No, I mean, seriously,' Felix says, glancing at me and shrugging. 'None of this'll be worth worrying about if the song's as crap as the Frog Chorus.'

'Stop it, you bully!' snaps Jane.

'Oh, get a grip on yourselves,' Felix moans.

Brian pants a little and wipes some tears away with a handkerchief.

'They were here within five minutes. But they were nothing like those nice boys I saw back in '81. These people were... horrible... clinical... cold...'

'White lab coats?' I offer.

'White lab coats,' Brian nods. 'One bald, one...'

'... with shit hair and heaps of dandruff,' completes Felix. 'Okay, we know the guys. Skip the description, what did they do?'

Brian looks out of the window. He looks desperately sad but appears to have temporarily exhausted his supply of tears.

'They appeared in the doorway. John had his back to them, still playing the guitar. I jumped a little with the shock, then I realised who they were and stood up to welcome them inside. I thought they were going to talk to John, but the dark-haired one just sneaked up behind him and held something to his neck, like a staple gun. It clicked, and John was frozen, catatonic. The guitar slipped out of his hands and crashed to the ground.'

I can see Jane's eyes have started to leak a bit, but then she sees me looking, sniffs loudly and sits up straight.

'I screamed at them, but they told me I'd be getting the same if I complained. One of them asked where my rendering machine was. How did they know I had one?'

'They know many things,' I murmured.

'Well, I told them it was in the bathroom, and the black-haired one led John out of the room, leaving me alone with the bald one. And, oh God, he was so horrible. Cold, arrogant. Kept calling me Mr Epstein, which no one's called me in years. I asked him what they thought they were doing, but he refused to answer. All he did was give me a pill, which he ordered me to wash down with some water and then go to bed. I tried to protest, but he reminded me what had happened to John. He said the pill would help me sleep. So I took the pill and he escorted me to the bedroom. I could hear the rendering machine working in the bathroom but I felt more and more sleepy and I hadn't the energy to do anything about it. Then I lay down and was asleep instantly.'

'Crafty bastards,' Felix whispers.

'When did you wake up?' I ask.

'Early,' he says. 'Perhaps seven. I still felt very, very tired, but I wandered into my sitting room and thankfully the men were gone. John was sitting out by the pool, smoking, staring out at the view. I asked him what had happened and he said he couldn't remember anything.'

'This would've been the Rendering talking to you,' I tell him.

Brian eyes me gravely.

'No.'

'It must have been.'

'At the time I didn't know whether it was or wasn't. Whenever I've made Renderings before they just seemed... you know. Fake. Plastic. Good for the afternoon, but not much else. But this seemed just like lovely John... slightly sleepy, shocked, but nonetheless John.'

'And then what?' Felix asks impatiently.

'Well,' Brian says, swallowing another glug of coffee, 'I reminded John he had a show to play, then we hugged goodbye, and off he went. I felt so miserable after that, but by the afternoon I was better, perkier.'

Felix looks over at me ruefully.

'The power of the Numbness,' he whispers.

'What was that?' Brian frowns.

'Nothing.'

'So... all day I kept popping into the bathroom to look at the machine, but I remembered what the bald one said – "If you try to tamper with our work, the same fate shall befall you" – oh, what frightful people they were... I would never, never have called them, had I... had I...'

He looks like he's going to start sobbing again more.

'Brian, stick with it,' I tell him. 'What's the last thing you remember?'

We can see him thinking hard, a painful expression on his face.

'I... I was thinking about going to the festival, but... I don't know... I was filled with a powerful urge to just... stay here, somehow. I had a swim... I had some drinks, I called a friend. I watched some of the show... that nice boy Kurt and that handsome Australian chappie... and I found myself forgetting about everything and just enjoying it... and then during Donna Summer my phone was ringing… I could see that it was George, which I thought was odd… I tried to answer, but I was feeling sleepy again, and I didn't get there in time… I remember finding it hard to move quickly… and then…'

'Then what?' Felix barks.

'That… *thing* came onstage…'

'What thing?'

'I don't know… but it wasn't my John… I knew immediately because… he was wearing different clothes and they'd given him a haircut… the Hamburg haircut and the clothes… you see, when he left here he was in his US Army shirt and his white slacks… and his glasses…'

We're all gazing at Brian now, all our mouths hanging wide open.

'Yes,' Brian nods. 'They'd already taken the Rendering with them. And I knew… I'm sorry, Felix… I couldn't… I just couldn't watch it happen… I had to… I had to turn it off. The rendering machine. I had to turn the damned thing off.'

Felix gapes at us for second, then emits one of his loudest roars and throws his coffee across the room; the cup smashes against the one of the drinks machines. I get up to remonstrate, but he's already stomped out of the building.

Standing there stupidly, I look at my watch again. Quarter past midnight. Honestly. By some distance, this is the most miserable Friday night I've had in years.

'Why is he always so cross?' Jane asks, watching Felix pace up and down the pavement, on his phone again, a near constant plume of smoke steaming above him. Sometimes it's hard to tell if this is from his cigarettes, or simply the anger steaming out of his ears.

'Felix likes being cross,' I reply. 'It's the only thing that keeps him going.'

Jane pads over to the drinks machine and pours herself a little more hot chocolate.

'Well, I learned a long time ago that there's absolutely no point getting cross about anything around here.'

'The Afterparty is a big deal, though.'

Jane takes a little sip and lets out a tiny yelp and a hiccup.

'We work on it all year,' I add.

'Why do you bother?'

'Good question,' I sigh. 'Music, mainly.'

'Why don't you ever get anyone to play some decent music, then?'

I frown at her.

'We're not doing too badly.'

'I've never heard of any of the people.'

'Are you serious? Kurt Cobain? Donna Summer? Whitney Houston? Michael Hutchence from INXS?'

She shakes her head.

'That last one's Australian, even,' I add, hopefully.

'Nope,' she shrugs, swigging the last of her chocolate. 'Ooh, that did the trick.'

'Well… John Lennon's obviously managed to cross your radar.'

'Not on account of his music.'

Now she's foxed me. How can you have heard of John Lennon, but not because of his music? Was she some massive fan of his short stories and sketches? Or maybe she used to be deaf, and just admired his politics?

She crosses the room towards me. It's impressive how perfectly red her lipstick is, even after this whole sorry evening. For the umpteenth time, she fixes the loose strand of dark hair and straightens her glasses. I can't deny that she is very pretty, in a sort of Moneypenny-ish way, but there is something... wrong about her. 'Wrong' is the wrong word. Not right, perhaps. Or rather... it feels like it definitely wouldn't be right to find her attractive. I can't quite put my finger on it.

She stops in front of me and raises her eyebrows.

'Hey. You wanna take a look at something?'

'Um... sure.'

'You gonna be okay here, Brian?'

'Oh, yes, thank you,' he snivels, 'quite all right, thank you...'

I follow Jane as she heads back out of the door onto the quiet street. At least, it would be quiet, if it weren't for Felix shouting '*Fuucck*!!' across the road, and the occasional *clank* as he kicks a lamppost.

'Didn't his mother teach him any manners?' Jane tuts, leading me to where the van is parked. She yanks open the back doors and pulls out an old battered Gladstone bag. 'Get in,' she commands, jumping in the driver's side.

She shuts her door, so I follow suit. I feel a bit peculiar, like we're going to have an illicit snog in a car park on a Saturday night. Jane switches on the van's cabin light, opens the case and starts rifling through a large stack of paper. More paper than I've seen in a long time. Like I said, you don't see a lot of paper around here. All of this paper is covered with scribblings, little pictures, diagrams and – astonishingly – what look very much like maps.

'What's all that?'

'Things you don't deserve to see,' she mutters. 'Practically a lifetime's work. Maybe two lifetimes.'

She continues to scrabble through her arcane filing system and I notice for the first time that – unlike her close-to-immaculate hair, face and clothes – her fingernails are a right state. Bitten and a little bit dirty, with some untidy flecks of variously-coloured nail polish lingering here and there. Also, now I realise, the fingers themselves are most peculiar: knobbly and a bit twisted, with more wrinkles than I've seen on anyone recently. They look like they belong to a different, and far older, person.

Jane notices me studying her and stops rifling for a second.

'What?' she says.

'Nothing.'

A few more minutes of frantic searching and she pulls out a single sheet of paper and holds it up to the light. She takes off her specs for a second and squints at it.

'Do you really need those glasses?'

'Never mind,' she snaps. 'Now. You were quite impressed with my zone-to-zone antics earlier, weren't you?'

'Um... well, I...'

'I heard you. I'm not deaf. You and old spivvy-face had a right yack about it while I was in the bathroom with Brian. So... where to begin. Did you know that almost half the journeys you take on that clunky old rust-bucket are twice as long as they should be?'

'The Trav?'

'Got it, Poirot. Your journey earlier tonight, for example. T109 to T136. Takes almost an hour. You probably think it's some crazy distance, like a flight across the whole wide world, which the wonderful Trav lets you accomplish in record time. Well, it ain't. Look at this.'

She shows me the piece of paper, which on closer inspection is one of those squared sheets we used in maths class for doing graphs. Drawn on it is a complex diagram of figures, arrows, single lines, double lines and large black dots. After studying it for a few seconds I begin to recognise some of the numbers.

'Okay,' she says. 'You ever wondered why some zones are S and some are T?'

'Um... not much...'

'Well, allow me. All the zone groups are pairs of letters... A and B... C and D... and so on. The pair that we can access is S and T. So... in T you've got all these numbers, all the usual numbers, from 023 to 829, and they're all linked in this criss-cross pattern like this. See? Some of them, like this... look here... T136 and T134, where we are now... they're linked by this tiny arrow here, which means they're physically next door to each other. But this black dot is where the Trav goes, so you take a Trav from T134 to T136 and they've got you going all the way round here... see these lines going round the edge, all the way round, all the way round, so it takes about half an hour. Same goes for the journey you took earlier, from T109, all the way over here' – she points at a little mark in the corner of the page – 'and then all the way over here to T136… that's a long way, right? But it's actually linked by this double line here, which is like a passage, or a tunnel sort of thing. So you can drive there. All you do is go from T109 to T110, on land, like we did before, then up a certain hill, which I've detailed on this page right… here! Look, it's a list of all the access points from T100 to T119… Now, where were we? Oh yes, right here, you get yourself up this hill, then into this passageway and it zooms behind all these other zones, T115, T119, T129, all the way over here to T136. Takes about fifteen minutes.'

I blink at her.

'You think you can drive from T109 to T136 in fifteen minutes?'

'I don't think you can, I *know* you can. I've done it.'

I blink at her a little more. She's smiling broadly at me, with the same sort of borderline-crazy smile as when we reached the brow of that inter-zone hill earlier. I toy with the idea of leaping out the car and dashing off, but then she starts yapping again.

'But wait… that's not what I wanted to show you. Look. Some of these passageways, when you get to a certain point in the slope, like the one we went up before… there's a turning, and these are the tunnels… or chutes, really… which take you to another level. So far I've only discovered one or two of these. One is between T487 and T341, and the other is' – she rummages through a few more papers – 'oops, sorry, can't find it, doesn't matter right now. But it's there. And we suspect there are more. They'll take you between T and S… basically they're chutes to different levels… physical levels. S and T.'

'Um…'

'S and T hang together, like all the pairs of letters. S is on the top, T on the… actually, it doesn't matter. They're like two halves of a circle. One's underneath the other, depending on where you're looking from. I guess because I started out in T, I think of T as being on top, and S underneath.'

'All of it?'

'The whole jolly thing. Although you'd never ever know that just by clanging about on the Trav the whole time. Anyway, like I said, I've only discovered two of these chutes, and it took me about thirty years to find the first one, and the second I found by accident, so…'

'Thirty years?' I exclaim.

'Yep.'

'How long have you actually been here?'

'Long enough.'

'And how have you managed to do all this' – I'm struggling to think of a word that won't be rude – 'um… this *detective* stuff… without being bothered by the–'

'Men in white lab coats? They ignore me.'

'Why?'

'Because I'm a girl,' she shrugs, still smiling.

'Ah.'

'There's nothing they really want from me, so they leave me be. Oh, I've had a few little run-ins with them over the years, though.'

I fix her with a curious look.

'How many years *is* that, exactly?'

'Why are you so obsessed with how long I've been here? It's not important. What's important is this.'

She thrusts a scribble-packed piece of paper under my nose.

'Look. Have you ever noticed that all the numbers you can't go to in T are all the numbers you *can* go to in S?'

'Um… what?'

'Have you ever been to S109?'

'Um… no, I don't think…'

'Cos the Trav doesn't go there. At the same time… well, you're a swinging sort of hipster fella, aren't you. I bet you like hanging out in S751, right?'

'Um, sometimes, yeah…'

'Groovy. Now, how about T751?'

'What?'

'You wanna go hang out in T751?'

'Can't say I've heard of the place.'

'Exactly.'

'All right,' I respond, shifting uncomfortably in my seat. 'So those are the missing zones. What's the relevance?'

'What's the relevance?' she hoots. 'Don't you get it?'

I shake my head.

'The relevance is… they're there! Those zones are there! You can't get to them on the Trav, but that doesn't mean they aren't there. And the connections' – she frantically grabs another piece of paper from the depths of her briefcase and thrusts it in front of me – 'are exactly the same in S as they are in T. I tested that out… wow, look at the date on that, 1976.'

She keeps dates. No one keeps dates. This is getting crazier.

'So,' she continues, 'if T134 is right next to T136, then it follows that S134 will be right next to S136.'

'I'm lost. You're talking about… getting outside of our local zone group?'

'No, dimbo, I already told you… outside our local zone group is the other letters, like P and K and whatnot. None of my lot have ever been there. I don't even know where they are. What I'm talking about now… are the missing zones, or as we prefer to call them, the "Minus" zones.'

A shiver runs down my spine and I reflexively check the car's side mirrors to see if Felix isn't hovering nearby.

'Shh, don't say that! Are you nuts?'

'What?' she frowns.

'Just… be careful not to say that in front of Felix.'

'Oh, boo and sucks to *him*,' she laughs, as loud as a foghorn. 'So, if you wanna go down to S487, you go down this long chute. It's long and steep and you don't even need to have the engine running, you can just freewheel, takes about ten minutes to get down there. Getting back is a right job.'

'Hold on,' I say, holding up my hand. 'Just bloody *stop* for a moment. I can't keep up.'

'Sorry.'

'You're trying to tell me… if I've understood any of your gibberish… that you've *been* to a Minus zone?'

'No,' she replies.

Ah, a nice warm feeling of relief.

'But my friend has.'

The nice warm feeling goes away again.

'Your friend?'

'Absolutely,' she replies, with a broad grin. 'I belong to a little society. We call ourselves the Curious. We meet every so often... once a year or so. In secret, of course. There's a girl there called Adeline who's been here even longer than I have. If you think I'm a bit crazy, wow. Meet her.'

'And she's been to a Minus zone?'

'Yup!'

'And what... what was down there?'

'Oh, it was horrific,' she smiles, as if discussing the food at a garden party.

'Um... in what... in what way?'

'Well, she didn't stay long, put it that way. It's a bad place.'

I blink at her. I so powerfully want to believe that she's talking out of her backside, but... it's weird. There's something horrifically plausible about her delivery. Or maybe it's delightfully improbable, I can't quite work out which.

'So,' I begin, carefully, 'the Minus zones are inhabited by...'

'Yup,' she nods vigorously. 'Bad people.'

I'd really like to sit in silence and think about this for a moment, but she takes a breath, brandishes yet another sheet of paper and rattles on.

'Anyway, the lucky thing is, T487 is just a short hop from here, and we know that T487 is linked very neatly to T109 by this little back route, down the side behind T300, T200, T168 and T142. And therefore, if my calculations are correct, the same should follow once we're in S. We descend the chute and we should be able to turn right and get to S109 within, ooh, about twenty minutes.'

'Sorry,' I frown. ' "We"? What on earth do you mean?'

She gives a little apologetic smile and shrugs.

'We're gonna have to go there.'

'Why?'

'Because that's where they've taken John.'

I so badly want to forget about this whole ridiculous business and head back to my dull little zone where I belong and continue my boring eternity being a bit miserable and a bit confused but generally okay and free from totally mad stuff. There is a look on Jane's face – eyebrows raised, eyes wide, mouth a little open and slightly curved into a smile – which Saffy used to give me when she'd just proposed some ridiculous domestic upheaval, such as the time she suggested swapping our entire lounge with our entire bedroom 'because the feng-shui is better.' She always got her way in these situations, but then regretted it a couple of months later when practical considerations like the TV socket being in the wrong room began to irritate. Looking in Jane's eyes now, I can tell I'm supposed to instantly say, 'Oh, fine! Great! Let's do it!' But I can't. In fact, I can't stay in this clunky old car with her for a moment longer. It has to be a fairly extreme situation that makes me go running back to Felix for some sanity, but this is one of them.

I wordlessly let myself out and bolt for it, run down the pavement and back into the coffee place where Brian sits with his head in his hands and Felix on the other side of the table, hammering a text message into his phone. He does look a bit calmer though, somehow more thoughtful.

'Let's go,' I tell him, without preamble.

'Eh?'

'I wanna get out of here. This is nuts. Let's just go back to 109 and get on with tomorrow's Afterparty.'

'Tomorrow's Afterparty?'

'Yes, Felix. Tomorrow's Afterparty.'

'What makes you sure there's even gonna be a tomorrow's Afterparty?'

'Of course there's going to be a tomorrow's Afterparty! Are you mad?'

'Nah. Word gets around. The most anticipated act in the Afterparty's history was a Rendering. We're practically finished, unless we return with Lennon.'

'Oh, who cares about *Lennon?*' I snap at him.

'I do.'

'Well, I don't!'

'Why are *you* getting so bloody spiky about this?'

'That nutty girl,' I reply. 'You wouldn't believe the shit she was coming out with just now. Come on, I'll tell you about it on the way home.'

'No.'

'Well, I'm going. You can do what you like.'

'No,' repeats Felix. 'I need you here.'

'What for?'

'Ideas. Back up. Communicating properly with Jane.'

I look questioningly at him.

'She knows something,' he shrugs. 'I hate to admit it. I've been here nineteen years, Podge, and no one normal has ever mentioned the Numbness like she did. Sorry. That means something. Plus, I've just been–'

'She thinks they've taken Lennon to the Minus zones,' I announce, flatly.

Felix blinks back at me. I suppose there are various responses I might be expecting. The one I'd most like is: 'Yep, she's a complete headcase, let's go.' I'd settle for: 'Um, I don't think she's quite right about that', or: 'I'd like to see full documentary evidence for her theory, after which I'll make a considered decision as to her bonkersness.'

But I'm very, *very* definitely not expecting him to say what he really does say.

'So do I.'

Going on a mission ain't what it used to be. Back in the real world, you prepare for it. You have a decent night's sleep. You set your alarm clock. You wear the right clothes. You pack some refreshments: fruit, sandwiches, crisps, chocolate, water. You make sure the car is full of petrol and you have a decent breakfast and a cup of coffee. You check that you've remembered an umbrella and/or some sunglasses; that your phone is fully charged; that you've got some decent CDs and that everyone's used the loo.

Not here.

Here, you just *go*. It can be any time of day or night. You just decide to go, and leave immediately. Similar to my slight pang of regret that the Trav is so endlessly instant and user-friendly, I some- times miss getting ready for a trip. To any announcement of a sudden departure I have a sort of knee-jerk reaction that I'll need to do some- thing before we go, but of course I end up just standing there, usu- ally with Felix shouting at me, 'What? What? Let's get the fuck outta here!'

As in this case. Actually, we did have one thing to do before leav- ing, and that was escort the mess of tears and shakiness that is Brian Epstein back to his apartment, but after that we simply piled into Jane's knockabout vehicle: me in the back this time, Felix riding shot- gun, reflecting his renewed – and slightly irritating – status as the Man In Charge. So, with a few grumblings, another terse instruc- tion not to smoke in the car and another brutal sounding yank of the ancient handbrake, off we go.

And what, you must quite reasonably be wondering, is the theory?

Well, it hangs on many, many complex bits and pieces. Some of these I already knew, others most certainly not. To explain in any kind of a fathomable fashion, we have to go back – as you quite often do, when trying to understand Felix – to Camden Town.

At school with Felix was an abrasive character by the name of Ben- jamin Mulnick, who Felix described as possessing 'heaps of front, but no back'. School being school, Felix started to call him 'Benny Bumlick', and a sworn enemyhood was forged. This being the second half of the 1970s, a lot of the more rebellious types became involved with the great punk boom, and if you couldn't actually play the music, you did something else, which is why Felix ended up promoting gigs. Unfortunately, so did Mulnick. Felix promoted a load of bands in north London, Mulnick in the south, and whenever they rubbed up against each other, which happened frequently, it was bad. To give two fairly minor examples, Felix arranged a massive, unfixable power-cut to occur in the middle of one of Mulnick's all-day gigs in the early '80s, featuring names as big as Echo & The Bunnymen and The Cure. To return the favour, Benny diverted a few truckloads of staging and backline equipment to a different county when Felix organised an outdoor show headlined by Simple Minds in 1984. All highly sophisticated, clash-of-the-promoting-titans stuff. But this rivalry turned nastier towards the late '80s when both of them began promoting acid-house events. Felix laid on a massive-such night in Bristol, and the story goes that Mulnick planted a load of stolen drugs backstage and then anonymously called the police. Not only was Felix's event shut down, but Felix was fined, bankrupted and briefly jailed. Upon leaving prison, he received an early visit by the gang of dealers from whom Mulnick had pinched the gear. Felix was in hospital for several weeks, after which – in a rare display of good sense – he resisted the temptation to retaliate. Felix's fortunes managed to recover, but Mulnick's activities became more and more desperate as the '90s broke. By the Britpop era, Mulnick was less music impresario and more out-and-out criminal, organising made-to-look-accidental house fires for crooked landlords and full-on gang murders. He was jailed for sexual assault in 1995, and was found dead in a Camberwell flat shortly after his release a few years later.

Much of this I already knew. But I had no idea Felix suspected their merry rivalry would, given half a chance, someday rear its ugly head again.

'What gave you that idea?' I ask, as Jane speeds us towards some distant hill and, I assume, inter-zonal access point.

'A feeling,' Felix says. 'But now I bloody know it for sure.'

'How?'

'Because I just spoke to Malcolm.'

'Oh, don't tell me. He's part of the grand plot?'

'No. But he had a visit from the lab-coated twats too.'

'When?'

'Two weeks ago. He said they'd asked if he knew someone called Benny Bumlick.'

'And?'

'Well, it's not the first time they've mentioned him. That dandruff-ridden Sherman once signed off a meeting of ours with, "Benny Bumlick says hi, by the way." '

'That doesn't mean anything.'

'Of course it does, man! Where d'you think they got that name from?'

'Oh, I don't know… Whatever system they've got in whatever zone Bumlick's ended up in. He must be somewhere, mustn't he?'

'Yeah, of course he's *somewhere*, Podge. But the point is… they couldn't possibly make the connection, unless they'd been talking to Benny himself. And anyhow, they wouldn't know him by that name.'

'Oh, for Heaven's sake.'

'Podge, seriously,' Felix says, turning and looking at me with his infuriating I'm-trying-to-calm-you-down face. 'They only know real names. Not the nicknames. Did they call you "Podge"?'

'Can't remember.'

'Bet they didn't. They didn't call me "Felix" at the start either… they called me Leonard.'

'Your real name is Leonard?' asks Jane.

'Yeah, Felix is just my middle name,' he shrugs.

'Wow,' Jane beams. 'My old cat was called Leonard.'

'Look,' I snap, 'we're wandering from the point here. Those lab-coat men know loads. They knew where I went to university, Saffy's surname, the works. If you think they couldn't find out something as simple as your school nickname for Benjamin Mulnick, you're insane.'

'But they have limits,' Jane says.

'That's true,' Felix nods.

I turn to the back of the van and take a deep breath, smouldering with fury. I can't bloody believe how quickly Felix has gone from finding Jane really annoying to thinking she's the bloody oracle. And now I'm supposed to accept any outlandish bollocks they hurl in my direction. Like the concept of Benny Bumlick languishing somewhere in the Minus zones. Until about half an hour ago the Minus zones, to me, were like something you scared children with at bedtime. Oh, I suppose I had half a notion that some place probably existed where Hitler could be seen drinking schnapps and playing knock-out whist with Pol Pot, but now everyone – well, everyone being Felix and Jane – is calmly telling me the Minus zones are as much a solid part of our reality as the asphalt on the ground or the metal in the Trav. Felix admits, a bit weakly, that he preferred not to discuss them because he'd always been afraid of the very idea of the Minus zones.

'Why?'

'Just a feeling,' he replies. 'Can't explain it, really. Sort of a… morbid curiosity, really… wondering who might be down there.'

'Like who?'

'People.'

'Which people?'

'People I knew.'

'Like Mulnick?'

'Yeah… and others.'

He drives me bonkers when he's this vague.

The other factor I'm totally bamboozled by – but which Felix, again, is now justifying as the most normal thing in the universe – is why our lab-coated friends would choose to help some frightful, malevolent dickhead resume his music promotion career in a place stuffed with scumbags? I mean, who's he going to be putting on shows for? Jack the Ripper? Harold Shipman? Even less believable is that they'd facilitate a pathetic game of tit-for-tat against someone like Felix: who, despite his shortcomings, is a hard-working public figure who actually does a small amount of good, providing entertainment in this dull place.

'Simple,' Felix says. 'They hate me.'

'And they like *him?*'

'Who knows.'

'These lab-coated beings are not pleasant,' Jane explains. 'They used to be nice. Now they're not. They're scheming. Unhelpful. Sly.'

'When did they change?'

'A while back,' Jane says. 'I don't know why. Something must have happened to make them more… tricky.'

Once again I'm tempted to ask Jane how long she's been here, but I think another truth-dodging answer would irritate me, frankly. We drive on – a few much-needed moments of blissful silence – and once again I can feel the hill inclining steeply. A flurry of butterflies rushes into my stomach. We're not supposed to get butterflies in our stomachs, but I damn well get them anyway.

'This is nuts,' I exhale. 'We're going to just show up in a random Minus zone and see what we find?'

'Don't worry your little head,' Jane replies. 'I do have a plan, you know.'

'Which is?'

'They like their symmetry here, don't they? So… using that logic… if they decided T109 was the place to hold your festival, it might just follow that in the Minus zones they chose S109.'

'Hold on,' I say. 'The Afterparty is only held in T109 because that's where Felix is.'

'Well,' responds Jane, patiently, 'you're half right. Actually it's the other way round. They put Felix in T109 because that's where they'd decided to have the Afterparty.'

I glance frantically at Felix, who I'm quite surprised hasn't already leapt in to call bullshit.

'Um… sorry… the Afterparty was Felix's idea!'

And that's when Felix turns round, with a very-rarely-seen guilty look on his face.

'No, it wasn't, Podge. It was theirs.'

In 1990s Britain, you had to get a prescription from a doctor for the morning-after contraceptive pill. No regular doctors being open at the weekend, a Friday night 'accident' meant a trip to a hospital emergency unit on the Saturday morning. Funnily enough – and obviously that's just an expression because it was one of the least funny experiences imaginable – the very first night I ever spent with Saffy resulted in such a mishap. And I remember thinking, on that rainy Saturday morning: this time yesterday I was on my own, having been on my own for a few years, sleeping alone, waking up alone, mooching about on my own, often going to the cinema on my own, sometimes drinking on my own; but perfectly happy, all things considered. And twenty-four hours later, I'm sitting on a hard green plastic chair, fixed to a hard linoleum floor, during the third hour of my wait in the casualty department at St George's Hospital in Tooting, while a strange red-haired young lady reclines with her head in my lap. I remember gazing at her as she rested – her lightly tanned skin, her freckles, the way her hair turned from red to golden as it reached the back of her neck – asking myself, as Talking Heads suggested, how on earth did I get there?

Well, similarly, this morning I woke up, expecting the day to hold nothing more dramatic for me than meeting a massively famous rock star and escorting him to our festival. But no. I'm now being trundled up a hill in a sixty-year-old minivan, driven by an increasingly peculiar, era-less woman, on the way to a place I hitherto only thought existed in the realms of myth. Felix is with me, of course, but he's hardly a calming presence at the calmest of times, especially now he's revealed himself to be the concealer of several key truths, not least the origin of the Afterparty.

Does it matter? Yes, it does. I suppose I'd never come out and directly asked him whose idea it was in the first place, but his relentless pride in the thing suggests it's his own baby, rather than him fulfilling some contractual obligation. He also continually paints the picture of the Afterparty being this grand act of rebellion, uttering boisterous sentences like, 'they don't want me to do this, but that's their tough shit', followed by his familiar coda that the whole thing has become so popular, 'they' have no choice but to help him out. And this vibe has informed our entire partnership: the feeling that we're colluding towards something invigoratingly mutinous. But now I know it is, in fact, anything but – I can't help feeling a bit swindled.

'But dude,' Felix insists. 'You've been working for me long enough. Have you never wondered where I get all the stuff from? The stuff for the Afterparty? The equipment, the staging, all that? You think I swap it all at Memory Swapshops?'

'Never really occurred to me. I guess I just assumed it all sort of... appeared.'

'Yeah, that's what happens *in the end*. But someone's gotta make it happen, innit?'

'I'm confused. If it's all their own plan, then why are they suddenly bursting the bubble?'

'It was their idea to put it on,' Felix explains, 'never that it would get this big. They just wanted a couple of quiet little concerts, to give people something to do. Now it's huge, and they're nervous.'

What Felix might really mean is: 'Now *I'm* huge, and they're nervous.' And I must admit an air of megalomania has surrounded Felix recently, and it's becoming a bit much. Perhaps it really wouldn't be such a terrible idea to take him down a peg or two.

We've crossed several zones in the course of all this debating, Jane as usual hammering the van up the hills until it creaks and crawls, then charging down the other side. She's been chattering throughout, but now her incessant jabber has thinned a bit as we approach the no man's land between T487 and T341. As usual, the houses have stopped, the hill is getting crazy-steep and there's a thin layer of fog.

'Spooky,' Jane says.

'Even the fourth time?' I ask.

'Just knowing it's nearby,' she says in a mysterious voice, leaning forward and peering at the darkness in front of her.

'What?'

'The chute.'

She looks back at me strangely through the gloomy light, and I have the bizarre notion that in the last few seconds her eyes have actually become a little bigger: wider, deeper. Sensory overload. I used to suffer from it after staying up for a few days on the trot back at Glastonbury, when Saffy's face would turn into a dripping zombie in the stone circle half-light. I've never seen it happen here, though, until now. I flash a glance at Jane's hands, and rather wish I hadn't: they now look even more mangled and lumpy than they did earlier, like they've been attacked by arthritis or, worse, leprosy. Just as I realise I've been staring too long, Jane reaches down and turns her radio up. It only seems to be churning out the one record, *Now That's What I Call Jazz & Big Band Classics* or something, and right now we're on Glenn Miller doing 'Pennsylvania 6-5000', sounding even more frantic and unruly than usual; the higher up we drive, the faster the music sounds. I'm forced to grip the seat in front of me as I've no seat of my own and no seat belt to hold me in place. Alarmingly, the road now seems to be flanked on either side by walls of some description, and I realise with a shudder that we're probably inside one of the tunnels Jane described before. Holy shit, this record is now stupidly fast, as if it's skipped 45 and 78rpm and is heading straight for 100. Just when I think it can't get any weirder, Jane changes up to first gear and emits a funny sort of moaning, which first makes me wonder whether she's attempting to sing along with the radio, but then she ups an octave and starts wailing. She still has that ridiculous smile on her face, as if she's experiencing some sort of driving ecstasy, and her eyes are now so huge she looks like a Manga character. I daren't look at her hands again. Felix leans forward and places his head between his knees, so I follow his lead and do the same, partly to block out all this batshit crazy racket. Then, with an almighty metallic crunch, we lurch rightwards, and the descent begins. The floor of the car is slamming into the bumpy ground; I'm terrified it's going to disintegrate and I'm going to get flattened into the tunnel wall and – worse still – left behind. We've accelerated, it feels like we're up to around sixty, but oddly the music is now slowing. It skips past normal speed and starts to elongate all its notes to a grotesque degree; the Glenn Miller chaps were singing '6-5-oh-oh-oh...' – but the final '*ohhh*' stretches out, continuing indeterminately as we race down the chute with sphincter-loosening velocity. Now the '*ohhh*' is morphing into something else… a different voice, a slowed down voice, and the '*ohhh*' becomes a deep-throated '*oohhhhd… fell dooowwn on maaahh kneeees…. Ahhh went to the crosssroooaad… fell down on maaahhh kneeees…*' I risk taking a look upwards and I can see light; light shining through the walls of the tunnel, the same sort of refracted light as when someone's shining a torch through their fingers, a bit of red, a bit of orange, and then a yellow glow in the middle… but then I must be hallucinating as the whole thing changes into a face… the face of a man who, incredibly, appears to be singing the warped song we're hearing… a cheeky-looking impish face… an old fashioned hat on his head… what the fuck, is this Robert bloody Johnson? And is he actually trying to burst through the windscreen? We've been looking for this guy for years… Felix scoured the local zone group for any sign of him… and now we find him *HERE*? '*Ahhh belieeeeve to maaahh soooul, nowwww… pooooor Bob is sinking doooowwwwwwwwwwwwwwwwwnnn…*' His face twists into hysterical laughter, all the red bits become blue, then all the yellow bits turns to white, and the white spreads and engulfs the orange and the blue bits, then the red bit, until it's all just white, and then white and the white, but if white, white or white

Minus

We wake up lying in a ditch. It's daylight, although a quick glance at my watch tells me it's supposed to be 2.30am. We're in some kind of sandy, dirty trench, about ten metres wide, seven or eight metres deep, with scrubby weeds and what looks like an electricity cable running down the centre. Random pebbles and clumps of granite are scattered here and there, but the first sign of anything more profoundly unusual is the worm. A little grey worm, about three feet away from my face as I open my eyes. It's wriggling around, darting into the earth, darting back out again. This is strange. There are no animals in our zones, unless you count the humans. The worm has a little face, and I realise it's actually more of a snake than a worm. But it's tiny, about the length of my little finger, and only a couple of millimetres thick. I stare at it for a few seconds, and it stares back. It looks friendly enough. Then I spot another one. And another. All things being equal, I think I'd prefer to be standing up. So I stand up.

Wow. It feels like someone's replaced all the blood in my body with burnt treacle. A couple of the worms drop off me. Yuck. I think my head might have hit a rock or something, as I can feel a pain in my temple such as I haven't felt in... I don't really want to know how long. I took strong painkillers for the last year of my life, so a good while before that, at least. But my limbs work, which is something. I've got grit in my eyes and I'm covered in so much dust, it's as if I've recently completed a paint-sanding job on someone's entire house. All of which is mildly uncomfortable and moderately surprising, but I can probably deal with it. What I might not be able to deal with, and is certainly very surprising and extremely uncomfortable, is the sun, directly above me in a television-studio-bright white sky, baking hot and burning the shit out of my face. There's a sheen of sweat on my forehead, drips of hot salty water running down my nose, cheeks and into my eyes, drenching my entire body. But by complete, extraordinary contrast, inside my mouth and throat there's a dryness and a... what's the word? Wanting? Yearning? Um... a hunger? A hunger for liquid? What do you call that again?

Oh, yeah.

Thirst.

Holy shit, what a thirst. This is thirst the like of which I haven't felt since... Oh, look, you get the picture. It's not just my throat, it seems to be everything inside me, my entire respiratory and digestive system and even my extremities, suddenly all feeling witheringly and shockingly free from any moisture whatsoever, as if I only exist in powdered form, like one of those meals I saw astronauts eating on *Blue Peter*. My pounding head feels like it's going to explode if I don't get any water within the next twelve seconds. Twelve seconds pass and I don't get any water. *Christ*. I wonder if the others feel the same? Maybe not, or Felix would already have–

'Bugger me,' comes a gravelly voice from further down the ditch. 'Did anyone bring a bloody bottle of water?'

22

'Fiddlesticks,' Jane rasps, somewhere behind me. 'Water. I knew I'd forgotten something.'

'Perfect,' I hear Felix grunt. 'Just perfect.'

Jane is standing a few feet behind me, coughing, dusting herself off, shaking the sand (and a few worms) out of her hair. Felix is kneeling a few metres in front, retching a little, while pointlessly trying to tidy his hair. He's similarly dusty and dirty, but more alarming is what I see when he finally stands up.

'Shit, Felix!' I exclaim. 'Your scar!'

'What about my scar?' he frowns, looking down at his chest. 'Ah, fuck!'

The previously clean, round blemish above his right nipple has transformed itself into a bloody gash, like someone's squeezed a giant's zit and it's gone rather horribly wrong. There's a big smear of blood on his shirt, and the whole thing – still being rather sarcastically pointed out by Cupid's arrow – is showing no sign of drying or healing. We don't see this sort of wound very often. I look away, then look back a few moments later, and it still hasn't healed. In our zone, unless someone had literally chopped off Felix's entire arm, it would have totally cleared up by now. Felix dabs it rather uselessly with his shirt, but merely succeeds in making another bloody smear.

'Does it hurt?'

'Big time,' he winces.

'Shit,' I mutter. 'Jane, where the fuck have you brought us?'

I squint at the top of the ditch, and decide to clamber up. It's harder and steeper than it looks. I slide all over the place and need to grab onto a few clumps of weed here and there, but I make it. Panting a little, I survey the scene. The ditch runs alongside a road. More than a road: a massive eight-lane motorway, which I bet looked really nice when it was new, but that's now littered with potholes and festooned with scrubby grass and shrubs poking through the asphalt. The landscape traversed by the highway is an immense, featureless desert. Actually, a desert has more features than this. Completely flat, the sandy, dirty, gravelly wasteland stretches off into the distance, punctuated only by the occasional stubborn weed and knobbly bush, until it vanishes into a hazy mess of dust and whiteness at the other end. There is no discernible horizon; no point where you could be sure the land ends and the white sky begins. The only things here – and I'm being generous in my description – are dryness and brightness. And worms. I can see them going about their business. I'm sure they'd gross some people out, but in this incredibly characterless place the worms actually manage to give it a tiny bit of character. Nevertheless, the sight of this vast, waterless expanse, and the feeling of another vast, waterless expanse within me, is fostering a sensation in my head that can only be described as panic.

'Jane?'

On closer inspection, the motorway only stretches off in one direction. Ahead of me it streaks across the panorama, in its bumpy, green-splattered way, disappearing into the haze after… what, fifteen, twenty miles? Impossible to tell. But when I turn away from the sun, the road limps along for about two hundred yards, then peters out. Then I see some grim metallic shapes lurking nearby. Ten, no, twenty of them, dotted around in the immediate distance, which I shortly realise – with a little shiver – are abandoned, burnt-out cars.

'Jane!'

'Huh?' comes her weak reply from below.

'Have we really come to the right place?'

Even my voice sounds weird: different in pitch somehow, like someone's playing me back on a broken Dictaphone.

'You what?' shouts Jane.

'Come up here and look at this. There's absolutely nothing here.'

'Is my car there?'

This question is so ridiculous I feel like laughing. I don't, mainly because I don't want to waste any precious molecules of liquid that could be hanging around my vocal cords. Nor do I honour Jane's question with a reply. Of course her bloody car isn't here. Unless it's one of the…

'Arrgh!'

Felix comes stumbling up the side of the ditch and trips onto the flat plain, then rights himself and marches forward until he's facing the central reservation of the highway with its bent and rusty barrier. There, without a further word, he unzips and urinates against the fence. It's a urination that continues for quite some time, so much that I toy with the idea of advising him to save a bit for later. But sheer fascination at Felix's behaviour silences me. Apparently involuntarily, he throws back his head and roars with a kind of relieved laughter, as the stream of deep-yellow liquid cannons out of his willy with a force and splatter that, even at this juncture, reminds me of the gigantic Edwardian bath tap at my great aunt's house in Knaresborough. It's an epic display; the piss Felix has been anticipating for nineteen years. Then, as the great amber waterfall finally subsides and his peals of manic laughter die down, Felix turns to me with, it transpires, an identical thought to my own.

'Jesus,' Felix splutters. 'Are we actually back on Earth?'

'Of course we're not back on Earth, you pair of loonies.'

Jane has now also dragged herself out of the ditch and is busily studying a little notebook she's extracted from a pocket. A pillar of concentration, she glances up at the sun, then paces forward. She seems to be calculating some sort of relationship between the sun's whereabouts and the direction of the motorway. Then she refers back to her notes, once again removing her glasses to read the scribblings. She takes one look back at the sun, then snaps shut the notebook, dons some shades she's produced from somewhere and strides off in the direction of the motorway's dead end.

'What are you looking for?' I yell after her.

'What do you think I'm looking for?' she snaps.

Felix stands next to me, watching Jane go.

'This is totally weird,' he observes.

'Yup,' I nod. 'How's your scar?'

'It's covered in shit,' he says, examining it, 'but I can clean it if we get hold of some…'

'Some water,' I shrug.

We wait in silence for a moment. The heat is oppressive. I badly need a sunhat or something. Goodness knows where my sunglasses are, they're no longer in my jacket pocket. Must have left them in HQ. Christ, HQ. Feels like a lifetime ago. Jane has reached the end of the motorway, now she's curving downwards and vanishing into another ditch. A few seconds' silence, then:

'Hey, fellas!' comes her muffled shout. 'Give me a hand!'

Neither of us move. Felix pulls out a cigarette.

'She's a strange one,' he says.

'Speaking of strange, have you seen her hands? They're like an old person's.'

'Hmm,' Felix comments, lighting up. 'Death defect.'

'You reckon?'

'Of course, man. Smoke?'

As Felix hands me one, he suddenly breaks into an avalanche of coughs and splutters.

'Fuckin'ell!' he growls.

'You all right?'

'These are like the strongest fucking…' He breaks off as he squints at the cigarette packet. 'Usual type, man… What the fuck is going on?'

I diplomatically tuck my own cigarette behind my ear.

'Okay,' I ponder, 'so it's like we're… back to being alive again.'

'Judas fucking Priest,' Felix rasps, gobbing on the ground.

'Hey!' Jane yells. 'What are you pair of dingbats up to? I need help!'

We start heading towards her. Slightly concerned, I break into a trot.

'Save your energy, mate' Felix says.

I ignore him and continue running. After five seconds I get a stitch and feel short of breath. I revert to a walk, shortly reaching the edge of the ditch. I gingerly peer over.

'Help me shovel the sand off this thing,' Jane puffs. She's grabbing big handfuls of the stuff and hurling it away from a dark-green metallic object half-buried in the far side of the ditch.

'Wow! It's the car!'

'Not "the" car. *My* car.'

'How did you know it was gonna be here?'

'Because I'm clever. Now, get down here and help me.'

I totter down the slope and start to dig. It's buried deeply and I'm not too sure how we're going to extract it from the ditch once we've freed it from the sand, but I scrabble and scrape as best I can. The sand is gritty and rough and starts to rip at my nails and sting my fingers after just a few moments. Felix appears above us.

'What the hell are you lot doing?'

'What's it look like?' I wheeze. 'Come down and help.'

'Oh, er…' Felix mutters, fiddling with his sunglasses. 'I'm just going to see if…'

'Get yer flamin' backside down here,' Jane bleats at him. 'Or you can forget about a ride into town.'

'Town? What town?'

'You'll see.'

Felix joins us and in a rather lacklustre way starts to assist. Although his sand yield is less than half of mine, which in turn is about half of Jane's, Felix is soon gasping and cursing the whole enterprise. He sits down after a minute and takes a break.

'Gotta get hold of some fucking water, man.'

'Yep,' I nod, throwing a dead worm away and pulling a sharp stone out of my thumb. 'That's gonna be an interesting one. They will have water where we're going – right, Jane?'

'Not answering any questions until we've finished.'

Felix rolls his eyes. 'What a cow.'

Gradually, the great metal machine starts to reveal itself. Thankfully it's facing the correct way, so having undug about two-thirds, Jane decides now is a decent time to jump in the driver seat and attempt to use engine power. She turns the key and, after a couple of misfires, the van bursts into life.

'You little beauty!' Jane hoots.

'Crazy,' comments Felix, leaning on the side of the ditch and taking a few unusually dainty drags on his cigarette. 'It'll never make it out. You wanna keep digging.'

Jane puts her foot down and, with torrents of sand, dirt, rocks and the ever-present worms, the great beast's strong rear wheels heave itself out of the hole.

'In you get, boys,' she smiles. 'Next stop, downtown S109.'

If getting the car out of the hole seemed relatively easy, getting it up the bank is another thing entirely. So for the time being we're heading along inside the ditch itself. We've been at it for about twenty minutes now. I'm riding shotgun again, Felix clearly deciding he prefers languishing in the back, free from any responsibility. Plus, I suspect, he also wants to be shielded from whatever awaits at the other end. I'm still thirsty beyond all reason, and so is Felix, although he's managing to smoke. Jane has given up trying to stop him, which on reflection I reckon is a good move; he's grouchy enough as it is. I tried a few drags of mine but it felt like inhaling a burning oven so I threw it away. Jane's car progresses slowly but steadily, despite the rocks and the large cable running along the middle, into which we veer occasionally.

'What is that, electricity?' I ask, but receive nothing but a shrug in response.

The worms are still everywhere. They're also in the car. I studied one of them as it crawled around my trouser leg before. In addition to a minute face, I notice it also has four tiny legs, one pair quite near its head, the other right the way down near the end of its tail.

'Hey, these are more like little salamanders, you know?' I announce.

'Caecilians,' Jane replies.

'Say what?'

'Didn't you study evolution at school?' she asks.

'Um… probably.'

She chuckles disparagingly and puts her foot down a little more. I flick the worm out of the window and then look around for more distraction. The sides of the ditch are boring, as is the ground in front of us, as is the sky. Periodically we see something sticking out of the sand – a bit of rusty metal, a piece of car tyre, a loose length of cable – but nothing really exciting enough to stop and look. I glance around the inside of the van, taking in its immaculately preserved doors, and the dashboard with its comfortably analogue dials. Even in this nasty, bumpy channel, Jane's managing to do about twenty-five. Then I notice something I'm sure wasn't there last time I looked.

'What's that little dial over there for?'

'Where?'

'Over there, underneath the rev counter.'

Jane lifts up her shades and squints at the dash.

'Ooh,' she says. 'Petrol gauge.'

'Petrol gauge?'

'Mmm hmm.'

'That wasn't there earlier, was it?'

Jane shakes her head.

'You're having a laugh,' Felix comments. 'Are we running on bloody petrol? How much have we got left?'

'Just under half a tank,' I tell him.

'Sorry to put a dampener on this happy party,' he says, 'but... exactly what happens when we run out?'

We both look at Jane, who is doing her usual eyes-fixed-straight-ahead thing.

'And how are we getting out of this ditch?'

Still no reply.

'I see,' Felix says. 'Anything on the radio?'

I lean forward and click the wireless on. A burst of static. I fiddle with the tuner for a few moments this way and that but there's just varying pitches of hiss.

'It won't be an Infonet radio down here,' Jane states.

'Great,' Felix replies. 'I was getting kinda sick of your Dixieland choices.'

'There's nothing,' I mutter.

'Go right down the end, man,' Felix says. 'You might be able to pick up some pirate.'

'You are of course joking.'

'I'm not. You never know, dude.'

I start twisting. It's just fizz and crackle. I reach the end and turn back the other way.

'Bingo,' whispers Jane.

'Bingo?' I answer, still turning the dial absentmindedly.

'We're in business,' she adds.

I look up. About half a mile ahead, on the left, there's a little glitch in the ditch: a lighter brown flash in the continuously dark brown side of the trench. It feels a bit optimistic to think it could be an exit – but it could be an exit.

'See the ramp?' Jane says.

'I see the ramp.'

Jane accelerates to a G-force defying thirty. Meanwhile, in radi-oland, I've almost reached the other end of the tuner, but just before the pointer softly bumps into the end of the frequency range, I hear a tiny snatch of something: a tone of some sort. I flick the dial back-wards.

'Hear that?'

'Yup,' Felix responds. 'Go easy, you'll find it.'

I creak the dial back the other way by a fraction of a millimetre, and suddenly we are listening to a male human voice. It is not, however, English.

'What fucking language is that, man?'

'Dunno,' I frown. 'Sounds like… German? No. I heard a snatch of French.'

'I heard something Spanish.'

'Shh, let's listen for a second.'

Whoever he is and whatever he's saying, he doesn't sound terribly enthusiastic. It's a low, slow drawl, like he's leaving a rambling voice-mail for someone. I hear numbers, in German – '*ein*' something – but then it continues in a tongue more like Spanish… or perhaps Por-tuguese? I was no language expert in life. He again repeats the num-ber – '*einhundert*', perhaps? – and then moves on to something more closely resembling Dutch. His tone seems to have changed too: he's getting slightly more cheerful, as if his cup of coffee is finally kicking in. One final time: '*einhundertneun*'.

'Hang on!' I shout. 'He's saying "109"! In German!'

'Yes!' grins Felix. 'Genius. Well done, dude.'

Jane is almost at the ramp; she changes gear, looks languidly over at us, rolls her eyes, then speaks in a flat, emotionless stream of words.

' "This is the rebel broadcast from S109, the sound of freedom, the sound of a new day dawning. This is the day all of us brothers and sisters here in S109 have been waiting for, the day of our Freedom Concert. It will happen this very day, my friends, this very day, in just a few hours, right here in S109. The countdown has begun." '

Felix and I blink at each other, then back at Jane.

'What on earth are you burbling about?' Felix scoffs.

Jane nods at the radio, then looks back at the ditch.

'You mean, you *understand* that?' I ask.

'Yup,' she replies. 'It's Hybreed.'

'Hybreed?'

'Hybreed. The unofficial language of the Minus zones.'

Felix and I remain silent for a few more seconds.

'But how do *you* understand it?' Felix asks, in that affronted tone of voice he always employs when he thinks someone is cleverer than him.

'Boys,' she smiles patiently. 'I've been here for many, many years. What do you think I do with my time? Knitting? Reading Enid Blyton books?'

'But,' I splutter.

'But,' Felix sneers.

'Excuse me,' she says, with a crafty smile. 'I have to drive up a ramp now.'

The ramp is steeper than it looks, and as bumpy and sandy as the ditch floor. Jane has to ram the car into first gear to climb up. Even then, it's a struggle. Much like its human occupants, Jane's van has definitely shown its age since we got here. Jane's ramming her foot down as far as it'll go, but halfway up the slope, the engine stalls.

'Fiddlesticks!' she shouts, yanking on the handbrake. 'You boys are gonna have to push.'

'Aw, really?' comes Felix's predictable moan.

'Oh, just get out and push. Gosh, I'd have hated to be your mother.'

'Funny that,' Felix snorts, 'because my mother hated being my mother too.'

We're both at the back of the van now, gamely clasping each side of the van's rear bumper and hunkering down for an almighty heave. Jane leans out of the window and shouts back to us.

'Ready? One... two... three... *push!*'

She hits the gas, we thrust from behind, and a blast of sand and dust and worms comes squirting out, covering our clothes and our faces. I close my eyes, trying to devote every atom under my remit to getting this lumbering hunk of metal up the ramp. Soon enough I feel a crack of movement, and finally the car surges upwards away from me. I collapse against the slope, sand in my mouth and up my nose. I cough up a couple of gobfuls of dirt, extract a worm from behind my ear and attempt to clean my eyes with my filthy hands.

'God,' I spit.

'Nope,' I hear Felix's voice say behind me. 'He's not gonna help you now.'

He's standing a little further down the hill with a cursory smear of dirt joining the bloodstains on his yellow shirt.

'Did you actually push at all?'

'A bit,' Felix nods.

'Bullshit.'

'Podge, you're forgetting I'm injured.'

'Oy!' Jane hollers from the top. 'Children! Stop gossiping and let's get a move on!'

We struggle to the top of the ditch. The van is parked sideways a few metres from the motorway, with Jane standing next to it, leaning one hand on the side of the door, shades on, gazing up at the sun like she's modelling for a 1950s American car advert. Felix stares straight ahead, a cigarette halfway to his gaping mouth. I follow his gaze. This time, the great highway is running fractionally downwards. The featureless landscape runs down with it: we are looking at a giant basin. Right where the hazy, horizon-like vanishing point would have been, there is a thing. A very large thing. We are alerted to its presence by its colour, a touch darker than the sky, a kind of greyish blue, like a rain cloud. But once my eyes have adjusted a little to the sheer madness of what I'm seeing, I can see that the thing's shape – unlike the cheerful, disorderly nature of a cloud – is regular. It starts way over to the left, as far away as I can see, and stretches all the way over to the right. It towers almost as high as the sky itself, and its complete form is a vast half-oval. The sun can be seen hovering in the sky to its left;

stretching out over the land in front of this gigantic object, for what could be as many as fifty miles, is an epic shadow. And within this shadow, I first assume, is a sea of rocks. Then I realise they are actually dwellings: shacks of some sort.

'You like it?' smiles Jane, casting an arm in the direction of all this lunacy, as if showing off her new ranch.

'Do I like... what, exactly?'

'Downtown S109,' she replies. 'With surrounding suburbs. Or... to use the local lingo... *favelas*.'

'Fah-what?' Felix frowns.

'Shanty towns,' she says. 'Slums.'

'Who the fuck would hang out there?'

'People who can't afford to be in the Dome.'

'Dome?'

'That's right, Dome. Ready? Let's go.'

And with that, she leaps into her van and starts the engine.

Felix and I remain standing, staring with mouths open at this vision before us.

'Dome?' Felix repeats, giving me an endlessly quizzical look.

I don't reply because I have no idea what to say. I suddenly want very much to go home. Failing that, I want an armoured vehicle and several firearms and heaps of ammunition. I also want a retired six-foot-six paratrooper who worked for many years in Baghdad, and maybe some sort of magical energy shield.

'Come on, slowcoaches!' Jane yells.

With the enthusiasm of someone being encouraged into the dentist's chair for root canal treatment, Felix and I shuffle into the vehicle. Felix bangs his door shut, then his worried face appears between Jane and me, like a toddler whose parents have just refused to get him a bag of Maltesers. He isn't wearing his shades any more and I can see genuine fear in his eyes, perhaps for the very first time. Jane, who seems as unfazed as a Labrador puppy chasing a parkful of pigeons, grins at both of us and hits the accelerator. We speed off, the enormous foreboding blue item beckoning us like an apocalyptic tidal wave. And just when I'm thinking things aren't quite nuts enough, Jane turns up the radio.

'You are having a fucking laugh,' murmurs Felix.

Some familiar electric guitar chords are joined by a punchy drum-beat. The singer's hoarse voice tells of reckless abandon and apathetic freedom, leading to a simple chorus that contains just one sentence.

'What's this claptrap?' Jane winces.

Yes, my friends. We are driving across Minus zone S109 listening to AC/DC's 'Highway To Hell'.

It's a long, boring journey, so I bombard Jane with long, boring questions, most of which I don't get satisfactory answers to.

'I don't know,' she says for the umpteenth time. 'The place Adeline came to was a bit different.'

'So it didn't have a Dome?' I ask.

'It had a Dome. But when she arrived, I think she was already inside the Dome.'

'So how did she know it was a Dome?'

'Because she eventually had to leave the Dome, to get back.'

'How did she know how to get back?'

'We already knew.'

'How?'

'We mapped it out together.'

'How?'

'Over the years,' she shrugs. 'We kept our ears open. We made notes. We're not the first people to make this journey, you know. Word gets around. Among the…'

'The what?' Felix asks.

'The Curious.'

'It's a society she belongs to,' I aside to Felix.

'Sounds like fun,' he mutters.

'It *is* fun,' Jane snaps.

'So how did they build that thing?' I demand. 'When?'

'I told you, I don't know. Anything involving sums and words, we could work out. Other things – hows, whys and whens – they were more tricky.'

And so it continues. As we get closer, the outline and texture of the grey-blue monstrosity becomes more defined. Far from being completely solid, it looks like it's billowing gently, like an enormous marquee. But with every mile, more of a ridiculous feat of construction it seems. It's much taller, by a factor of about five, than any earthly skyscraper, and it's as wide as a city. Put a five-thousand-metre-high tent over the whole of Los Angeles, and you're probably getting there.

'What's holding it up?'

'Enough with the questions, mate,' Felix sighs. 'What's holding any of this up? What makes the Trav run? Why do Renderings work?'

More concerning is our rapid approach towards the edge of the slums. Like in our own zone, the sun doesn't move, so the Dome's shadow is static. Therefore the little buildings begin abruptly where the shadow begins – about ten miles away, at a guesstimate – but the surrounding land is still completely barren, apart from weeds and worms. The three of us have lapsed into stunned silence now; personally, I'm busy wondering exactly what we're going to do when we get there, whatever 'there' is.

'Shit,' says Felix suddenly. 'Look.'

'At what?' I reply.

'Over there.'

He's pointing ahead but slightly to the left. Just the other side of the central reservation is a grey, dusty shape, like a piece of tarpaulin, but with something coming out one end, maybe hair, and perhaps a leg emerging from the other. As we trundle past, the leg shifts under the grey material and another one appears.

'That fucker's moving!' comes a raspy shout from Felix, followed by Jane slamming on the brakes. She yanks the car into reverse.

'What are you doing?' I gasp.

'Taking a look, of course.'

'We're not giving it a lift,' Felix snaps.

'Well, it's my van, so I'll decide that, won't I?'

She jumps out and climbs over the central barrier.

'Go with her,' Felix says.

'Why?'

'In case it's some total freakshow.'

'You go.'

'You!'

'Hey, boys!' comes the predictable shout. 'Keep me company!'

We sit still for a moment. I've never been so reluctant to get out of a car.

'Incredible,' Felix observes, shuffling his way out the back. 'More physical work than I've done in years, hotter than I've been in years, thirstier than I've been in years, and no access to water. All simultaneously.'

We climb over the bashed up barrier – I'm not sure who or what bashed it up, but it's dented and bent along practically its entire length – and trot over the bare, scruffy middle bit. Now I realise that in addition to being completely barren, the ground also looks a little scorched: there are traces of black, as if the land too suffers from the constant barbecuing by the overhead sun. We hurdle the next barrier and join Jane, who is kneeling next to this barely twitching, sun-baked item. Once again, she is flicking her little syringe and preparing to plunge the needle.

'You're gonna waste that stuff on it?' Felix rasps.

'Don't worry, I've plenty,' Jane mutters.

'Didn't think it would work around here,' I frown.

'On the contrary,' she says, reaching down to grab one of its ankles. 'Okay, stand by, you two. Get ready to…'

She pauses.

'To what?' Felix barks.

'Dunno,' she shrugs. 'Watch. Help. Escape.'

In goes the needle and down goes the stopper. Instantly, whatever it is under the tarpaulin emits some sort of unholy roar and rises up, as if summoned by a séance. The tarpaulin drops and the leaping, screaming form of a very peculiar looking – man? – comes bolting out. I'm assuming it's a man because it has a deepish voice and seems to be covered in hair. But it's not particularly tall; just over five feet, I'd guess. It's quite a sight: this dirty, sandy, sweaty, long-haired and bearded phantom tearing around the flat of the road in a circle, hollering, jumping, occasionally hopping and clutching the ankle Jane has just speared with her syringe, but all the while shielding itself from the brutal glare of the sun. In fact, it's the sun that triggers its first intelligible utterance.

'*Le soleil!*' it seems to be saying, which even my crap French can understand.

'Ohh, sweet Mary, sweet Jesus, Mary mother of God, *le soleil*' –

and then a whole stream of nonsense I can't comprehend. Jane, however, is soon talking back to him. They have a strange conversation, in between his hyperventilations, his screams, his leaps and his sprinting fifty yards down the road. Amid the hullabaloo Jane has dropped her syringe, which Felix picks up and studies. He looks for a moment like he's considering trying a shot of the stuff, but Jane snatches it back. Felix shrugs and lights another cigarette.

'What's he saying, then?' Felix grunts, after a few minutes of the bizarre exchange.

'Oh, nothing much,' Jane replies. 'Just that he's trying to get away.'

'Get away from what?'

'The giant blue demon.'

The man screams something from the central reservation, where he's currently trying to hide underneath the metal barrier.

'What was that?' I ask.

'Something about us all perishing, and how we need to escape quickly in our green metal horse.'

'Ask him if he knows whether there's a John Lennon gig happening this evening,' Felix deadpans.

Jane frowns, bites her lip, then mutters a few last words in the peculiar tongue. She pauses at the end of the sentence, and the man stops leaping for a second. She completes her sentence by saying 'Lennon, John' in a mildly questioning, apologetic tone. The man blinks at her, his eyeballs looking surprisingly bright and blue amid his filthy face. Then he lets out the mother of all bloodcurdling screams and races off down the road. This time, he doesn't stop. That's the last we see of him.

Back on the road, the radio is treating us to Andrew Gold's 'Lonely Boy'. Jane taps her strange hands on the steering wheel along with the beat.

'Music improving?' I suggest.

'This one's at least got a tune,' she replies. 'Look, there's more.'

A few other bodies are lying next to the highway as we pass, each of them covered with similar bits of material.

'All facing the same direction,' Jane quietly notes. 'All trying to escape the same thing.'

'So what else did our guy say?' I ask. 'How old was he?'

'He kept raving about Jesus and Mary and the God of the sun and the seven angels. My Hybreed's a little rusty, but a lot of what he said was definitely complete twaddle. He seemed thoroughly nutty. Adeline did mention that a lot of them had gone mad...'

'A lot of who?'

'The Dwellers.'

'Dwellers?'

'These medieval-looking people. The Domers call them the Dwellers.'

'Who are the Domers?'

'The people from the Dome, silly.'

'So do you think they're... *literally* medieval?'

'Could be,' Jane shrugs.

'But they can't have been out here for that long.'

'Why not?'

'Because they'd be...'

'What? Dead?'

I blink at her, then look round at Felix. He's lying back with his shades on so it's impossible to guess what he's thinking. Then he looks up.

'What's your definition of hell?' he says. 'If you told me it was an eternity in the burning sun with no shade, no water but with the constant feeling of thirst, hunger and an everlasting dryness, without the power to escape or even die properly, I think I'd probably believe you.'

I look back at Jane. She smiles happily at me, pops her sunglasses back on and turns the radio up.

The number of roadside bodies increases as we near the edge of the shadow. I suppose I shouldn't call them bodies any more. Roadside dwellers. Anyway, there are roughly five or six of them per minute. One turns its head upwards and cries out as we pass. I feel weird not telling Jane to stop and help, but I know it would be pointless. After ten more minutes the count increases and they seem to be wriggling about more and more, then finally – just before we hit the shadow – they're actually crawling, in a slow, desperate escape from the blue monstrosity rearing up ahead of us. I see one character shoving a handful of worms into his mouth before continuing to creep along. The way he's moving reminds me of something, but I can't imagine what it could be. The heat in the car is still stifling and I've been desperately thirsty for so long now it's almost become the new normal, but I suppose I'm holding out, as ridiculous as it sounds, for the hope of finding some sort of liquid when we get to the slums. We're now close enough to see a few of the buildings' details: they're assembled like shacks, but not with the traditional sheets of corrugated iron, cardboard and plastic one might expect. Instead, it's loose white bricks; rather familiar loose white bricks as a matter of fact, and rather familiar grey roof tiles. It's like some demented property developer has come along and smashed up all the houses in T109, then built five times as many with the rubble.

Two minutes away from the shadow we're presented with a macabre parade of oddities: a wrinkly guy standing, rifle in hand, next to a tunnel entrance, which I soon realise is his house, built entirely underground, out of the sun's glare. He frowns a deep, troubled frown as we pass and cracks off a few rounds into the air. Two men are beating the shit out of each other in the middle of the opposing highway carriage, then another pair of fighters can be seen a little further along, one trying to chop the other's head off with a broken piece of metal. Another, somewhat better-dressed chap is streaking across the desert on a shiny motorbike, holding his own gun aloft and firing a couple of shots as he goes, while two of the wrinkly, diminutive beings sprint hopelessly away from him. And finally, on our side of the road, a pair of women pedalling a large, wheeled engine, upon which is stacked a pile of light-blue plastic buckets. One of the buckets is placed right at the front of the machine, catching a little trickle of water.

'The fuck is that?' Felix asks.

'Water generator,' Jane states.

'What, the water generates electricity?'

'No, dummy. It generates water.'

'Why would they want to do that?'

'Do you see any other water anywhere?'

Of course, this is perfectly true. There is no water anywhere. No lakes, no streams, no ponds, no puddles and definitely no roadside shops selling ice-cold bottles of ice-cold anything. In our zone, this wouldn't be an issue – in fact we'd barely notice it. Down here, it's a major problem. The raging, plate-throwing thirst I'm experiencing everywhere from my throat to my toes is getting worse by the second. As we pass the ladies pedalling along their strange contraption, even the little stream of water that dribbles into the bucket looks endlessly appetising and I find myself making a funny, almost yearning, little sigh. To top all the fun I'm also starting to need a piss, which gets worse every time Jane changes gear – and in this old banger and on this road, that's quite often.

I tear my eyes away from the dribble of water and tell myself the only way to survive is to concentrate on other things. Fortunately, as we're now within seconds of hitting the shaded area, there are a lot of other things. A couple more underground dwellings with assorted wrinkly Dwellers standing outside, squinting at our car as we trundle along. A bunch of khaki tents, empire-style, none of which seem to contain people, but supplies: sacks of grain, rice maybe, provisions. I crane my neck to try to see if, wonder of wonders, one of them houses pallets of bottled water, but this is wishful thinking in the extreme. The crawlers along the side of the road have now become walkers, some of them veering into the road itself, Jane deftly dodging a few. Strangely, one or two of them seem to be wearing winter clothes. One man is taking off a large overcoat and a woman has a woolly hat and a scarf which she's unwinding. A couple of other cars roll along,

174

all of them filthy, all missing a vital part like the windscreen, the roof, the headlights or one of the wheels. And now, finally, like we're crossing into a different dimension: the shaded area.

The sunlight vanishes so dramatically it's as if we've just entered a tunnel, and the effect is as immediate as it is unexpected: it's bloody freezing. I had mentally budgeted for a pleasant, Mediterranean-evening drop in temperature, but it's like driving into a giant fridge.

'Clever,' observes Jane, taking off her sunglasses. 'Too cold in here, too hot out there.'

'The ideal limbo,' I nod, fishing around behind my seat and grabbing my jacket.

'Bugger me!' shouts Felix, the cold snap waking him up. 'Who set the air-con to Arctic?'

The cautious upside to this situation is that the road is still relatively clear. I had expected some teeming masses to come out and teem a little, check out our vehicle, aggressively try to find out who we were, what we wanted and whether we had a few bottles of Evian stashed somewhere, but I guess most people are sitting around a fire inside their shacks. And shacks there are plenty. Crammed into every available millimetre of ground that isn't the road, sometimes creeping slightly into the road itself, they are one-storey huts with barely a window in sight. Occasionally we can see a candle, a fire or – more rarely – an electric light flickering inside one of the dwellings.

'Holy shit,' Felix gasps. 'I wonder what it's like here at night?'

I glance at my watch. Approaching 4am, our time.

'Do they even have night in this place?'

Jane shrugs. 'Not if no one's bothering to make it night.'

It's difficult to imagine night time being any gloomier than what we currently see. It's different to simply being in the shade. As we pass a rare pedestrian – a straggler bobbling along near the central reservation, squinting up at the forbidding dark mass in front of us – it hits me: it's very much like an eclipse, the remote removal of both the Sun's light and its heat from the atmospheric equation. It's as if this looming blue blob isn't just a giant construction, but like... a planet.

A little shiver runs down my spine and I clasp my jacket around me. My body is feeling bloody weird. And so it should. Two minutes ago it was sweating in forty-five degree heat, but now it's being swiftly packed in a thin layer of ice. I glance at the dashboard to see if there's anything resembling a heater in this banger; of course there isn't. Jane, curiously, seems unaffected by the change, still just in her smart shirt, still ploughing onwards like a trooper without any chattering of teeth or anything.

The radio finishes its current selection – Big Country's 'In A Big Country', curious choice – and the DJ continues to blather in his strange tongue.

'Has he mentioned what the local time is?'

Jane listens for a moment. 'I'm not sure if they really *do* time. He's mainly talking about the revolution.'

'Has he mentioned the Freedom Concert again?'

'It's *all* about the Freedom Concert.'

'Does it say where it is?'

'If you'll stop yapping for a moment I might be able to listen.'

Amid the ensuing gobbledegook I can decipher the occasional number, and the word '*concert*' is indeed repeated quite often. They seem to use German for numbers, French for nouns, and perhaps Portuguese or Italian for everything else, but I'm speculating wildly. Strangely, after a few minutes of this I hear the words 'Jimi Hendrix' and 'Ramones'. Felix, unsurprisingly, pricks up his ears.

'What? What was that bit?'

'Wait.'

'He just said Jimi fucking Hendrix!'

'I said belt up, numbskull!'

Jane pulls the van over for a second, intently listening. Finally we all hear, very clearly, repeated three times: '*gran sorpresa*'. Even my non-existent Italian tells me what this could be.

'What,' growls Felix, never the linguist, 'is the grand suppression?'

'Big surprise,' Jane says, slinging the van back into gear and moving off. 'The concert will feature…'

'Jimi Hendrix,' I recite, 'the Ramones, and…'

'A big surprise special guest.'

'Lennon,' I mutter.

'Screw Lennon!' yells Felix. 'What about Jimi fucking Hendrix? When did those bastards swipe *him*?'

'He might be a Rendering,' I reason.

'No,' Jane says. 'Renderings won't work down here.'

'How do you know that?' Felix snaps.

'I just do.'

'And what about the Ramones? I thought they were playing for Tony Wilson.'

'Maybe he's done a transfer deal.'

'This isn't bloody funny, Podge.'

'It wasn't supposed to be funny.'

'Anyway, it's not possible,' Felix announces, a statesman-like tone audible in his voice. 'I would have been informed.'

Jane giggles. Everyone finds it funny when Felix is being pompous.

'So when's this bloody concert taking place?'

'Today.'

'And where?'

'Didn't say.'

'Useless,' growls Felix, sinking back into his hole.

We drive on, past shack upon shack, with the occasional filthy-looking alleyway in between. From time to time we see a heavily dressed person standing by the roadside, eyeing us with dubious interest as we pass. The faces, from what I can see, are all very similar: wrinkled, darkened – whether through dirt or sun – with two bright eyes twinkling out from under matted hair. The clothes are a curious mix of very old and new: shawls, blankets, jeans, overcoats, oversized jumpers, what might be animal skins, smart suits, dirty trainers, army uniforms. It's like a peasant from the Dark Ages has been let loose in a theatrical costume shop and then ordered to roll around in some mud.

Abruptly, there's a sharp increase in people trudging along in the same direction we're travelling. Gazing up ahead, I see a vision on the left hand side that can only be described as a crowd.

'Well, how about that?' Jane observes. 'I think we probably have ourselves a market.'

'A market?' I blink. 'Selling what?'

'Who knows? Wanna take a look?'

'Not really.'

'Come on, chicken,' Jane smiles, slowing down the van again.

'We're not leaving the car,' Felix instructs.

'Suit yourself.'

Jane turns the engine off and leaps out. Against my better judgement, I follow.

'Can you get me a bottle of water?' Felix yells after us. 'And, I dunno, some crisps or something?'

We must have temporarily lost our minds. Seconds ago we were riding along in a perfectly nice car (I wouldn't have said that three hours ago, but never mind) and now we're choosing to leave it and go exploring deeply uncharted and profoundly unwelcoming territory in the freezing bloody cold. Jane is already fearlessly charging across the highway towards the various swarming groups of Dwellers; it does indeed look like a trading post of some sort, although Christ knows what they're bartering with. Once I've caught up with Jane I can see three 'stalls': raised platforms, each with a person standing on it – the traders. They are considerably neater in appearance than everyone else, without the wrinkly complexions or matted hair. Domers, I assume. One of them wears a smart, dark-grey overcoat, a burgundy scarf, a bowler hat and a self-satisfied look on his face as he hands out shoebox-sized packages to the herd. Next to him, collecting small white objects from the 'customers', stands a security-guard figure straight out of a Cold War thriller: bomber jacket, fur hat, bored expression. About ten yards to the right of this performance, another stall is in full swing. The trader – khaki parka, also with accompanying Soviet-era security dude – hands out slips of paper to another clutch of punters, while rightwards ten yards further, a rather peculiar-looking woman presides over the busiest stall of the lot. She's working the crowd like a commercially-minded banshee, screaming numbers at people, frantically handing out dark bottles and snatching the small white items from outstretched hands. She appears as some sort of witch: purple cloak, voluminous black boots, but scrappy dyed-blonde hair poking out below her pointed hat. Intriguingly, she also seems to require no security guard. I have the strangest sensation of having seen her before, although I've not the foggiest idea where. It's this supposed merchant that we head for; or rather, Jane heads for her, and I uselessly tag along behind.

We pitch up, and lurk behind the muttering throng. A couple of customers turn to look at us, but most are far too intent on grabbing whatever there is to grab. The woman on the platform is speaking very loud English, with – if I'm not mistaken – a slight Mancunian accent. There's the slightest smattering of Hybreed, for the occasional word like *aqua* or *cerveja*.

'You there,' she barks, 'you haven't paid. Six dollars. That's right. *Sechs*. Okay, you. *Aqua*? Four *aqua*. Twelve dollars. You, over there in the blue hat, you still haven't paid. What? I don't care if you've lost it, give me back the bottles then. Okay, you. Whisky? Twenty-five bucks. Right, you. Six waters and four… no, we have no vodka today. You hear that, people? No… vodka… today. Got it? Tomorrow. *Cerveja*, yes. Fifteen. You there, you still haven't paid. No, I don't care. Give me the bottles back now, dickhead, or you're going to make the demon very angry.'

These words have an immediate and dramatic effect on the witch's patrons. About half of them utter a terrified sort of wail and back off. A few drop to the ground, clasp their hands together and begin a low, eerie moaning. Witch-woman cackles with laughter at this, but in doing so she looks up and spots Jane and me. We receive a nasty glare.

'All right, piss off everyone,' she shouts, sweeping her arm across the throng. 'That's enough for today.'

The customers quickly disperse and we amble up to her. She looks profoundly unhappy to see us, like she's been well and truly caught with her pants down.

'Who the devil are you?'

'We were about to ask you the same,' Jane replies.

'None of your God-damned business.'

'Charming. Can we have some water?'

'You can *buy* some water.'

'Well, you see, we don't have any local currency.'

'That's your tough shit, then. Why are you Australian?'

'Why am I Australian?' Jane smiles sweetly, looking at me for assistance.

'Oh… because you like kangaroos?' I suggest.

'That's right, because I like kangaroos. Why are you pretending to be a witch?'

'Joe!' shouts witch-woman, over at one of her colleagues. 'Come and get rid of these reprobates!'

The security guard in the middle raises his eyebrows and starts moving through the crowd towards us, shoving people out of the way with his large gun.

'Anyway,' continues Jane, unfazed, 'we were hoping you could help us...'

'Well, you hoped wrong,' snaps the witch, packing her bottles in a small trailer, which I can now see is attached to a motorbike.

'Because,' Jane continues, 'we're friends of... Benjamin... oh, fiddlesticks... Podge, what's his surname?'

'Bumlick,' I mutter.

'No, birdbrain, his real surname.'

'He must be quite a friend if you don't know his real surname,' comments the witch.

'Um... Mulnick?' I offer.

'That's it!' Jane whoops. 'Benjamin Mulnick!'

The security guard, who has now sidled up to us, frowns and speaks with a distinctly eastern-European burr.

'You are looking for Mr Benjamin Mulnick?'

'Indeed we are,' Jane twinkles.

'You're in luck,' he replies. 'My boss over there is selling tickets to Mr Mulnick's concert.'

I suppress a very large sigh. It's partly a sigh of relief that we're not totally pissing up the wrong lamppost, but also a sigh of gloom that we're going to have to go through with the whole silly mission after all.

'Ah, perfect!' Jane says. 'And where would this show be taking place?'

'In the Dome, naturally.'

'Wonderful. And I suppose you'll be heading there yourselves?'

'Yes, of course,' nods the guard.

'Excellent. Mind if we tag along?'

'No problem at all. Just purchase a ticket, and we'll see you there.'

'Ah,' Jane winces, 'that presents us with a problem... As we were saying to your lovely friend here, we have no local currency, and I... we're friends with Mr Mulnick, you see, and...'

'Not my decision,' shrugs the guard. 'You won't be allowed across the border without a ticket.'

'The border?' I ask.

'Yes, the border.'

'The border between what and... what?'

'It's all right, Podge,' Jane hisses. 'I can handle this.'

'Bloody foreigners,' mutters the witch.

While Jane is engaged in this protracted negotiation, I happen to glance over at our van. For some reason the back door is open. Why would the back door be open? Felix isn't standing nearby having a cigarette, and it's unlikely he'd open the doors if he were still inside. So where is he?

Jane, meanwhile, has been allowed to see the 'boss'. The security dude leads her over to the next stall where the man in the parka is flogging his wares. I am not invited, so I remain standing rather stupidly next to witch-woman, who is hurriedly packing. She really does look familiar. Big eyes, big nose, wavy blonde fringe poking out from beneath her absurd hat. I feel like I've seen her in a photo somewhere, possibly in a newspaper. But my brain's not connecting the dots. She catches me staring and scowls.

'Didn't your mother teach you it's rude to stare?'

'Can't remember,' I reply. 'It's been a while.'

She screws up her nose and scratches the back of her head.

'I'm curious. If you didn't know what the border was... but you speak English... and you haven't got any dollars... where the heck are you people from?'

'Um... we're from, ah... well, we're not really from round here.'

'I gathered that. Where, then?'

It's at this point that I spot Felix. He's approaching the witch's cart from behind, creeping along the edge of the highway. He's putting his finger to his lips, while with the other hand he's miming a circular motion. I get the message.

'Oh,' I say. 'Well... If I told you where we're from, I'd probably have to start from the beginning. You've heard of the singer and songwriter, John... um... Lennon?'

'Of course I've heard of John Lennon, are you stupid or something?'

'Well, you see...' – Felix makes it to the cart and swiftly extracts three bottles which he shoves in his back trouser pockets – 'we're representatives of Mr Lennon and he's actually going to be playing at the... um... concert this evening...'

She screws up her nose again. 'Don't bullshit me. John Lennon's not playing at the Dome concert.'

'Well, um... not officially, it's supposed to be a surprise, you see...' – Felix pinches another three bottles and stashes them in his front pockets – '... but the silly thing is, ha ha, we've managed to become separated from the rest of Mr Lennon's entourage...'

'Hang on,' witch-woman says, holding one hand up and closing her eyes in thought. 'You're telling me that *John Lennon*... as in the Beatle... is playing a show... in S109?'

Oh, bollocks. Have I gone too far?

'Um, yes,' I nod reluctantly.

'But that's impossible. He's not down here, is he?'

Felix, for his final trick, is now carefully removing a metal strongbox from the cart, which he secretes behind his back. I can't believe he's doing this. I could kiss him on both bumcheeks. He then tiptoes away, hunched over and desperately trying to keep his spoils out of sight, looking like some madcap cross between a Dickensian pickpocket and Quasimodo.

'Well,' I explain to the witch, 'he's visiting.'

'Honestly,' she snorts. 'I've heard some tommyrot in my time, but...'

'I know it's difficult to believe, um... I'm sorry, what did you say your name was?'

'I didn't.'

This conversational stalemate is then broken by a massive explosion from somewhere. I glance in the direction of the noise: I'd guess about half a mile away, in the middle of the sea of shacks. All the Dwellers scream and duck for cover. The witch rolls her eyes and mutters, 'Oh, Tuesday.'

Jane comes dashing over. 'Let's go.'

'Did you get the tickets?'

'No.'

Parka-man descends from his platform and starts shouting over at witch-woman.

'Okay, Myra, we're out of here!'

'Hang on,' mutters the witch, turning round. 'Where the devil did I put my...'

'Myra!' shouts the man. 'Didn't you hear me? We've gotta move. Now.'

'Which one of you horrible little thieves stole my box?' she screams. The Dwellers, the ones that haven't already hit the deck or scarpered off, all cower and whimper at the witch's movements. 'Right, you're getting the most powerful spell I can conjure, this very second, unless one of you coughs-up my box, or tells me who has it. Do you hear me?'

Jane and I dash back across the highway and leap over the central barriers as another explosion, similar in size to the first, blasts out from some other nearby location, this time on our side of the road.

'Maybe that wasn't such a good idea,' Jane says.

'Don't worry,' I reply. 'I think Felix has a surprise for us.'

We wait for a clapped-out Ford Granada to trundle past and then sprint back to the van. We leap in, slam the doors and Jane hits the gas. I turn to Felix. He's wearing a smile so wide it's making him look like Aphex Twin. He's holding aloft a large bottle of water in one hand and an ice-cold beer in the other. He laughs the laugh of a man who hasn't effectively deadened his brain in almost twenty years.

'Ha-ha... good health, my lovelies!' he roars. 'Bottoms up!'

You've gotta hand it to Felix. He has this amazing habit of suddenly being the hero, even if he hasn't a clue what's going on. We're speeding (well, fifty-five with Jane's foot completely hitting the floor) down the highway towards the Dome, a few more explosions renting the air nearby, and we're all of us overcome with childish giggles. Nilsson's 'Jump Into The Fire' is cannoning out the radio. We've chugged a bottle of water each and Felix is already halfway through his second beer, and it has to be said, he's drunk. Jane took one sip of hers and spat it out immediately. I'm tempted to join Felix on his way to oblivion but I realise I might need all of my marbles for whatever border fun awaits us. We yanked open the strongbox with a spanner Jane found in her glove compartment, so I'm also counting the cash, which is no easy task because I'm not entirely sure what any of it is. The coins appear to be made with some kind of ceramic, they're irregularly shaped – more hexagonal than round – and about the width of a button. There are no markings but I must assume they're a 'dollar' each. The box is full to the brim and it looks like we have in the region of five hundred bucks. How much that really represents around these parts, I'm not too sure, but if I make a crude calculation based on Myra the witch charging three dollars for a bottle of water, we've probably got... what... about a hundred and fifty quid?

'How much were they flogging those tickets for?' I ask.

'I didn't get that far in the conversation,' Jane replies, swerving a couple of large potholes.

We pass another bunch of stalls: a similar scene to before, this time minus the witch.

'Aren't we gonna stop and try to buy some tickets?'

'Nah,' drawls Felix. 'Less juss carry on... we can pay the border guarss...'

'Christ. You *are* drunk.'

'Fuckin' great, man. Haven' been thiss piss sinss... I dunno...'

'You'd better not do any of the talking at the border.'

'What? What are you sayin'…?'

Another huge bang rocks the car, this time coming from the stalls we've just driven past. A cloud of smoke engulfs the road behind and some figures can be seen charging out into the middle of the highway.

'Dweller terrorists,' Jane states matter-of-factly. 'Adeline mentioned all this. The Dwellers attack the Domers, then the Domers get back at them by putting all the prices up, then the Dwellers attack the Domers again.'

'And the Domers are selling tickets…'

'To a Freedom Concert on the inside of the Dome. Smart, huh?'

'Yeeeah,' Felix leers. 'Sounss like the sort of fuckin' shit Benny Bumlick would… gessa… euhhh…'

Then a loud clunk from behind; Felix has passed out.

'Great,' Jane smiles. 'A few moments without his verbal diarrhoea.'

I gaze around us, the diabolical shacks, the rising plumes of smoke, the occasional onlooker staring at our van as it rattles past. Then I look at Jane: her pretty, inquisitive face, her cardiganned arms, her weird hands. I'm having a rather confusing time of it, I must admit. Who is she, anyway? It suddenly strikes me that she might reveal slightly more about herself now Felix is out of commission.

'Jane…'

'Yes?' she beams, overtaking a juggernaut.

'Who exactly are you?'

'Wow, look!' she exclaims, pointing up ahead. 'That looks like a petrol station. We might be needing it on the way back.'

At last we approach the foot of the unfathomable blue monstrosity. The shacks have petered out and in their place are shabby canvas tents, and epic queues of Dwellers. Most of them are strewn all over on the ground, some of them lying in piles: a warming method against the intense cold. Guards, similar to those we saw back at the trading posts, parade up and down, prodding people with truncheons and occasionally poking rifles at insubordinates. The vast majority of potential border-crossers are on foot, but there is a short line of vehicles, thankfully moving forward at a reasonable pace. Most of them are dusty, bashed-up lorries and old tanker trucks, all driven by our wrinkly friends. The entrance to the Dome, looking so tiny about an hour ago, is actually an arch around thirty feet high, leading to a blackened tunnel of uncertain length. In a small hut, a team of officials examine papers and so forth, none of whom look like they'd enjoy being fucked with. Our plan is refreshingly straightforward: the happy product of having absolutely no choice. Having pocketed a hundred bucks for petrol on the way home, Jane is simply going to hand over the strongbox, with lid wide open, to the guards, and smile disarmingly. We're assuming that – here, of all places – money and a pretty girl's smile will do all the talking.

There are only two problems. One is that Felix is snoring like a washing machine full of potatoes. We've half a plan to wake him up when we're next in the queue, but then again, it'll be easier to get any negotiation done if he's asleep. The other problem is mine and mine alone, and it's this: in the last fifteen minutes, my need for the loo has gone from urgent to utterly frantic.

It's the weirdest damned thing, and at a time when things are already pretty damned weird. It started with a regular sort of tickle around my privates but quickly became more of a burn: a build-up of energy and pressure that thundered down my penis, like a dam about to burst. No, that's understating it; it feels like my urethra's about to give birth to a colossal water bomb.

I haven't a clue what to do. I can't recall feeling anything quite like this in my life, let alone my death. It's impossible to ignore; as debilitating as a bad hangover and just as immune to any remedies. I've taken deep breath upon deep breath, I've shifted my seated position till I'm practically hanging out the door, but nothing helps. Stationary as we are, I've also considered making a bolt for the back of some nearby building so I can quickly relieve myself, but I know this would be madness after witnessing a ferocious little scene just now.

From what we've been able to tell, there are two queues of pedestrians. One, moving at a slow but noticeable rate, must be for those who work inside the Dome, or have a ticket to the concert. They reach the front, a guard checks for a mark on their wrists or a ticket, and they're let in. The other queue barely moves at all; hence everyone sitting or lying down, and the queue being a couple of miles long and requiring the least fun looking campsite in history. At the front of this line, each applicant is taken away into a nearby building, where I dread to think what happens. We've been here for ten minutes now, and we've yet to see anyone coming back out of the building. That aside, there is at least some sort of order to the proceedings, until something goes wrong. And just now, something definitely went wrong.

A woman and a man, wrapped in the usual mud-splattered get-up, approached the guard at the front of the moving queue and presented their wrists. Whatever this guard saw was obviously not good. He shouted something, went back in his hut, and came out again with, of all things, a Brillo pad. Haven't seen one of those in a while, and I can't say I've missed them. Amid a fair amount of low-level moaning from his customers, he gripped the man's arm and gave his inside wrist a brisk scrubbing. Whatever was supposed to be permanent clearly started coming off, as the guard started yelling, the moaning altered to high-pitched whining, and without much ceremony the guard yanked a pistol off his belt and shot the man in the face. Rapid, shocked intake of breath from Jane and me, and even Felix emitted an extra loud snore. The woman wailed and knelt down to help her companion, but the guard, showing an almost laughable lack of mercy, reached out and shot her in the head too. He then turned to the rest of the queue, said nothing, but fired a shot in the air. The two Dwellers remained in a heap on the floor for about a minute, then started crawling back along the queue, a giant smear of blood providing the nastiest of vapour trails behind them. As they passed us, we caught a glimpse of the man's face: a blackened, bloodied hole about two inches wide filled the space between his nose and his cheekbones; I could even see a snatch of daylight through the other side.

So, all things considered, I don't think there's much point in acquiring an everlasting bullet hole for the sake of a swift piss, however urgent it seems. And, oh boy, does it seem urgent. Every time the bloody van moves forward, it hurts, it tingles, it burns. I take the risk of lightly brushing my flies with the back of my hand, just to check if anything's leaked out, and instantly regret it, as it sets off a surge of hidden drama that makes me think I could shortly be in trouble... Warm, damp trouble...

'Identification?'

We're at the border. A gruff guard sticks his nose through the window and surveys the van's interior. He's pointing his snout far too close to Jane's face for my liking, but she seems unmoved by it, smiling her usual dazzling smile and clutching the strongbox.

'Good morning, officer,' she says.

'But this is the afternoon,' he frowns.

'Well, there you go. Been a long day already. The thing is, you see, we don't have any identification. We're taking part in the Freedom Concert...'

'Freedom Concert,' the guard grins. 'Ha, ha. Is that what they're calling it now?'

'Ha, yes. We're working with our friend Benjamin Bumlick.'

'Mulnick,' I manage to squeak.

'Sorry, Mulnick. And we...'

'You are working for Benjamin Mulnick?'

'Ah, yes,' she twinkles.

'But that man is a crook.'

'Um... possibly?' Jane shrugs, giving a little giggle. I almost lose it. I turn to my door, resist the urge to punch the window and settle for biting my lapel instead.

The guard frowns dangerously. 'You are working for a crook.'

A terrible moment of terrible silence. Then, miracle of miracles, the guard smiles nastily.

'Everyone here is a crook! Ha, ha, haaa!'

'Of course!' Jane hoots. 'Aren't we all!'

She throws back her head and lets the laughter flow. I'm almost letting something else flow but I take a breath and pull back at the last millisecond.

'And,' continues the guard, his laughter vanishing, 'between crook and crook, there must be a little in exchange.'

'Ah,' Jane nods. 'Yes. Well...' – she opens the lid of the strongbox to reveal the pile of money – 'in that case... would... this be of any use?'

The guard's eyebrows shoot up and I know we've made a schoolboy error. Or a maybe a schoolgirl one.

'How much is this?'

'Oh... we're not entirely sure... but we think about... four hundred?'

Instantly you can see him clocking up what four hundred bucks is going to get him on the inside. He smiles a broad, sinister smile and fingers the coins.

'I may have to check with my colleague, but... are you sure, four hundred?'

'Yes,' Jane replies, dumping the entire box in the man's hands. He gazes down at the booty and attempts the slightest expression of bargaining, which he swiftly abandons.

'Well... oh, who cares. It's a sunny day.'

'Indeed,' Jane agrees.

'Not here,' grins the guard, showing a few horrid metal teeth. 'Inside! Ah-ha, ha haaa! Never out here!'

Jane joins him in a burst of joyful laughter, the car rocks slightly and my time is nearly up. An utterly involuntary celebration is about to take place beneath my trouser zip, and this time, there ain't no stopping the party.

'On you go,' he booms, 'and send my greetings to that crook for me! Ah-ha-ha!!'

Jane yanks off the handbrake, shoves the gearstick into first, presses down the pedal and shoots me a relieved look and a smile. I stare back at her, mouth open, eyes drooping, head nodding like one of those bloody stupid puppy dogs you used to see in rear windscreens, and then the dam explodes, the volcano erupts and I'm unable to contribute to the proceedings any further. My body sinks back against my seat as the van thrusts forward, and I just let it happen. Jane looks back at the road, drives into the dark hole, and for me, one nightmare is neatly replaced by another.

'Fiddlesticks,' Jane says, after we've been driving through the bumpy, barely lit hole for about two minutes. 'We should have offered him two hundred, haggled a bit.'

I'm desperately trying to keep the top of my dry trousers separate from my sodden underpants without it looking weird. I'm failing miserably.

'Are you all right there?' Jane asks.

'Yeah, just a little restless,' I reply. I'm terrified my soggy mess will soon start to smell. Mind you, there are other concerns. Like what the blazes awaits us on the inside. It must be relatively good, if so many people want to get in. However, I've stood in enough long queues for shitty nightclubs to know this rule doesn't always carry.

Whatever it is, it's well protected. Only after we've been driving through the tunnel for about ten minutes do we see a little tiny chink of light in the distance. Our lane of traffic is alone – there must be a separate tunnel going in the opposite direction – and it's almost completely pitch-black, not even a wall or a barrier to the left or right of us, although periodically we pass a gaggle of Dwellers wandering haplessly along, or a stationary Land Rover with a bored-looking guard sitting inside, chain smoking and vaguely fingering his weapon.

'Did I miss anything?' comes a sudden groany voice from behind.

'Damn,' Jane says. 'I forgot about him.'

Felix starts moaning about having a headache. The fool even asks if we've got any headache tablets. Then he asks a few desultory questions about where we are and how we got here and where all this darkness has come from; we give him a brief rundown of all the nice things we've seen in the last hour while Jane continues charging through the tunnel. The chink of light soon becomes a fistful of light and then an archway reveals itself about half a mile ahead. A white building and a palm tree can be seen through the arch, and some blue sky. We get closer, and we can still see the large white building and the palm tree. And the blue sky. Trundling through the arch itself, we can see... a large white building and a palm tree. Blue sky. That's it.

'What's...' I begin.

'Hmm?' Jane responds.

'What's the appeal?'

The road becomes even bumpier – they actually seem to have stopped bothering with asphalt – but the air temperature has returned to bearable, and the sun (which, strangely, is in a totally different position to where it was outside the Dome) is pleasantly warming. There's one big house near us, and after a few moments we spot another one off to the right. Both are surrounded by ugly white walls topped with vicious spikes and barbed wire. Neither of them look like places I'd want to rent for a holiday.

'What's so bloody great about it in here?' Felix grumbles.

Jane pulls the car over and we get out. The air seems fresh – but a little too fresh, like the air on a plane. Then I turn around to see where we've come from, and I finally see what's so bloody great about it in here.

'Water!' I gasp.

Beginning about half a mile away is a lake, stretching as far as the eye can see. The tunnel we've just driven through is housed in a dyke-like grassy structure which, we now realise, has water lapping on either side of it. I can't make out the distant edge of the Dome, just a hazy horizon, but water is all around us; in fact we're on an island, with various access roads and bits of reclaimed land jutting out into the middle of the vast pool. But in case anyone thinks a refreshing drink or a dip in the lake might be a nice idea, a metal fence – more of a steel wall, really – has been brutally installed along each edge of the water, with an electricity transformer every couple of hundred yards.

Jane claps her hands like she's just remembered the capital of Paraguay in a pub quiz.

'That's it! Water! I knew Adeline mentioned something else!'

On what little land there is, houses of differing design and dimension are built, all substantially larger than the bungalows in our own zone. Compounds would be a more accurate term: each has a high, fortified wall, a main house, a few palm trees and a couple of outbuildings. The one nearest us has a faintly Greek theme – a portico and statues of God-like figures can be spotted poking up above the wall – and another residence about a quarter of a mile behind us has tried, and pretty much failed, to look like an English stately home. Picture the sort of ostentatiously vulgar house you'd see shown off in a gossip magazine by a lottery winner, but then imagine it'd been recently converted into a prison. Here and there we can see vehicles driving from place to place: a black 4×4, a sports car, a Bentley, a couple of white vans. A tanker truck comes thundering past us, a couple of dead-eyed Dwellers in the cab, then clatters off along the top of a dyke. After a minute it stops next to a bedraggled group of pedestrians traipsing along; they clamber on board and the lorry steams off again into the distance.

We're about to get back into the car when some sort of altercation can be heard. A scream, a shout, some crashing and smashing, then gunshots. It's all coming from the nearby house. We hear a male, English voice, speaking very loudly and aggressively to some unknown offender.

'I don't give a shit what you needed to do! Don't go in there, you little piece of shit! Now get the fuck out of my house!'

'No... no... suhhh...'

'I don't give a fuck!'

The large wooden entrance gate in the centre of the white wall swings open, to reveal a well-dressed, tanned man with slick blonde hair and sunglasses, beating the shit out of a cowering Dweller with the butt-end of a large gun. Draped around the man, even while he's exacting this violence, is a wafer-thin dark-haired girl in a bikini. Following a particularly vicious blow to the abdomen, the Dweller tumbles out of the gate and falls to the ground. Not content with this expulsion, the well-dressed man advances on the heap of dark cloth and bones, delivering a brutal blow to the head.

I take a breath to mutter something at Felix, but he urgently puts his finger to his lips.

The girl smiles in a fucked-up, druggy sort of way, then reaches down and unzips the man's trousers. Jane, Felix and I are rooted to the spot, flabbergasted by what we see. As the girl pulls out his erect penis and begins to suck, the man whirls the gun around as if it's a drumstick and blasts a couple of rounds into the Dweller, to a whimper of pain and not much movement. The man then raises a bottle of something to his lips and takes a few gulps, liberally allowing the liquid to spill over himself and the girl. It's only when he unclasps the bottle from his lips that he spots us.

'What the fuck are you plebs looking at?' he roars. Jane and I free ourselves from our frozen poses and leap into the car, but Felix remains glued in position, staring helplessly.

'Felix!' I yell, as the man raises his gun towards him. Felix recovers from his trance and hurls himself into the back of the van. Jane fires it up and hits the gas, and in the sideview mirror I can see the man taking aim at one of our wheels, but thankfully he's distracted by what's occurring in his nether regions and lowers the gun.

'Jesus,' I splutter, finally.

'I feel bad,' Jane says. 'We should've picked that poor man up.'

'Come on,' I reply. 'What could we possibly have done?'

'Shot that idiot with my pistol.'

'You've still got it?'

'Of course,' she says, tapping the glove compartment.

I whirl round to look at Felix. He's leaning against the side walls, panting, staring back in the direction we've come from.

'You okay?' I ask.

He doesn't answer.

Jane's heading along one of the wider dykes. She remembers she has a pair of binoculars in her never-ending glove compartment and hands them to me. If I thought our previous scenery was depressing, this takes the cake. The water is, well, watery, but the metal power-fence ensures that every drop is beyond anyone's reach. The stretches of land have the same blank, dry cheerlessness as outside, but with the added bonus of seeing these giant houses, doubtless mostly inhabited by similar specimens to our friend before, serviced and maintained by these pathetic little slaves. Here and there we can see a novelty: an uninviting but relatively spacious block of flats, a large carbuncle with adjacent car park which is perhaps some sort of shop, and several factories on the edge of the water with queues of Dwellers and rows of tankers parked outside.

'Water plant,' Jane says.

'They work there?'

'Yup.'

'So they slave away in the factory, then the Domers sell the water back to them...'

'For a fuck-off price hike,' Felix adds. 'I wonder where they got that idea.'

'Ingenious,' Jane nods.

'Appalling,' I gasp. 'I feel like... I don't know... trying to help them.'

'Good luck with that,' Felix mutters, lighting a cigarette.

'There must be something we can do.'

'Nah, fuck it, Podge. They're here for a reason.'

'What reason?'

'Same reason we're *not* here.'

'What, they're bad people and we're good people?'

'You got it.'

'So how do you explain the Dwellers and... the others? Different levels of badness?'

'It's the difference between a petty criminal and a gang boss,' Felix improvises. 'These little fucks just look clueless, but the Domers look evil. The kind of brain that says "screw everyone else." It's like Benny Bumlick. He never gave the slightest toss about anyone but himself. And if he needed to screw or murder people to get what he wanted, that's what he did. And now he pays the price.'

'What price?' I ask. 'Having everything you want, fleecing the locals and lording it over everyone?'

Felix sits back, for once looking thoughtful.

'You're both wrong,' Jane shrugs. 'I think it's just plain old bad luck. The Dwellers died at the wrong time. The newcomers discovered how to fiddle the system and protect themselves, so they wouldn't end up with a baked brain and a body like a dried prune.'

'So what are we going to do?'

'What we came to do,' Jane says. 'Find John, go home.'

'How?' I blink, looking around at the desolate assortment of armoured houses, scrubland and epic plains of water. 'There's nothing here. Who would we ask? Without getting a massive hole blasted in our heads by some depraved, violent moron? So we drive around like clueless twats and attempt to find the gig ourselves, but where would we even start? Do you see anywhere at all where they might possibly be putting on a bloody rock concert?'

My companions are, for once, unable to disagree. But then, amid the ensuing silence, a strange noise. A noise we've probably only been without for five or six hours, but considering everything we've been through, it feels like weeks. Jane looks at me curiously, I look at Felix. The noise is a tune, and that tune is the flute part to 'Ghost Town' by The Specials, crudely bleeped from somewhere. Felix starts patting his various pockets.

His phone is ringing.

Felix finds the phone clattering around in the back of the van somewhere, then holds it up and stares at it for a moment. I expect it to go
to voicemail, but it just keeps ringing.

'Well, answer the damn thing?' I suggest. 'Who is it?'

He doesn't reply; he just carries on squinting at the phone.

'Who is it?' I repeat.

'Podge, just shut up for a second!'

He looks genuinely concerned, as if he's weighing up at least five
or six different pros and cons of taking the call. Meanwhile, 'Ghost
Town' keeps on bleeping. Finally he holds the phone to his chest and
closes his eyes, gritting his teeth.

'Pull over the car,' he says, suddenly.

Jane pulls over the car.

Felix honestly seems to be experiencing some sort of psychological
crisis. He wipes his eyes with his sleeve. Then, finally, he bursts out
the back doors and picks up the call, hurrying away from the track
with a finger in one of his ears. He walks almost all the way to the
metal power-fence and I'm hoping he doesn't forget it's a power-
fence and get himself electrocuted. I can hear him speaking in the
kind of low, calm voice he usually reserves for Death Missions. I'm
straining my ears to work out the occasional word, but it's hard. 'Well,
we just thought we'd... you know... come down,' is one of the only
complete sentences I'm able to decipher. His demeanour suggests he's
being strangely apologetic and cagey, so he's either talking to someone he doesn't trust, or someone he's naturally used to lying to. Maybe
both. It's impossible to be certain, but I have a strong suspicion he's
talking to a woman.

I take the opportunity to leap out of the vehicle myself and finally
finish my wee a few metres behind the car. My jeans are soaking
wet. Never mind finding John Lennon, I just want to find a Memory
Swapshop so I can maybe cadge some new trousers. Jane also gets out
of the van, exchanges her glasses for shades and leans back, briefly
enjoying the sun and what passes for a slight gust of warm wind. I

admire how positive she's managing to remain. She has a lightness to her, if that's the word; perhaps an innocence. Oddly beguiling, but in a very particular way. I generally never find myself attracted to other women while Saffy looms so unrelentingly vital in my mind, but all the same, I'm perplexed by what a tiny amount I fancy Jane. It's more how one might feel about a beloved sibling. Dunno. I can't quite work it out.

Felix is signing off. 'All right,' he says, 'see you there' – so casually, as if he's just arranged to meet a friend in a bar.

'What happened?' I demand, as he hangs up.

He shrugs, a little guiltily.

'I've just arranged to meet a friend in a bar.'

11

There's something fishy about this, and to make it even fishier, I'm the only one who seems concerned. Felix, typically, doesn't want any pesky rational thought to get in the way of his plan, and Jane is maintaining a suspiciously disinterested stance, though perhaps she's just concentrating on the road. Felix is riding shotgun again, as if to give himself and his slightly altered mission added kudos, while I languish in the back, strongly considering necking one of these strong beers and fucking everything off. To explain why all this is happening, we once again have to delve into Felix's past. You'll recall the tale of how Felix's Rendering girlfriend Suzi came into being, although perhaps I gave you the impression that the original person, i.e. the *Playboy* model who was rendered, was selected largely at random. This wasn't the case. In fact, Felix searched and searched the entire local zone group until he found someone who accurately resembled her. And who is 'her'? One night last year, Felix told me who 'her' was. It was on a very strange day when all the Locals broke down; they stopped moving abruptly at about four in the afternoon and didn't start again until eleven the next day. No one knows why, but it was one of the more interesting occurrences of the last few years. Perhaps things should break down more often. Felix and I were on our way back from Scott Weiland's Death Mission in T134, so we had to walk all the way to the T134 Trav station, then all the way back from our station in T109. On the trudge home Felix embarked on the whole sorry story.

'Her name was Kim. She was born in St Lucia but her parents came over to Britain when she was a baby... grew up near Kilburn. I met her through a friend of a friend... She was a backing vocalist... had loads of hits with various people... Bananarama, Thompson Twins... plus a whole bunch of also-rans. Used to hang out up Primrose Hill, Chalk Farm way. But there was always something... I dunno... a bit tricky about her. Didn't have just one drink, had nine. Couldn't take just one pill, had to take five. But fuck me... I just fell. Head over flip-

pin' heels. Never knew anyone or anything like her. Just… the sexi-
est… oh, man, I can't even describe. We went out for… oh… almost
five years… before she got put away.'

'Put away?'

'Yeah, Holloway. She was accused of murdering her flatmate. Well,
I say flatmate… she was really her landlady. She owned this gaff up
near Wembley Park and Kim… I dunno… She was pissed out of her
mind back then, but the official story is that she kidnapped the landlady, nicked a load of money off her… then bumped her off. Made it
look like suicide.'

'Shit.'

'Yeah. But Kim always insisted it was the landlady's daughter, who
was a fuckin' horrible piece of work. Kim had a shit lawyer, and the
daughter's team based the whole prosecution on Kim being off her
nut the whole time… which unfortunately was true. Anyhow… she
got life, of course… suffered a load of racist shit in prison… then she
managed to do herself in with a bottle of bleach she nicked off one of
the cleaners.'

'Terrible.'

'Yeah, man… I was a mess. I never thought I'd be the sort of person
to… y'know? To feel like that about someone. I don't think I ever
really got over it.'

I must admit, I didn't give this story much thought at the time. But
now I realise Felix must have been right. He never got over it. If he
had, there's no way he'd believe the phone call he's just received. A
phone call from Kim. This Minus-zone-residing ex-girlfriend of his.
But I'm not buying it. How can this possibly have happened? The
phone system, like I've said before, is delightfully simple. No number,
just the name, but we only have the names of the people in our local
zone groups. That's why we can't call Abraham Lincoln, or Winston
Churchill, or Archimedes. Or, following the same law, it's also why
we can't phone Hitler, Stalin, Fred West or King Leopold II of Bel-
gium.

A few more minutes down the road, I test this theory. I grab my
phone and try to call Benjamin Mulnick. Nothing. I type in Myra
Hindley. 'No user found.' Then I stick in Felix Romsey, and it won't

202

even let me connect to my next-door neighbour, currently sat two feet away from me. So, in order for this lady to have phoned Felix, not only would she need to already know he was here, but someone, somehow, *somewhere*, would need to connect the call. And that, to me, suggests fishiness of the highest order.

'I know what you mean,' Felix smiles, shaking his head in amazement. 'Coincidence, huh?'

'No, not a coincidence.'

'Why not?'

'Felix…'

He turns round, grins at me, and gives my shoulder a friendly little shake.

'Come on, man. At least we know where we're going now, eh?'

Where we're going, incidentally, is what Felix describes as a 'leisure facility' about fifteen minutes' drive away, in which this blasted concert is happening. It involves us heading back towards the tunnel and driving along the top of the dyke for a bit, after which, says Felix, we'll apparently not be able to miss the place. The leisure facility in question is called – of course – the Seventh Circle. I mean, really. What else would it be called?

'Felix,' I insist. 'This is wrong. Sorry. I know you're excited about… you know… seeing Kim again and all that… but… this isn't happening.'

'Podge, why are you being so negative about this, man?'

'It's a trap.'

'A trap!' he hoots.

'Come on,' I insist. 'Don't you think it's odd?'

'I dunno, man… I'm trying not to overthink it. I'm going with my heart, not my head. You know?'

I can't believe what I'm hearing.

'Jane?' I demand. 'What do you think?'

She shrugs. 'Do you have any better plans?'

Oh, screw all of it. I reach over, grab a bottle of beer, pop the cap with my lighter and glug half the bottle in one hit.

Seventh Circle, do your worst.

10

With a symmetry even I have to admit has a certain dry wit to it, the Seventh Circle is a mini-version of the Dome. It's the same shape and appears to be made from exactly the same shade of industrial tarpaulin, but it's about the size of a sports arena. It's surrounded by the kind of barbed-wire-topped white wall that's so popular around here, some jolly-looking snipers standing at various vantage points around the perimeter, a large outside area within the boundaries, and an ornate French-villa-like construction at the back with outhouses and prefab cabins. A water tanker-truck is parked at the back, where we can see a couple of Dwellers messing around with a giant hosepipe, and various other vehicles milling about delivering this and that. At the front, there's a pair of the Minus zones' most popular amusements: queues. One is a leisurely line of well-dressed Domers walking pretty much straight into the arena, with only the most fleeting checks from the security dude at the gate. Then, unsurprisingly, there's a long, oppressive line of Dwellers, some standing, some sitting or lying down, a belligerent-looking guard strolling up and down with a large gun, while his bored colleague at the front takes his sweet time checking tickets and occasionally letting a few of them in. Far from being the vivacious, liberating experience they've perhaps been expecting, the Dwellers – the ones that have probably spent their life, sorry, death-savings on a ticket – are merely herded into the pen-like outdoor area, where they're apparently going to watch the whole show on a medium-sized video screen.

Jane parks among a few other vehicles at a safe distance from the whole shebang – slightly up the incline towards the dyke – then carefully locks the van and we traipse over the scrubby, bumpy land towards the complex. Or rather, Jane and Felix traipse, while I waddle. I waddle and stumble and tumble and trip and do just about everything but walk normally. Dear oh dear – was that bloody beer strong. Or maybe I'm just weak. I haven't been this pissed since my thirty-third birthday, roughly two months before the diagnosis. Happy days.

I'm expecting Felix to laugh at my predicament; some kind of conspiratorial wink maybe, seeing as he was in a similar state himself only two hours ago. But nothing. He seems to be on a thoroughly different plain now, preoccupied and – more to the point, I suspect – nervous in a way I have rarely seen him. Bloody women.

Speaking of women, Jane has also been sporting a more serious mantle in the last few minutes, and seems in an equally anxious state. The two of them have a quiet conversation about the plan of action, like they're a flipping team all of a sudden; neither of them bothering to include me. They're becoming an utter drag. I didn't want to come on this stupid mission in the first place, so frankly, once inside, I'm considering finding a bar and getting obscenely plastered, maybe with a few perfunctory glances at whatever peculiar entertainment might be on offer. I'm particularly intrigued to see whether they really have nabbed Hendrix, and what motley crew is going to be masquerading as the Ramones.

Oh yeah, and whether Lennon shows up.

We approach the entrance: and what a peculiarly dark atmosphere there is, despite the sunshine and the promise of music. The line of Dwellers is as energetic and festive as the queue outside a Seattle methadone clinic, and the hard-cases lining up at the Domer's entrance are radiating hatred from every pore. They're all wearing holsters and ammunition belts and emit a general pig-headed vibe that wouldn't be out of place on a National Front awayday. Just for a laugh (it would seem), someone tosses something over at the opposing queue, resulting in a medium-sized explosion. I mean, really. Who throws a hand grenade at a queue to get into a rock festival? A couple of wounded Dwellers shuffle off, nursing bloody holes in their sides.

'Hey, Jane,' I ask. 'Did you bring your gun?'

Actually that's not quite what comes out of my mouth.

'Eyy, Sshhane. D'you bwwing the g-gun?'

She turns to me and frowns.

'Can't believe you've got yourself into this state. I'm ashamed of you.'

'Aww, fuck off,' I find myself muttering, to a withering look.

The guard at the head of our queue can't even be bothered to ask us for tickets, which is just as well. He waves me through, and I stagger in. Inside the compound is pure poison. Whoever designed the place had a good idea when they separated the two classes of punters. We troop down a little walkway between two chicken-wire fences, watched by herds of curious Dwellers who shuffle about, wondering what to do with themselves now they've paid through the arse for an afternoon in a prison courtyard watching imposters on a video screen. Even through the wire fence, our charming Domer companions can't help taunting the Dwellers, one guy beckoning them with the promise of a swig of whisky, then punching a gullible fool through the wire fence when he gets close enough. The mischief seems to be executed solely by the men; the women display an impassive stoicism, laughing occasionally but generally remaining inert. Another wave of drunken dizziness washes over me and I find myself stumbling, so I steady myself by holding onto the fence for a moment. I'm just glancing around to see where Jane and Felix are – they've moved on ahead, nice of them to wait for me – when there's a massive blow to the left-hand side of my face and I find myself eating a mouthful of chicken wire. I topple to my knees and taste fresh blood. Wow. That's not a taste I've tasted for a while, and I haven't missed it. I'm stunned, rendered totally useless, and it's all I can do to turn my head to see who did it: a chattering, toothless, filthy, blanket-wrapped oaf on the other side of the partition. He's still chortling when he gets clunked over the head with a nearby security guard's truncheon, dragged along the pockmarked concrete ground and then hurled – quite literally hurled – out of the gate. As if to prove some already fairly obvious point, one of the snipers on the arena roof takes aim and shoots my assailant as he crawls away. This incident produces a few little shocked gasps but not the same cowering and whimpering we saw by the border, and it strikes me, even through my shock and stupor, that the Dwellers inside here are of an appreciably higher stripe than those we saw outside.

I take a moment to regroup, still on my knees, a few people barging into me as they pass.

'Get up, ya fuckin' wimp,' comes a Scottish voice from above. I look up, but he's blundered on ahead.

'Brother...' comes another voice, from a different direction. I warily look over to my left and realise another hunched creature has bent down next to me on the other side of the fence. '*Vive la revolution*,' he hisses, followed by a wheezing bout of toothless laughter.

'I don't... speak... your...um... hybrid... thingy...'

'I know,' he says, smiling a smile that includes – despite my previous toothless assessment – two or three green and yellow teeth. He then points to his wrist. There is no watch there, but his next sentence nonetheless concerns time.

'Four o'clock, brother.'

'Wha... wha'sappening at four-clock?' I slur.

'Four o'clock,' he whispers. 'You outta here.'

And with that, off he sods.

I look at my own watch, but of course it's still rather uselessly set to T109 time, currently hovering near the 6am mark. I struggle to my feet, lurch forward and follow the herd of Domers into the vast oval marquee, in the vague hope of chancing upon a clock somewhere.

Inside, there are normal things and there are decidedly non-normal things. On the normal side, it really is a gig arena, with low-lighting, cattle-market seating, a couple of bars and a big illuminated stage from which a ramshackle rock tune is blaring out. From that point onwards, normality largely ends. Despite the Seventh Circle being big enough to accommodate, at a quick drunken guesstimate, ten thousand, there is hardly anyone here: five hundred at the most. But these five hundred are certainly making sure this is an afternoon to remember. Everyone is in various varieties of fucked-up-ness, to say the very least. A smell of filthy, chemical smoke pervades the entire place, as people seem to be starting fires with whatever they can lay their hands on: plastic, polystyrene, the occasional Dweller they've smuggled in for their own amusement. I see people shooting up, smoking various pipes, three or four couples having violent sex and plenty of other orgiastic activity, men beating up women, women beating up men, at least four other fights between random groups of people and two guys being shot: one of the victims remains on the floor while his extremely drunk lady-friend calmly mounts him, the other simply wipes off the blood with his shirt and stumbles to the bar for another drink. I witness one of the bartenders – not a Dweller, but a younger, rather more pleasant-looking Domer – being hoisted out from his stall by a chunky gangster-type, and then mercilessly beaten.

But officially, I don't care about any of this stuff. If I started caring, I'd be quickly driven barmy. I only came in here to find out what the time is: an incongruously quaint mission in such a place. I look behind the bar that recently lost its tender, but no clock is there. I try to flash a look at a female passer-by's wrist, and almost get punched by her primate-resembling geezer. Then I have a brainwave. Hey, I work at a festival, I know where to bloody well find a clock when I need one. At the Afterparty, there's always a clock by the side of the stage. As chaotic and apocalyptic as this shit-show is, there must surely be some infinitesimal degree of order to the side-of-stage area. So, praying that I don't blunder into anyone, I summon all my remaining sobriety and traipse down towards the stage.

At this gig, no one is rubbing shoulders with anyone; everybody's too scared that some face-deforming fight will break out. Edging myself forward in the crowd is therefore quite a palaver. I weave and slide as delicately as I can, but it's so taxing that after a few minutes I need a breather. I come to a halt behind a pack of people, and only now do I turn my drunken attention to the uniquely awful racket being produced onstage. It's a band, a four-piece rock band – that much I'm certain of – but the noise emerging from the musicians sounds like a school covers band after they've broken all their instruments and consumed their entire booze rider. They're dressed in black leather and vaguely look the part, but it's like the four instruments are being played in different time zones. Anyway, never mind all this: the clock, the clock. I'm only here for the clock. I need to get nearer the stage, but as the Pet Shop Boys once sang: how am I going to get through? While I'm standing there wondering, I receive a smile from a nearby girl.

The actual smiling isn't the only unusual part. She looks... quite nice. You know, like a nice person. She has a pretty, cheerful, open face, tousled light-brown hair, flower-power dress and a pair of long black boots. I'm well aware that looks can be deceiving, but she certainly wouldn't be my sure-fire candidate for an eternity in the Minus zones. The only unattractive thing about her is the ubiquitous holster

209

and gun combo, but needs must, I suppose, when you hang out in a dangerous dystopian dump. Chancing my arm, I smile back.

'Hey, how are ya,' she says. American.

'Hello,' I mumble.

'Want some?' she says, passing me a joint.

'Um, yeah,' I reply, then sort of wish I hadn't. Drunk *and* stoned might make a quick getaway tricky. Nonetheless, I allow myself a quick toke. Sweet, creamy. Ten times better than the stale shit Felix sometimes gets hold of. It seems to sort my head out too. I hand the joint back to her, and I swear, I haven't a sodding clue why the next sentence emerges from my lips.

'What's a nice girl like you doing in a place like this?'

She stares back at me, shaking her head sadly.

'Is that really the best you can do?'

She laughs, and goddammit, my cock hardens within my sodden pants. Now *that* hasn't happened for a good long while, I tell you. Even in our zones, most people are quite promiscuous – I mean, what's the worst that can happen – but it's never been for me. Usually at this point, a little flag flies up somewhere at the back of my brain, telling me I shouldn't be going any further with this escapade; then the face of Saffy appears like an internet pop-up window, and my willy shrinks to the size of a cocktail sausage. Not this time. Today I get the flag, but not the pop-up, and the cocktail sausage is rapidly turning into a butcher's banger. Squeezing the last droplets of sense from my brain, I manage to at least ask the girl for the vital bit of information I'm seeking.

'Er... have you got the time?'

'Why,' she grins, 'somewhere you gotta be?'

'No, I... um... wanna know what time the Ramones are on.'

'What are you, nuts?' she chuckles. 'They're on right now.'

I squint at the stage and listen to the din.

'*That's* the Ramones?'

'Yeah!' she says.

'No, it isn't.'

Just as I've said this, the song stops, the drummer clicks his sticks and the band tumble into another discordant blast, but this time there's a fraction more detectable rhythm and some recognisable words.

'Hang on,' I ponder out loud. 'What was that he sang? I *don't* wanna be sedated?'

Tommy the drummer – if that's really him – is playing one handed and, with the other, is swigging from a bottle of whisky; in fact, pouring most of it all over himself. A woman is kneeling down in front of Joey, giving him a blowjob as he sings. Various members of the audience periodically invade the stage, pushed aside and kicked by the other two guys in the band as they blunder through the song. Security hardly seem interested. It sounds like utter crap, but – and I can't believe I'm actually admitting this – there's something grimly captivating about it. If the slick, positive, high-energy shows at the After-party are delivered through a glove of Numbness, then this is raw: bare-knuckle boxing raw, a wild animal ripping meat off the bone raw. It's like they're playing outside their own skin. They want to feel everything. They don't wanna be sedated... and I believe them.

'Wow,' I comment. 'I can't believe the Ramones are actually playing this toilet.'

The girl looks a little downcast.

'Best thing we've got, isn't it? Mind you, there's a rumour going around...'

'Oh?'

She leans forward and whispers in my ear. I can feel her warm breath on my face and the whisper makes my whole left side go a bit tingly.

'... they've managed to bag a *big name* for later.'

'Never,' I respond.

'True,' she grins.

'Um, anyway,' I continue, the tingle spreading all over my body in a surprisingly distracting manner. 'D'you think you could answer my, you know... question?'

'Oh, yeah!' she laughs. 'What's a nice girl like me doing in a place like this? Okay. *Right*. Well... it's a long story, but I suppose the short version is... I started life as a happy sort of person, y'know... liberal type, late 60s, peace rallies, Woodstock, that kinda thing... then

I started working in pharmaceuticals in the mid '70s, one thing led to another, and I started doing really well and became a... y'know... executive... then the '80s being what they were, the money began to get the better of me... I started to cheat... I offered bonuses to our staff if they cut corners to boost profits, which specifically meant... kinda... not disposing of our waste water properly, but dumping it into the municipal water supply and... some of the public got really sick, but we got even richer, and then we got sued, and I lied in court, which took away compensation payments from the victims, and I got richer still... but then... I got really sick myself, and then I... y'know... died. So... here I am!' she says in conclusion, with a sad little smile and a 'ta-daa!' wave of both hands.

I gaze at her for a few seconds.

'Sorry,' I mutter. 'I meant – have you got the time.'

'Oh!' she says, laughing. 'Sure. It's... ah... quarter past three.'

'Thank you.'

She laughs again, reaches up and brushes my cheek with the back of her hand.

'So... you wanna fuck?'

Before I can make any swift and sensible decision, she wraps her arm around my waist and pulls me in. We're suddenly kissing. Or rather, she's kissing. I'm just standing there with my mouth open. That said, in the absence of my usual Saffy pop-up window, there's no denying I'm as randy as Newman and my private parts are, you'll have gathered, a total tiswas. Her tongue and lips feel soft and hot and I find myself moving eagerly into her, while my right hand investigates her breasts. My cock is going nuts down there and my nuts are going, um, cockers, and I know with a racing certainty that this'll all be over quite ridiculously soon.

'Don't worry,' she whispers. 'Everyone has the same problem around here.'

Despite her brazenness, she has so far exhibited the most tender of touches, so I'm a little surprised when one of her hands, previously caressing my lower back, now grabs the back of my hair and pulls, hard.

'Hey,' I exclaim. 'Easy!'

But the pull turns into a yank and I find myself stumbling backwards. How can she be doing this? Has she got extraordinarily long arms or something?

'Podge!' shrieks a voice.

Oh shit.

I grab the pulling hand and somehow manage to recover my footing. I whirl around and there stands the livid, eyes-ablaze gorgon that is Jane.

'Ah. Jane.'

'Don't "ah Jane" me, sunshine. We've gotta go. You've gotta come. *Now.*'

I turn back to the girl, who is glaring darkly at the intrusion but thankfully not getting her gun out. I'm about to embark on some half-arsed apology when Jane grabs my arm and frogmarches me towards the exit. Her grip is amazingly strong, but then my current state is pitiably weak. After we've made it out of the busier area, my legs catch up with the rest of me and I uncouple myself from Jane's furious clamp.

'All right, I'm coming, I'm coming! Can you just chill out? I was only having a brief…'

'I'm not interested in any pathetic explanation… just get your head together. We've got a big problem here.'

'Right… so you heard about the four o'clock thing too?'

'What four o'clock thing?'

'The bad thing that's supposed to happen at four o'clock.'

She stops marching and turns to me. We're a few metres from the exit now. A man wearing a dinner jacket and a monocle enters the arena pushing a wheelchair, in which sits a lavishly dressed girl with both legs missing. I wouldn't mind hearing the backstory to that one, but obviously now isn't the moment.

'How do you know?' Jane says.

'One of the Dwellers told me to be out of here by four o'clock.'

Jane bites her lip and thinks for a moment.

'Well, that could mean a number of things, but we'll need to be gone by then in any case.'

'Why?'

'Because Felix is being *converted*, that's why.'

'Converted?'

'No time to explain, just come.'

She turns and dashes through the exit. I hurry after her as she runs around the perimeter of the arena for a few minutes. We come to a security fence where a bored looking guard stands around looking at his phone. He doesn't even look up, just waves us through.

We dash on a few metres, to where the arena is connected by a makeshift tunnel to the garden that stretches out in front of the white villa. There's a long, large curtain of tropical reeds that we're about to walk through, into whatever den of iniquity lies on the inside. I can hear laughter, splashing, enjoyment. Then Jane stops and turns to me with a concerned expression on her face.

'Podge,' she whispers. 'What did you say your real name was?'

'I don't think I did.'

'Well, what is it?'

'Adrian. Adrian Jones.'

'Okay,' she murmurs, a slightly pained look on her face. 'But does anyone call you that any more?'

'Not really.'

'Good. Remember that. And… Podge… what do you want out of all this?'

Strange time for such a philosophical question, but I play along.

'Um… from this… mission, kinda thing?'

'Yes.'

'Um… I suppose… to get back home.'

'With John?'

'Yeah.'

'And with Felix?'

'Of course with Felix,' I frown. 'Where are you going with this?'

'But what's the most important thing?'

'Um… home, I suppose. To get back home.'

'To T109?'

'Yeah.'

'You don't like it here?'

'Of course not.'

'All right. Remember that, okay? Remember who you are. Remember the Afterparty. And remember... the name that people call you... is Podge.'

I frown at her, then nod.

'Okay,' she pants. 'Ready?'

'Yeah.'

'Then let's go in. And one last piece of advice. Walk fast.'

Walk fast. Okay. I think I can do that. Jane walks through the reeds, fast. All right, then. Fast. So, with my fastest walking head firmly, if a bit drunkenly, screwed on, I march in my best walking-fast manner through the curtains. The reeds are surprisingly heavy and, even walking as fast as I am, they put up a fair bit of resistance as they drape themselves all over my face and body.

And then we're in.

We're hurrying through an immaculately manicured continental garden: partitioned lawns, perfect flowerbeds, a vast variety of trees, both
tropical and European, some in a strict arrangement, some forming
little copses and jungle glades. There's an abundance of water features:
small dive pools, hot tubs, lagoons, fountains, and a larger, more regular swimming pool in the middle of the scene. Dotted here and there
are entwined couples, most of them completely naked, drinking, popping delectables into their mouths, smoking this and that, and, mostly,
fornicating. Waitresses of quite astonishing beauty, all naked, carry
around trayfuls of various items: more drinks, more food, sex toys,
bongs, pipes, syringes, you name it. In the background, somewhat
absurdly, we can still hear the pounding disaster-punk from the Seventh Circle. One wonders why they bothered with a rock concert at
all, when they could just spend their whole time getting fucked in a
garden. I'm about to share this musing with Jane when a girl – nude,
of course, dark hair, gleaming brown skin, so gorgeous I find it hard
to even contemplate – grabs me by the hand.

'Adrian,' she purrs, with a smile that could melt breezeblocks. 'Not
so fast. Maybe you'd like to stay here with me for a moment… have
some fun…'

She reaches down and lightly touches me between my legs.

'Podge!' shouts Jane. 'Let's go, Podge.'

'Adrian,' repeats the beauty. 'Stay with me…'

Utterly transfixed by this vision, I hesitate; but then I close my eyes
and, using every joule of energy I have at my disposal, wrench myself
away. We carry on striding.

'Well done,' Jane murmurs. 'There'll be more of that.'

Then I stop again, and gasp. Over the other side of the pool, I spy
the immediately recognisable Jimi Hendrix. I'm assuming Felix hasn't
also spotted him yet, as his limbs are all still attached. He's warming up
his fingers, not on a Stratocaster, but with what looks very much like
a household broom. He has a delirious smile on his face as he exhales
a vast plume of smoke.

'Podge!'

'Sorry,' I mutter, moving off again. 'This is unreal.'

'Exactly.'

'So where *is* Felix?'

'The villa,' Jane replies worriedly.

'Why don't we just find John now and worry about Felix later?'

'Well... John's never met you, has he?'

'No. Well, not the real one, anyway.'

'There you go. And me... well... I'm not completely sure what he'll say when he sees me.'

'He'll know you, though, right? I mean... you're friends?'

Jane gives her familiar evasive look.

'It's, um... been a while, let's say. So we definitely need Felix.'

Then another apparition floors me. She's sitting butt-naked on the edge of a scarlet velvet couch, incongruously parked in the middle of a leafy glade. This time she's blonde – not usually my bag – but they've added a twist, in that she's gently crying. She looks up at me, and with teary although still piercingly beautiful eyes, delivers her opening gambit.

'Adrian. Please love me? No one will love me.'

It's difficult to believe a line like this, uttered by someone who'd have a queue of people eager to love her stretching across the entire zone, but nevertheless I falter for a second, and as I do, she moves her hand to her neat blonde bush and gives it a delicate stroke.

'Adrian,' she sobs, 'just a little love from you, that's all I need.'

'Podge!' Jane snaps. Just as sofa-girl starts to fondle one of her pert breasts and beckon me with her other hand, I again manage to painfully extract myself from the picture.

It's worth mentioning that there are also fantastic-looking naked men parading about the place, but Jane isn't batting an eyelid.

'How come you're not affected by any of this stuff?' I ask.

'Perfection is boring,' is Jane's only comment. 'Now... I need to concentrate... '

We pass the entrance to what looks like a small maze. Inside the entrance I can see a flash of pink material, which then vanishes. Jane, who has been striding along at breakneck speed up until this point, stops short. She tilts her head to look through the gap in the hedges, and – of all things – a little curly-haired girl in a pink party dress jumps out.

'Ha!' she squeaks, smiling in Jane's direction. Jane gasps, puts her hand to her mouth, and then a look of unabashed delight spreads across her face.

'Oh! Hello!' Jane beams.

'I'm Bonnie,' the little girl announces. 'What's your name?'

'Jane.'

'I'm ten and a half,' the girl volunteers. 'Want to help me find the middle of the maze? It's a bit tricky...'

'Yes, of course!'

Okay, so she's good with kids. But aren't we in a desperate hurry? And what the hell is a ten-year-old kid doing here anyway?

'Um, Jane...'

'What?' she exclaims, whirling around, frowning at me.

'Don't we need to... um...'

Jane looks down at her feet, blinks hard, then looks back at the little girl.

'Sorry, Bonnie. Maybe another time.'

Jane sighs deeply, then dashes up the steps to the villa. Goodness knows what that was all about.

The villa itself is a reasonably authentic take on a French manor house: rustic magnolia walls, sash windows, blue shutters. Jane throws open the wooden double garden doors while I take a second to look behind me. Thankfully none of my tempters are following; they're probably being boned already by some other randy chumps. On either side of the arena two more tanker-trucks are arriving, all staffed by our Dweller friends, while the original tanker can be seen on the right hand side of the house. That's one heck of a lot of water.

'Podge, come *on!*' Jane yells.

I give my head a little shake and trot inside the house.

Inside ain't so pretty. All the work has clearly gone into making the outside look nice, while now we could be in the lobby of a municipal office block. In here we see a bunch of workers: Dwellers who've smartened themselves up just a tad – jeans, polo shirts, trainers – but their wrinkled complexions and matted hair are always a giveaway. They hurry to and fro, carrying towels for the pool, food and drink to hand over to the waitresses. They eye Jane in a shifty sort of way, but they don't pay me the slightest mind. One of them is coming down the stairs as we start to head up, and he actually stops to give Jane an elaborate sniff as we pass, just as one might smell a rare flower.

'That's enough of that,' Jane snipes at him. Nonetheless his gaze follows her upwards and he puts his hand on his heart in a strangely innocent gesture. It's almost as if, in this palace of blatant debauchery, Jane and her understated 1950s secretarial chic becomes the beacon of desire. I guess it'd be natural to find yourself immune to all those oiled body parts after a while.

Once at the top of the stairs, Jane runs along a wood-panelled landing and chooses one of the rooms on the right. She puts her ear to the door and winces.

'He's in this one,' she whispers, turning the handle and pushing.

I press my ear to the wooden door myself, and predictably enough there is much moaning, sighing, grunting and giggling. There is music too: some obscure '80s sounding pop-soul track. I glance back at Jane, with a cringe.

'Um… I'm not too sure about–'

'Podge, stop pussyfooting around! Just knock on the blinking door!'

I knock very cautiously. Jane rolls her eyes.

'Podge, we're here to snap someone out of an infernal trance, we're not visiting the headmaster's study.'

I glare at her and bang three times, hard, with my fist. All we hear is an enormously long, loud groan; a deep, cavernous unleashing of some sort, followed by more giggling. Then there's a ferocious pounding sound, like someone whacking a table with a cricket bat, and the music increases in volume.

'Shit,' I whisper, banging on the door again, 'Felix! It's Podge! I need to talk to you, like, now!'

No reply. More laughing, pounding, squealing. The music is reaching some sort of soulful crescendo, and then it stops.

'Now!' Jane snaps. 'Before the next song starts!'

'Felix!' I holler, thumping the shit out of the door. 'Snap out of it, for fuck's sake! We've got half an hour to get out of here!'

'Uhh?' comes a confused sounding grunt from within.

'Felix! It's me! Podge! What are you thinking? We've got to—'

Then the next track starts: some awful goth-rock sounding thing with a team of caterwauling backing vocalists. It's loud. I'm inaudible.

I turn to Jane and feign powerlessness.

'We break the door down,' she decides, reversing across the landing towards the bannisters. 'Come on.'

I'm about to protest but I realise this is pointless. Jane has the fire of destruction in her eyes and she ain't stopping now. I taxi backwards a good few metres and we prepare ourselves to run.

'Ready?' Jane yells. 'On three. One… two… *three*!'

We sprint towards the door and both shoulder-barge the thing. It refuses to budge and we collapse, Keystone-Cops style.

'Bloody shit!' I yelp, clutching my shoulder.

'We need a big thing,' Jane decides, apparently unfazed by any pain.

'A big thing,' I repeat.

Jane searches around the landing, spying, miraculously enough, a long wooden bench up at the other end by the front window. 'Here, Podge! Grab this and let's barge it.'

I hobble over to the bench and we pick up one end each. But when we turn around, we hear someone stomping up the stairs.

'Someone's stomping up the stairs.'

'So what?' Jane whispers. 'Let's do it.'

I can see the stairwell from here, and the top of someone's head as they ascend. I hesitate for a second to see who it is. In fact three heads come into view, one with an elaborate, jet-black quiff, and on either side two crew-cuts. The crew-cuts wear security guards' bomber jackets. The quiff has a long leather coat and, we soon see, leather trousers.

'Podge, pick up the bench, will you? Let's go!'

'No. This is gonna be trouble. We should leave.'

I drop my end of the bench and try the handle of the nearest door. Locked. I leap over to the room on the opposite side. Also locked. Jane is taking no notice of this performance whatsoever, instead hauling the bench along towards Felix's door by herself. The three men reach the top of the stairs and turn the corner. The two security dudes hang back near the bannister while quiff bloke slides along towards Jane.

'Can I give you a hand with that?' he says. 'Hate to see a girl struggling.'

Old-fashioned London accent: Jonny Rotten meets one of the Great Train Robbers. Jane looks up, smooths her hair back and gulps. She drops the bench with a clatter and stands up straight.

'No?' chuckles the guy, retrieving a packet of cigarettes from his pocket and flicking one into his mouth.

And what a sight he is. There's the aforementioned quiff, leather coat and trousers, but now he's facing us we can see some ridiculously cumbersome, ornate gothic boots, a Charles Manson T-shirt and heavy, Satanic jewellery. However, this is not the part of the man Jane and I find ourselves helplessly gaping at. One side of his face, his right-hand side, is normal, the heavy eyebrows and sideburns reminding me of a bizarre crossbreed between Marty Feldman and Eddie Tenpole. But on the other side, starting just beyond his lips, is a void, a vacuum, a flesh-exposing, muscle-uncovering, bone-protruding horror-fest stretching all the way to beyond where his ear might have been. His left eye has survived, but, disgustingly, the hole exposes some of his eye muscles, so you can see them bulging and contracting as he glances from place to place.

And they do indeed skip from place to place, because he also suffers from an assortment of twitches, perhaps a nod to years of earthly drug abuse, but in all likelihood brought on by whatever terrifying terrorist incident gave rise to his gaping head hole. Towards the back of this chilling arrangement, just before his hair starts again, there's a metal plate that curves around, linking the back and side of his head; presumably required to keep his brain in place.

He lights the cigarette and laughs at our horrified expressions.

'Ahhh... the look of love. It's all right. I'm used to it.'

He offers me a smoke and, calculating that it couldn't harm our situation any further, I accept.

'And for the lady?'

'No,' Jane says stiffly.

The guy shrugs and then looks back at me.

'Hope you don't mind me disturbing your little rescue mission. You see... I know Felix pretty well... and I know he won't want to be interrupted right now. It was quite an emotional reunion.'

We hear another colossal groan from within the room. Quiff-bloke does a strange sort of twitch-and-grin combo, and the collection of gubbins within the left side of his head squelch and flex in quite the appalling manner.

'Heh heh... they're definitely making up for lost time. Gave 'em some viagra and some of my finest coke too, so they'll be at it a while. Not hurrying off anywhere, are you?'

Jane and I keep schtum.

'Good,' he smiles. 'Y'see, we like sharing the love around these parts. Sharing the love, that is... not the hate, as some of those slanderous little cunts often say.'

Jane clears her throat.

'You're Benny Bumlick.'

Benny closes his eyes, grits his teeth and takes a deep breath.

'Motherfucker,' he whispers, then twitches, exhales, and finally nods. 'Yes, my Australasian heroine, I am Benny Bumlick. Look on my works, ye mighty, and despair.'

He cackles in a Disney-villain manner, which I assume is supposed to be funny. I take a drag of the cigarette. Remembering Felix's coughing and spluttering routine earlier, I summon all my strength not to do the same.

'Well,' Benny says, turning his attention to me, 'I must say, I'm impressed. I thought you'd be busy sampling the delights of my little paradise right about now. You must have some willpower, young man.'

'Perfection is boring,' I mumble.

' "*Perfection is boring*"?' he drones, copying my still rather drunken delivery. 'My, my... you are a damp blanket, after all. Felix told me he'd hired a young star. Not quite the flamboyant mogul, are you?'

I shrug, looking around dejectedly. Nice to be back in the school playground.

'What happened to you two being arch-enemies?' Jane asks.

'My dear girl,' Benny replies. 'Any intelligent company is welcome around here. And you know… Felix and me… it was always a love-hate thing, rather than a hate-hate thing. There was always respect.'

'Apart from when you were burning down houses and murdering people,' Jane shrugs.

'That,' Benny snaps, 'was circumstantial.'

'So where's John?'

'John?' Benny frowns, heralding an all new selection of bendings, bulgings and wrigglings in his skull. 'First name terms, is it?'

'We're old friends.'

'Oh, old friends. I see. Well. If you're old friends, then I suggest you do what a friend would do, and leave him the fuck alone. You see… he wanted to come here.'

'No.'

'Yes. They all did. Jimi, those Ramone boys, Bon…'

'Bon?' I ask, finding my voice from somewhere. 'As in, Bon Scott?'

'The very same.'

Cheeky bastard. I spent ages last week trying to find out where he'd vanished to.

'I think,' continues Benny, 'he wanted to find out whether hell was a bad place to be or not… ah-ha ha haa!!'

Jane and I stare at him silently.

'Oh, come on. That was quite funny. Anyway… where was I? Oh, yeah. John. John was practically *begging* to come. I never take anyone against their will. What would be the point of that?'

'John would never–'

'Oh, yes he would, sweetheart. Stuck in that crappy little collection of greenhouses you call home, he was miserable as a dry Christmas… hanging out with those numbed-up losers, unable to create… artistically mute.'

'That's not true,' I put in.

'Oh?'

'He was writing again.'

'Yeah, *right*,' Benny laughs nastily. 'After thirty-five fucking years, he writes one verse. One… sodding… verse. Have you any idea how… *excruciating* that must be? For the world's greatest ever song-writer?'

'I always thought Macca was better, actually,' I mutter.

'That,' Benny leers, 'doesn't remotely surprise me.'

An ecstatic female scream now rings out of the locked bedroom and across the landing.

'Heyy, that's my fucking *boy!*' Benny hollers, clapping his hands. Then he turns back to us. 'Look. I'm an empathetic guy, despite what you might think. I can see how soul-destroying it's been for John. And now he's here… and he's been here for just *twelve hours*… do you know what he's been doing?'

We both shake our heads.

'Sitting in a room with a guitar, and some paper, and a pen… *writing songs*. I checked in on him, about two hours ago. Happy as a pig in shit. Three, four complete new songs. Not a drink, not a drug, not a bird in sight, but he was bouncing around the room. Completely rejuvenated. His mind… unlocked. Free from whatever junk they pump into the air in your boring Plus-zone shithole. And now, in a few hours, he'll be playing a full-on, kickass rock gig in front of an adoring crowd…'

'Um… now, hang on,' I begin, finally reaching a subject I have a clear opinion on. 'You mean that horrific bunch of gun-wielding, over-testosteroned, violent psychos? Lennon won't want to play his music to them.'

Benny rolls his eyes.

'Oh, my gawd. Who ordered the bleeding-heart, fucked-up-the-arse liberal? You bloody people. You only see the few dickheads who ruin it, don't ya? And then you paint everyone with the same brush. I bet you were a *Guardian* reader back in the day.'

'The *Independent*, actually.'

'Same fucking difference. Anyway… look. I ain't got all day to stand around and chat. You seem like nice people, in spite of every-thing, so I'm gonna make you a deal. And think about it carefully, because it's the only deal you're gonna get.'

He takes another drag, all the better to make his point.

'You get the fuck out of here. *Now*. My friends' – he indicates the two security guards – 'will very kindly escort you from the premises, all the way to your wonderful vintage motor... which is a nice touch, by the way, I might have to find out where you picked her up before you leave... and then you fuck the fuck off, back to the city of dreams that is T109. I'll call the border guards, get them to let you out swiftly... not that they ever give a shit who leaves the Dome... and then you never... *ever*... come back.'

'Without Felix and Lennon?' I ask, in a smaller and weedier voice than I intended.

' "*Without Felix and Lennon?*",' he mimics again, in a nasty nasal whine. 'You wet little turd. Oh-ho, yes. Definitely without Lennon. And as for Felix, well... let's ask him, shall we?'

He steps forward and thumps hard on the door.

'Romsey? Hate to disturb you, my brother... but your chums are heading back to T109 now... You wanna join them?'

The cacophony of banging and moaning ceases for a couple of seconds, although the musical din continues.

'Romsey? You hear me? It's home time. You interested?'

Another mega-groan is unleashed followed by a female giggle, then the volume of the music increases and the banging resumes. Benny delivers a wicked grin, holding out his hands as if to say, 'Well?'

I shoot a glance at Jane. She's glaring at Benny with an almost palpable hatred. Me, I'm thinking about John Lennon. I wonder what he's really up to right now. I think about the song he was starting to write. It was a bit weak and underwhelming, I have to admit. I think about the sobbing mess that was Brian Epstein. I even think about George Harrison, and what a pain he was, but how he ended up being correct about everything. I think about Felix, and how utterly typical this is of him. And for some reason, my mind also flashes to Suzi... Felix's Rendering girlfriend. Yes, she's a Rendering. But she's never been anything but sweet to me, and she will – in her artificial Rendering way – be devastated.

Benny holds up his wrist, to which a chunky watch is buckled. He taps the face. 'Tick-tock, tick-tock. Decision, please.'

I catch a glimpse of the watch face, which is of course set to Minus zone time. We've managed to waste twenty minutes with all this malarkey and it's now 3.35pm. Benny seethes and looks up at the ceiling, as a large drip of blood seeps out of his gash, rolls down his leather shoulder and splashes upon the floor.

'Come on!' he snaps. 'You're taking the fuckin' piss. What's it to be?'

I take one more look at the fierce, unwavering Jane, and back at Benny. Then I say two words, nice and loudly so he can't accuse me of being a damp blanket ever again.

'*Fuck. You.*'

He rolls his eyes, throws down his cigarette, spins his repulsive head around and roars at his guards.

'Aarrgh, these fucking people! Put them in the fucking cellar, will you, lads? One that hasn't been cleaned in a while... cage four or something. And make sure you turn the fucking lights off, yeah?'

Without a further word, he stomps off down the stairs, gnashing his teeth and twitching like a trenches veteran. The two guards take us both by the arm, sullenly but quite gently. We all troop off the landing and descend towards the cellar. One of the guards even says sorry.

However. The place where they stick us is something else. The basement area has various lockup cages that they use for booze and so forth, but there's a terrible smell down here, a rotting stench of disease and faeces, the provenance of which I don't even want to think about. And the worms are back: our little grey friends from outside the Dome, thousands of the tiny blighters, squirming all over the place, being squashed in their hundreds as we all stomp along the sticky concrete floor. The guards show us into one of the cages, about three metres by two; they lock the door with a hefty padlock, and then, as instructed, switch off all the lights and depart. A couple of worms run up my trouser leg and I bat at them furiously. Jane fumbles forward and tries the lock, but she judges it resistant to any picking she might attempt. The cage, we soon discover, also has a roof, and after a feeble shot at trying to bend the connecting cage wires, during which I manage to spike my finger, we decide this is also a non-starter. So, apart from a couple of occasions when a Dweller worker comes down to grab some more bottles (we plead for him to let us out, or even to leave the bloody lights on, but to no avail) – that appears to be that.

'We should have just gone,' I mutter.

'No, you did the right thing.'

'But we're no use to anyone here. We should've pissed off while we could…'

'No, you did the right thing.'

'… headed back to T109 and returned with the cavalry.'

'Nonsense. Can you imagine anyone agreeing to come back with us?'

I picture our highly motivated office staff at the Afterparty, and me bursting into HQ saying, 'Quick, everyone! Felix has been kidnapped and he's in one of the Minus zones! Any volunteers for a rescue mission? We'll head back down there in a clapped-out van, traverse a zombie-and-worm strewn desert, battle through a terrorist-laden shanty town, blag our way past murderous border guards into a giant artificial dome where slavery is rife and gun-waving psychos run free. Who's in?'

I concede that Jane might be right.

'Did you notice what the time was?' she asks.

'Yep… twenty-five to four, and that was… what… fifteen minutes ago.'

'What do you think might happen?'

'Um… Everyone goes nuts. Massive battle. Loads of fun for all the family.'

'But not a bomb?' Jane responds.

'How would anyone sneak a bomb in here?'

'How would anyone sneak a gun in here?' she counters.

I sigh, fishing a couple of worms out of my shoe.

'Poor Felix.'

'You're a loyal chap, aren't you?'

'He's done a lot for me.'

'Well, I wouldn't feel too sorry for him. Sounds like he's having the time of his death.'

I hear her fiddling vainly with the padlock. When she speaks again, her voice sounds just a touch more vulnerable.

'May I ask you something?'

'Sure.'

'You know… the things you were doing… before?'

'What things?'

'You know. With the girl, inside the arena. Before I came along.'

'Oh… that.'

'Was it… nice?'

I sigh.

'Well, yes. In its own way, it was.'

'Sorry I interrupted, then.'

'No, no. She was awful, actually.'

'She looked very nice.'

'Oh, yeah… but I mean… who she actually was.'

More jingling with the lock.

'How about you?' I ask.

'What about me?'

'I mean… do you ever indulge in that kind of thing? Back home?'

'Me?' she sniggers. 'Oh, no! Not me… Ha! Not likely.'

'Why?'

No reply.

'Seriously,' I continue. 'Why? And… why haven't you been tempted by any of this stuff? I know you said perfection was boring, but… really.'

A moment's more silence. Then, finally:

'Podge… oh, fiddlesticks. Look. I'm not… I'm not supposed to be here. I don't mean *here*… of course I'm not supposed to be *here*… I mean… there. You know, S and T. I'm not supposed to be there. I'm a mistake.'

'What… you mean you shouldn't have died?'

'No, not that. Goodness, the place'd be half empty if… no, no.'

'Then what?'

'Well, there are zones where the likes of me are supposed to go, and I'm not there.'

'The likes of you… meaning?'

'Look, Podge… you're not a fool. You know how the local zones basically work. People from the same part of the world, more or less, are grouped together. The same language… grouped together. People who died around roughly the same time are grouped together.'

'Jane, it's okay. I know you're a little older than most of the people around us. I get that.'

'No, no.'

She stays quiet for a few more seconds, as do I.

'Oh, for goodness' sake, Podge. I thought you'd have cottoned on quicker than this. You saw what happened in the garden just now… with the maze?'

She takes a deep breath, then sighs again.

'I'm a child.'

'You what?'

'I'm a child. I died when I was eleven years old.'

Silence.

'I was born in 1940, I died in 1952. We moved to Australia when

I was nine, then a year or so later I caught malaria and I died. I never made it beyond eleven.'

'Ah.'

'Yes,' she confirms, a few little sobs creeping into her speech now. 'And there's a place, of course... like everything else, there's a place where all the children who died young are supposed to be, and I'm not there. Some big... I don't know... some big mistake must have happened, because I'm not there. And that's why I've been trying, for sixty-four bloody years, to find out where the place is. So all this stuff that I do... all the exploring, all the mapping, all the nonsense I spend my whole time doing... it's all because I want to find the place, but I've never bloody found it...'

She dissolves into tears. I move towards where the sounds are coming from. I don't have to go far, obviously. I find her shoulder and give it a squeeze, then she falls into my arms, crying her eyes out. I hold her tightly, wondering what I could possibly say next. After a few moments something occurs to me. Not overwhelmingly sensitive, but it'll have to do.

'Um... where are your parents?'

'Oh, I don't know,' she whimpers. 'I've looked them up a billion times, but just my luck, I think they're probably still alive. They'd be well into their nineties by now... crikey, almost a hundred. I had hoped – God, it sounds horrible to say – but I had hoped, for about thirty years, that they'd die soon. But they must be living a nice long life, which is... well, it's nice isn't it? Good. They'll appear eventually. So I had to let it go. Instead I started to look for others... other people that I'd known.'

'Any luck?'

'Yes,' she croaks, 'a few. Grandparents, cousins, a few friends. But it isn't all it's cracked up to be.'

'No?'

'Ah-ah. You've no idea how *boring* people are.'

'You'd be surprised.'

'I knew you'd say that,' she laughs. 'But really... it's bad enough being eleven, forever, in a sea of people who are all at least nine, ten years older than me. And everyone thinks I'm a little bit weird, but really, I'm just...'

'Eleven.'

'Yeah,' she sighs, a great relief audible in her voice. Perhaps she's never told anyone this before. Impossible. She must have mentioned it to someone in sixty-four years. Still...

'But also,' she continues, 'people are just so... *numb*. It's unbelievable. I just wanna... ooh, I just wanna shake them sometimes!'

'Yeah, absolutely. Me too.'

'So, in the end, I just spend an awful lot of time on my own. And I get so lonely... you wouldn't believe...'

We're still holding each other, in case you were wondering. And I'm pleased to say, it's been an entirely platonic experience; Jane's revelation having completely thwarted any other ideas. And with the lights being off, it really does feel like I'm talking to an eleven-year-old. Now the natural time to unclasp seems to have arrived, and when we do, it's an entirely effortless movement.

'Have you ever wondered why you're not affected?' I ask.

'By the Numbness?'

'Yeah.'

'It's because I'm different.'

'That's it?'

'Uh-huh. Whatever it is they're doing, it's designed for people who should be there. And I shouldn't. So it doesn't work.'

'How about me?'

'Oh, you're more numb than you think you are.'

'Eh?'

'Remember that chat we had about the hill at the other end of your street?'

'Um...'

'How come you've never explored up there? You've been here long enough. But you accept the world you've been given, just like everyone else. Felix too.'

I'm trying not to be, but I'm offended.

'Well, I've tried to... um...'

'Oh, don't get me wrong,' she chuckles. 'All people are numb, but

233

some are more numb than others. You're definitely a little bit different, too.'

'Ah. How?'

'Well... this is just a theory... but... you're longing for something.'

'For what?'

'A girl... you had a girl, in life. Didn't you?'

'Yeah,' I croak. 'Saffy. How did you know?'

'You can tell a mile off. I may be only eleven, but I'm also seventy-six, remember? And I reckon... when your longing is strong enough, it changes you. One thing I've realised over the years is... very few people die when they're in love. Really, properly in love. And those who do, they're different. Love is very powerful. I've learned that much. It's real.'

'You're sounding like John Lennon now.'

'Ah yes,' she says. 'John.'

'Wonder what he's doing now?'

'I don't even want to think about it.'

'So what's the story with you and him?'

'Oh, I—'

BANG.

Well, all I can say is: I'm glad we were in the bloody basement. And I'm also glad we were locked in a cage. Benny, unpleasant dickhead that he is, inadvertently provided us with the ideal bomb shelter: a thick layer of concrete and a strong wire box which kept us free from any dangerous shards of metal or falling masonry. Not that we aren't completely covered and near-suffocated by a dense cloud of foul-smelling dust, a horrible flood of grit, shit and pieces of worm finding its way into our mouths, eyes and ears for the second time on this exasperating expedition. Our cage has been knocked over onto its side by a ton of brickwork toppling down from somewhere, the upside of which is we now have a small shaft of light. A very small shaft of light, because of all the crap in the air. Through the coughing and spluttering and finding (once again) the two of us involuntarily holding onto each other for dear... oh, dear death, whatever... there is nonetheless just the teeniest, tiniest ray of hope that the top lid of the cage has miraculously become unhooked.

'Is it open?' Jane growls, the dense dust lending her voice the qualities of Bonnie Tyler after a night's drinking with Rod Stewart.

'The wires are all bent,' I reply, 'I just have to find one that's maybe... yep, here we are, one of them's undone... have you got anything hard or sharp at all? Like the heels of your shoes?'

'Yeah,' she sighs, scrabbling around and handing one of them over. 'My precious shoes. Swapped a gold-plated cigarette holder for these.'

I insert the heel into a loop of wire and start pulling furiously.

'I meant to ask you,' I rasp, 'what sort of crazy clothes did they give you when you arrived?'

'Oh, it was ridiculous,' she whispers. 'Military uniforms and posh dresses from the 1920s. But at least it wasn't a wardrobe full of children's clothes.'

'An irony too far,' I splutter, yanking the shit out of the wires. Weakened and bent by the blast, they seem to be yielding to my efforts. There is all sorts of commotion upstairs: screaming, yelling, running, gunfire. And the smell. Beyond the dust, there's a ghastly industrial stench of some sort, like when you drive past a brickworks – thick, sweet and sickly – but enhanced by the charred aftertaste of an explosion.

Finally I've unhooked about seven of the wires: enough to squeeze out, I hope, so long as we don't mind getting scratched to pieces. I give Jane back her shoe and begin the tricky task of forcing my way out.

'Careful once you stand up,' Jane advises. 'The ceiling might not be where it used to be.'

With a few scrapes but nothing serious, I pull myself up, my hands instantly touching pieces of rubble on all sides. Then Jane emerges too; I grab her arm and help her out. Although neither of us is particularly certain what 'out' is. The dust is so thick that we have only a faint idea whether this is still the basement or whether we're in a giant crater. Closing my eyes and putting one careful hand on my head, I scrabble through the breezeblocks and hoist myself up some steps, Jane following close behind. Then I realise the steps are going nowhere.

'Hang on,' Jane says. 'There's a ledge over here, I think it's the ground floor.'

'Can you reach it?'

'Give me a bunk.'

I push her feet north-ways and she vanishes up.

'Yup, this is good. Give me your hand.'

I reach out, she pulls, and soon I'm standing on something firm, with a crack of daylight visible to my left. We climb up one more ledge, and we're on the parquet floor of the villa's hallway. The light is still murky as fuck, but I can make out the strewn, blasted remains of the left hand wall of the house – broken windows and bits missing but still just about intact – while the other side of the villa has completely gone. The floor above us has half-collapsed too; it's a little difficult to tell which part Felix was in.

'Look,' Jane gasps, pointing towards the garden. We hurry to where the door used to be – past one of the waitresses, still naked, sobbing and clutching a rag to her bleeding head – and gape at the carnage. The garden is no more: it's now all blackened scrubland, yellowed, burnt plants and an awful lot of mud. Bits of tree every-where, flowerbeds on fire. And beyond, it is now obvious: a gaping hole where the Seventh Circle once was. To the right, the mangled and twisted remains of the water tanker.

'The bombs,' Jane murmurs.

'In the tankers?'

'The tankers *were* the bombs. They must have filled them with petrol. And the guards never thought to check.'

A deafening burst of gunfire shatters our attention, as four Dwellers come careering down the main stairs, one brandishing a machine gun. We leap out of the way and flatten ourselves against a nearby ruined wall, but they take little interest in us, instead running over to the cavity from where we've just emerged, and leaping over the edge towards the basement. I recognise one of them: the guy who came down earlier to stock up on booze.

'Looting,' I whisper.

'Good on them,' Jane nods, but then clasps one of my hands anx-iously. 'Hold on, did they come from upstairs?'

'Shit, Felix!'

We race across the hall and up what's left of the stairway. The ban-nister on the left side has gone, but miraculously the steps are still climbable. The rooms on the right look intact too, but – ominously – the door to Felix's room hangs off its hinges, and the handle has completely splintered away. Amid the various bursts of gunfire and screams from all over the locally audible area, I can still hear groans coming from within this room, but they are groans of a somewhat different nature.

We dash inside.

The room doesn't contain much: a large metal-framed bed, silk sheets, huge pillows. But I inhale quickly, deeply, unexpectedly, involuntarily, at the first bad detail that my mind succeeds in process-ing. An almost perfect circle of dark red, the circumference spanning practically the entire area of the mattress. Four human legs, two of them pink and hairy, two of them dark brown and slender. Two bod-ies wrapped around each other, one female, a perfectly toned torso obliterated by one shockingly round bullet hole, right in the centre of the stomach. A tragically beautiful face, a mouth stretched wide in the shape of eternal pain, eyes that have long-since ceased to harbour any life, and now also seem to have parted company with death itself. Next, glued to her figure with a mixture of blood, sweat and a muscular clinch that can only be described as desperation: a male body, hairless and tanned, a Banksy-style Cupid tattoo on the upper chest, pointing his arrow towards a large, horrific but mathematically precise bullet hole, through which I can already see the rapidly reddening sheets underneath. Felix's motionless face presides over the whole sorry scene, his bright green eyes wide and unblinking, his mouth twisted into a strange sort of smile.

'Fuck, fuck, fuck!' I shout, stumbling over to the bodies and searching desperately for any signs of movement.

'Podge, I'm so sorry,' Jane murmurs, standing by the door.

'Fuck!' I repeat, frantically looking around for any clean material with which I might fashion some sort of hopeless tourniquet. 'Felix, you stupid, stupid bastard! You weak, dumb dickhead! Look what you've gone and done to yourself! You even had a target for them to aim at, you moron!'

Jane arrives on Kim's side of the bed and dithers indecisively for a moment, nervously brushing her hair back and turning towards the shattered window.

'So… Jane… you know *everything*… what now? What happens now? They die *again*? How can they die again? Where do they go next?'

'I don't know…'

'Shit!' I cry, the tears appearing out of nowhere. Finally hitting upon a half-arsed idea, I grab the only pillow that isn't being laid upon, whip out the innards and hastily press the pillowcase to Felix's bullet wound.

'AAAARRGH! Judas *Priest*!! Don't press there, you twat!'

Felix has lifted his head fractionally off the pillow and his whole body has stiffened, then he inhales – the heaving noise is deafening, like a cow warning you not to touch its udders.

'What… you're alive?'

'Of course I'm fucking…' His voice then runs out of voice, and the

rest of the sentence is spoken in an agonised backwards whisper – '…
alive-you-utter-berk-well-not-alive-you-know-what-I-mean-
bugger-me-that-fucking-hurts…'

'Who did it? Those Dwellers?'

'Yeah,' he rasps, 'I-told-those-cheeky-fuckers-we-were-on-their-
side-but…'

His speech dissolves into an almighty heave.

'Don't worry, I get the idea.'

'Oh… ah…' Jane says, looking hysterically down at Kim. 'Are
you… erm… there as well? I'm sorry. It's just that I've never been
very good with blood…'

Kim yelps, then starts to breathe fitfully.

'You don't… have to… do… anything… I've been… hurt…
before… it… takes a while… but… it gets… better… a bit…'

'Okay,' I sigh. 'You're both… both okay. Relatively speaking.
Right. Let's not hang about. Jane, do you reckon your van's still there?
Do you guys think you can walk? We've gotta get out of here…'

'No,' Felix whispers.

I blink at him, incredulous.

'Whaddya mean "no"?'

He fixes me with a look I've never ever seen on his face before.
That's because the look's name – in addition to a sizable portion of
excruciating pain – is apology.

'You're *not* staying here,' I tell him.

'Yes,' he breathes.

'No!'

'Yes. I'd… made up my mind before… this shit… happened…'

'But you can't! You don't belong here! You have a house! You have
a' – I flash Kim a swift awkward glance – 'girlfriend!'

'Podge…'

'You run an enormous festival, for fuck's sake!'

Felix shakes his head gently.

'Podge… who cares… whether you ought to belong… where they
say you should… belong….'

He swallows painfully and takes a deep breath. I don't wait.

'Sorry, Felix. I can't let you do this! You said it yourself… these

241

people are here for a reason! And... Kim, I've never met you before, but...'

'I know,' she gasps, 'I know what you're thinking... but I never... I never did... those things. It was wrong... all wrong...'

'They might have got it wrong on Earth, but they don't usually get these things wrong here!' I shout.

'But sometimes they do,' Jane murmurs.

'Well, then! If that's true... then let's put it right! Come back with us, now, both of you!'

But I know this is a non-starter before I've even finished the sentence. There's an unshakable resignation on Felix and Kim's faces, and as I look around the room – the blood-stained bed, the various booze bottles, the vintage record player with some random '80s album still spinning around uselessly, some lines of coke chopped up on a nearby table, waiting to be sent brainwards, the smashed window letting in the noises of the gunfire and assorted shoutings and screamings outside – it all makes some kind of twisted sense. Squalor. Excess. Pleasure. Vice. Danger.

Absolutely bang up Felix's street.

And yet...

'What about the Afterparty, for goodness' sake?'

'Podge,' Felix says, even managing a crooked smile. 'Don't be so... modest. You could... run the damn thing in your... sleep.'

'No, I couldn't.'

'Bollocks. All you gotta do... is stride around getting... angry with people... bloody place practically runs itself...'

'Look, I'm not leaving you here like this,' I insist. 'I can't. No matter what you say. Look at this place, half the house has fallen down. You could get blown to pieces, even worse than now, any second... either by some pumped-up Rambo knobhead or these Rebel Alliance chancers. And even if you get out of here... what are you going to do, where are you going to–'

'Kim has a lovely place,' Felix gasps. 'By the... lake.'

'On which side of the terrifying electric fence?'

'Podge! Just stop... arguing and *go*... will you? You're in... more danger than… us. We'll just… slow you down. And you… need to find… John.'

'Oh, screw John. He's the fucker who got us into this mess in the first place.'

Felix shakes his head.

'No. You need to… find him.'

This is impossible. In eight long years, I've never seen such madness spouting out of his stupid moustachioed mouth. I look frantically over at Jane, whose face and demeanour seem very much to be saying, 'This ain't going anywhere… we should just split. Now.'

Felix grabs my hand and gives it a squeeze.

'Sorry, man,' he wheezes.

'I'm gonna record you saying "sorry" and play it to the Afterparty staff.'

Jane is almost jumping up and down with impatience to go, but Felix isn't letting go of my hand.

'Podge?'

'Yeah?'

'Look after Suzi for me… will you?'

'Suzi?'

'Yeah… keep an eye out.'

'But…'

'She is what she is. But… still. Turn her on from time to time.'

I look at him uneasily.

'Not like that, you filthy fucker…. switch her on, keep her going.'

'I'll see what I can do.'

I look at both of them, broken smiles on both of their stupid faces. Dear oh dear, what a bloody mess.

'Just one more thing,' I stammer.

'Podge,' Jane says, jiggling her legs about like she needs the lavatory.

'I know, Jane, I know… but this is important! Felix… remember when we were at Brian's place, and you asked me where we were, and I told you my theory?'

'Yeah…'

'Well, you never told me yours.'

He swallows again and fixes me with one of his deathly serious looks.

'Very simple,' he says. 'It's all an illusion.'

'Eh?'

'It's just one... big... illusion. How can it be anything else, man? And it's not just *an* illusion... it's whatever illusion you want it to be. It's *your* illusion.'

'Uh... right?'

'But as Guns N' Roses once said... it's up to you... how you use it.'

I stare at him, agog. Felix smiles a huge, toothy, bloody smile, and gives my hand one last squeeze.

'Now fuck off, you nutter.'

It's 'leap of faith' time. We are, amid all this chaos and destruction, to find John Lennon, pray he isn't in a similar state to Felix and Kim, make it to Jane's van, pray the van is even there, and get the merry blazes out of here. And that's not even the hardest part. After this entire hullabaloo, how can we expect the tunnel, border and slums to be anything other than a complete, snarled-up, dangerous bombfest?

Jane and I make it back downstairs and outside the house without an enormous amount of trouble, but now, surveying the Somme-like garden area, comes the tricky bit. On our left side, crouching down between some rubble and the still-standing perimeter wall, is a team of Dwellers, about five of them, who have themselves a mortar gun and a clutch of other weapons. Over on the opposing side of what was once the lawn, the right-hand wall has been completely blown apart. Behind various bits of debris are the pink-faced Domers, all wearing shades and waving guns of differing sorts, firing off rounds and behaving like they're on some bachelor-party paintballing trip, screaming various preposterous war cries ('Have some of that, you sister-fucking bunch of retards!' etc.), all apparently commanded by Benjamin Mulnick himself who is crouching behind one of the burning dressing-room prefabs, barking commands into a radio. In between these two factions lies nothing but body-strewn desolation, and – horrifically – a blood-red swimming pool, complete with bodies, torsos and even heads bobbing around.

'What happens when you lose your head?' I hiss at Jane.

She gazes at me and speaks in a low, spooky drone.

' "*A fiend is here behind, who with his sword hacks us thus cruelly, for first our gashes close, 'ere we repass before him.*" '

I blink back at her, perplexed.

'Not a literature student, then?' she sighs. 'Come on, there must be a back door.'

She pulls me back inside the house – not that it's really much of an inside any more – and we dodge bits of burning furniture and clamber over piles of blackened white bricks, picking our route to the rear of the villa. We scramble through what used to be the hallway, now looking like the sort of ancient ruin I might have seen on a geography field trip, in the centre of which the quartet of Dwellers we saw earlier are standing around, glugging from huge bottles of Champagne and Scotch while the wounded figure of a Domer writhes around agonisingly on the floor. We put up our hands as we pass by, but they pay us not the slightest attention. I've never been so happy to look weedy and pathetic.

'Where next?' Jane asks.

'The prefabs… the dressing rooms.'

'They're all flattened.'

'I know, but… he might be… oh, I dunno, let's just go and see.'

We climb through a collapsing hole in the perimeter wall, then instinctively run further outwards across the scrubland, turning around after about fifty metres to survey the scene. We can see now that all three tankers exploded; where the arena used to be is a giant burning pile of metal and blue plastic, unspeakable bits of bodies here and there, bloodied people wandering hopelessly about. And now that we're at a distance, we can see a horizon of figures surrounding the whole scene: a circle some two-hundred yards away of hollering, jumping, singing, dancing, partying, celebrating Dwellers, delighted at this latest and most triumphant instalment in the eternal battle between Dome and slum.

'My van!' Jane exclaims, with a little yelp of relief. 'It's still there!'

And indeed it is, patiently waiting a safe distance away. I'm amazed – but the urgency of the situation strikes home. When we parked it was next to about fifty or sixty other vehicles. Now it's quite alone.

'It won't be long before someone pinches it,' I tell her.

'I have the keys,' Jane says, jingling them.

'Someone will know how to hotwire it. We've gotta go.'

We set our controls for the heart of the burning prefabs and sprint off, dodging various bouts of gunfire and the occasional grenade as we go. The dressing rooms are, like everything else, merely blackened shells. There are a couple of wounded figures lurking underneath, but even in their hideous, distorted states we can tell none of them is John

Lennon. We move on to the field of devastation, where the blood is so widespread and the injuries so gruesome, I have to wait a minute while Jane runs off to be violently sick. I'm not quite sure how I'm managing to hold it together myself, but I keep replaying my earlier visit to this very area when it still had a roof above it, and the charming displays of humanity I witnessed, and remind myself that most of these people are total cunts.

Lennon remains conspicuously absent. There are various figures strolling around doing a kind of half-baked humanitarian thing, giving out bottles of water, smiling sympathetically, not administering any first-aid because of course we know that's a waste of time, but holding the hands of the injured and assuring them that everything – in a kind of nightmare-vision-from-Hades way – will be all right in the end, and I have it in my head that maybe Lennon would be one of those people, using his celebrity at this unusual juncture to cheer people up, spread a bit of peace and love, perhaps even drift about with his guitar singing a couple of soothing songs. But he ain't. Time is ticking away, and the distant Dweller mob are still boisterously leaping up and down; it's conceivable they could soon press their advantage, pile back in and do even more damage, if that's possible.

Jane returns, wiping her mouth.

'He's not here. Is he?'

'I have the strangest feeling,' I reply, 'that he has already left.'

Jane's lip wobbles worriedly. I manage to persuade her to at least take a moment's refuge inside her vehicle, in case anyone has designs on it. We sprint round to the van, traversing the whole pile of carnage as distantly as possible, keeping low, hiding behind clumps of weeds from time to time to get our breath back. It takes about ten minutes – but we get there, miraculously, neither of us taking a bullet.

Jane fiddles with her keys, opens her door, jumps in and leans over to unlock my side. I leap in too, and we shut ourselves in, taking a minute to savour the safe warmth of the car, the hot leatherette of the seats, the moment of relative quiet... before heading off somewhere, anywhere. A plan I still don't think Jane's fully onboard with.

'So...' I begin.

'Not sure,' Jane says.

'I understand.' I'm trying to be as tender as possible while at the same time illustrating how crucial it is that we sod off immediately. 'I mean... I still feel like going back for Felix, too.'

'But Felix doesn't want to go. I know John does.'

'How?'

'I just do.'

I think about this for a second, searching the vaults of my brain for any salient information about Lennon's wishes and desires.

'Yes,' I conclude. 'I suppose that makes two of us.'

'Make that three of us,' comes a familiar Liverpudlian voice from underneath the car.

5

How long would it take you to recover from finding a Beatle under your car? Jane and I take a conservative three minutes, after which we excitedly bundle him into the passenger seat and creep, thankfully unmolested, past the picket line of Dwellers, after which Jane floors it. Now we're speeding back along the dyke, the dyke which houses the tunnel, the very important tunnel which will provide our prompt escape from this squalid little watery suburb, while Lennon tells us how the buggering heck he managed to find himself with a green delivery van on top of him.

'One of those wrinkled little squirts came into my dressing room. He was pottering about, filling up the fridge and whatnot, then he asked me for the third fuckin' time whether I wanted a woman. He kept saying he could get me a woman, so I said, "No, I do not want a woman, mate." Then the weirdest thing. The guy stops what he's doing, looks me straight in the eye and starts singing, in his crazy accent, my song "Woman". Caught me right off guard. Before I knew it, I was singing too. We get all the way to the bloody chorus, and he bursts out laughing, so I laugh too. I ask him where he's from, and he shakes his head and knocks the side of his nose with his finger. I said, "Come on, man. You can tell me." He gives me this really sly look and says, "You no wanna play this concert, my friend. You wanna be away somewhere. You no stick around." Then he taps the side of his nose again and vanishes out the door. So I waited for the security geezer to fuck off to the loo or whatever, and I pegged it out of there. Underneath the cabin, round the back, I managed to find a little door in the side of the wall and then I just ran. All these people were arriving, but of course I'm wearing this helmet so they didn't recognise me.'

He looks nothing like his Hamburg-era Rendering, but instead is a dead ringer for his character Gripweed in *How I Won The War*: military helmet, military shirt and little round glasses. Another unnecessary specs-wearer, but hey, who's complaining.

'Why the helmet?' I ask.

'That revolting mutant running the joint gave it me... He said I might need it while I was onstage, the fucking tit. Anyway, I hid behind a bush for a while, then I spotted your van. Couldn't bloody believe it. They used to have these in Woolton in the 50s. Laughed my head off when I saw it. Ideal hiding place.'

The real Lennon's personality is incomparable: warm yet spiky, tired yet crackling with life, sincere yet as bright and witty as you'd hope, despite the shittiest of days he's had. He's understandably freaked out by the experience of the last forty-eight hours, not least the whole abduction bit.

'Last thing I remember, I was on the Trav heading to your gig. Then... nothing. Woke up with something over me head, banging along in the back of some car, and then after... I'd say after an hour... I got pushed into another car and they injected me with something... I went back under. Woke up with this banging headache, feeling hot and parched...'

'Yep,' I nod. 'I know that feeling.'

'And then they took the thing off me head... and that freak starts giving me the whole Bond villain thing. Such a stupid get.'

'So... you didn't have, like, a rebirth of creativity in the dressing room? Songwriting, I mean?'

Lennon turns to me and frowns, and for a horrible moment I think I might have overstepped the mark. I have only just met him, after all, despite it seeming like I've known him years.

'It's always hard, it's always easy,' he begins, cryptically. 'No matter where you are. You never know what you're going to get. And that's one thing Felix probably never understood. He goes barging around barking orders at people to write new stuff. Even back in the old days, we'd have hated that. Filo's a damn interesting fucker, but he's black and white, good and bad, heaven and hell. Life was never that simple. Neither is death.'

There's my answer to that one, then.

Only one naggingly curious box remains unticked in the back of my mind, but my mind is so befuddled right now, I can't presently recall what it could be. No matter, because we've soon got all sorts of other things to worry about. As we reach the entrance to the tunnel, the route, unsurprisingly, is blocked by a couple of sturdy barriers and a couple of even sturdier, armed security guards.

'Tricky,' Jane mutters.

'That our only route?' John asks.

'As far as we know,' I reply.

'Hold on. Let me see if I can work some magic.'

John takes his helmet off, lights a cigarette and gets out of the car. He strolls along towards the guards and raises a hand in greeting.

'Afternoon, fellas.'

'HALT!' they both shout, engaging their rifles and pointing them unequivocally in John's direction. 'You get back in the car!' adds one of them.

John tears back towards us and leaps into his seat. With a screeching of tyres, Jane zooms off in the opposite direction.

'Oops,' John pants. 'Beatles can't have been big in their country.'

Jane keeps up a frantic pace until we're at least ten houses away, then she slows to a stop and extracts her mess of papers from the glove compartment. I can hear her panting with anxiety as she searches for whatever vital link she's missing, and it strikes me that this is the most anxious I've seen her all day. She fingers her way through the pile of notes with their arcane scribblings, bizarrely detailed maps and crazy arrows heading all over the place.

'I can't… seem to find… oh, fiddlesticks! I thought I had it!'

'Fiddlesticks?' John scoffs. 'What a word.'

Jane glances up at him, blushing.

'Oh, never mind that,' she says. 'Expression of my mother's… I haven't been able to shake it off…'

'Why should you?' John says. 'I love all that. "Two shakes of a lamb's tail." '

' "Three sheets to the wind",' Jane grins, her face now almost as red as her lipstick.

'Ah, I dig it,' John laughs. 'My Aunt Mimi used to come out with all that.'

He stops, and looks wistful.

'Lovely woman, despite all,' he says.

'Oh yes, I remember,' Jane says, then she stops, gasps, puts her hand over her mouth and her eyes fill with tears. 'I'm so sorry!' she sobs, then dumps the pile of papers on the floor and dashes out of the car.

Lennon frowns and looks back at me.

'What's going on there?'

Naggingly curious box: tick thyself.

I'm sitting in the van alone while, about fifty yards away, Jane is sobbing into Lennon's shoulder. It's quite a day for people sobbing into each other's shoulders. Frankly I can't wait to get home, so everyone can calm down a bit.

At last they return to the car and fill me in. So basically, Jane and John were village friends between the ages of six and eight, stretching perhaps to playing 'doctors and nurses' occasionally. Lennon, understandably, probably never thought about the friendship more than a couple of times since 1948, and therefore it took a bit of mental filtering to unearth it, but for Jane, naturally, it has taken on rather a larger significance.

'You're silly,' John says. 'Why did you never just come and say hello?'

'Shy,' Jane replies, sifting through her papers once more.

Lennon laughs.

'Shy for thirty-six years?'

'I didn't want you to think I was just saying hello because... oh, look, never mind,' she says, removing her glasses to study a scribbled map. 'We've got bigger problems now. Like how to drive through twenty miles of water.'

I blink at her. 'Really?'

'Really. Unless they've built a dyke all the way to the hill.'

'Hill?'

'Remember I told you,' she says, 'that all the S zones are mirror-images of the Ts?'

'Um, sort of.'

'So what I'm expecting,' she says, 'is the entrance to S101 on the other side of this zone, just like the entrance to T101 is next to T109. Now... as you know... S101 is a regular zone, and not a Minus zone, so all we'll have to do is drive through about four or five access tunnels between S174 and S341, sneak through the gap, and then drive back normally on the T side.'

Lennon looks round.

'She's lost me.'

'Don't worry,' I tell him. 'Just accept everything she says, it usually does the trick.'

'The only problem,' Jane continues, 'is the water.'

'And,' I speculate, 'getting out of the Dome on the other side.'

'No.'

'No?'

'My calculations suggest that there *is* no other side.'

'How can there not be another side?'

'If this is basically a mirror-image of T109, there will be a hill… the dividing hill… starting in about ten miles. So I expect the Dome to only have one side. They just built it into the hill.'

'Sounds good to me,' Lennon deadpans.

We drive on, heading in as straight a direction as we can, via the network of dykes and reclaimed tracks that stretch out across the vast lake, nervously hoping – in my case at least, praying – that the track doesn't suddenly plunge into the water. If it does, I'm also praying that Jane's van has a kind of James Bond-esque aquatic conversion feature she's neglected to tell me about. Apart from the occasional erratically driven 4×4, a glimpse from time to time of someone sunbathing on their roof, or a few wandering, tired looking Dweller workers trudging along the tracks, we pass no one. It's a strange sort of watery, dykey road trip, punctuated by the occasional muffled explosion in the distance, and I have the weirdest sensation that we're driving across wartime Holland. With John and Jane's dreamlike catch-up chatter in the background, the 1940s picture is complete: names, faces and places from old Liverpool are flicked through like a dusty photograph album that's been hidden in some vault for almost a lifetime. After a while, bored of worrying, and with nothing much to do or think about, I begin to doze off. Two things wander through my mind before I conk out. One is, of course, Felix. Felix bloody Romsey. Who knows how long it'll take him to regret his snap decision? Maybe it's happened already. Maybe tomorrow. Maybe as soon as he discovers Kim has omitted some vital ingredient from her current existence, like – I dunno – that she and Felix will both have to work in the water factory too. Or perhaps it'll all work out. To paraphrase

Morrissey: he's not right in the head. But this is why I like him. Stupid bastard.

The other thing is a small but significant concern. Wasn't there something about needing fuel sometime? We've only seen one dilap-idated petrol station in this whole place, and of course it was on the other side of the Dome. Didn't Jane even hold onto some of those weird white ceramic coins for that precise purpose? But I'm sure Jane's got it covered. She always knows what she's doing. Still, it would suck so badly if we got within a mile or so of S101, the boundary line, the access point, the whatever-you-want-to-call-it... and the last drop of petrol glugged into the engine.

Why oh why do I even say these things?

3

I pick myself up off the ground for the third or fourth time and try to resume my grip on the rear bumper, taking small comfort from the fact that the clearly less-fit John Lennon has stumbled over a good few more times than me. He's changed from his previous chirpiness to a studied, stoical workmanlike slog, but to be completely fair to the man, he's complaining a damn sight less than Felix would have. In the dark now, saved from pitch-black by the thankfully still working headlights, we've reached the top of the hill and managed to push the van round the tight corner of what Jane seems convinced is the entrance to the correct tunnel. The ground feels damp and dirty, but not, as I'd feared, gross, slimy and riddled with Minus worms. Maybe they just can't be arsed to come all the way up the hill, and who could blame them. We're still going upwards and it's blindingly hard work, especially when the surface starts to angle slightly to the left. I put my left arm out to get some balance, and I'm surprised to feel the tunnel wall – cold, slimy and not particularly hard, almost like reptile skin.

'The tunnel's closing in!' I shout.

'Yes,' Jane yelps from the driver's seat. 'It's supposed to do that.'

We carry on pushing but the slope is getting steeper, the angle is getting more angular, and the walls are getting narrower. Soon we've slowed to the breathtaking rate of about five metres per minute, and Lennon's side is sloping upwards so much he's practically lying on top of me.

'Fuckin'ell,' he gasps. 'Haven't worked this hard since the Bermuda Triangle.'

'You were in the Bermuda Triangle?'

'Yeah, on a little boat, we had to sail through the fucker. Hardest thing I ever did.'

'Really?'

'Yep,' he puffs. 'Shea Stadium? A breeze.'

'Stop chatting and keep pushing!' Jane shrieks.

'Bloody slave-driver,' Lennon pants.

The tunnel is now less of a tunnel and more of a duct through which we're pushing this enormous hunk of metal. The twisting wall is holding the van on both sides and the wheels aren't even touching the ground any more. Lennon and I, both leaning sideways, are slamming ourselves against the damn van for what feels like half an hour, Jane hollering, 'Push! Push!', like some deranged Australian midwife. The two of us have abandoned all qualms regarding physical contact; we're rammed up against each other, heaving and shoving. I can no longer remember what the correct way up is supposed to be, whether I am currently on my side, or upside down, or what. We might have spun round more than once for all I know; it doesn't make any difference. Finally, the car stops moving altogether.

'It's getting narrower!' I cry. 'This isn't going to work!'

'Yes it is!' Jane hollers. 'I can see the other side! Just three more huge pushes and we're there!'

'Can we take a break?'

'Come on,' Lennon growls. 'Let's get organised… do it in counts. After one… three… two… *one*!'

A gigantic shove from both of us, which moves the car precisely a centimetre.

'Three… two… *one*!'

Half a centimetre.

But the strangest sensation is starting to hit me. I feel a sudden burst of energy, and – although I've had no water – a lessening of the frantic thirst I've had for hours. I also realise I can see the faintest glow of light through the tunnel walls. The next time we count three, I push with all my might and miraculously the car lurches forward a couple of feet.

'Yeah!' shouts Lennon. 'Now we're cooking!'

A couple more blasts of muscle from the two of us and we can feel the wheels finally connecting with the floor again.

'Jane!' I yell. 'Look at the dashboard, can you see the petrol gauge?'

'Yippee!' she screams. 'It's gone, boys!'

Lennon glances at me through the murky light and winks.

'*Yippee*,' he sniggers.

I don't know whether Jane heard but we're soon rewarded with a burst of exhaust in our faces as she fires up the engine.

'Shit,' I cough, opening the back doors and jumping in. 'You might have warned us.'

We leap back into our seats and Jane gives her car the slightest burst of gas, and we're off, freewheeling through the strangely lightening, plasticky tunnels. Soon we've swerved into another thoroughfare and the slope downwards begins to even out. We rattle on like this for quite a while, making a few twists and turns; then we're out of the tunnel and the mist is back. The mist of the old Plus zones. Never thought I'd be pleased to see it.

'How do you feel?' I ask.

'Happy,' Jane says.

'John?'

He stares forward through his small round specs, running a hand through his hair and sighing, not entirely contentedly.

'Normal,' is his eventual reply.

Finally the fog thins, and beyond it, the suggestion of a sunny morning. They're all sunny mornings. No one says anything for a while. It's just gone 9am. The identical white houses start to appear on either side of the road, along with the good old occasional trees. The sun hovers near the horizon for a while and then just plops itself into the sky, like someone's flicking a switch somewhere. Perhaps they are. Everything looks familiar, humdrum even. Halfway down the hill, passing a solitary Local working its way upwards, containing one bored-looking man in a flat cap staring out the window, Jane turns on the radio. I'm expecting to hear Jane's regular big-band clatter, but instead it's a familiar-sounding 1980s ballad, a ruminative synth pattern and reverb-slathered tinkling ivories, but with a drumless, slow-burning melancholy all its own. After a moment or two I realise it's George Michael. It's too new for John and it's certainly not Jane's cup of tea, so it must be coming from me.

Lennon sits back and listens. What does he think when he hears music from after he died? I wonder what sort of records he himself would have been making in 1986? The lonely-sounding song fills the car as we trundle towards downtown – downtown whatever zone Jane said this was – and of course my mind immediately meanders off in the direction of Saffy. Just like in the song, she's always been the only one to stop my tears. But for the first time, I find myself daring to wonder whether this is really true.

Could I be taken back in time? Could I forget, maybe?

Then I think of Felix. What am I going to do without him – without the Afterparty? He said I should continue to run it by myself, but that's impossible.

I'm so scared. I'm so scared.

How could I ever replace him? The relationships he had with the stars, the furious energy with which he pushed the organisation along, and not least – in fact, probably most – those special text messages he would receive. How could I possibly proceed without those things? The rival festivals – Malcolm's, Tony Wilson's, and so on – would grow rapidly with a trickle, maybe soon a torrent of new stars, and in the not too distant future the Afterparty would be Felix's greatest fear realised: an Afterthought. A nostalgia show, featuring merely the last few remaining faithful subjects. We might even have to start using Renderings. No, no. There's no way I could continue. I'll just have to take up some other pastime. There are a million things I could try. Hanging out with Jane a bit, reading some literature together. Maybe I'll try to bump into that sporty girl I saw on the Local yesterday morning: ask her if she'll take me surfing.

Or perhaps I, too, should go back to feeling lonely and confused.

Or perhaps not.

'Podge?'

It's Lennon, turning to me with a grave look on his face.

'Podge. You gonna put the Afterparty on today, after all this?'

My kneejerk reaction would be, 'Are you mad? Of course not.'

But I pause.

'Well... I could make a call...'

'Because,' John continues, 'I don't know what you're thinking of doing... but I feel like playing.'

'Playing?'

'Yeah. Playing the gig. The gig that never happened.'

I spend a second or two pondering the incalculable logistics of this. It can't be done. Or can it?

'Let me make that call.'

I turn my phone on, to something like twenty-five voicemails and thirty-six texts. I ignore all of them and call Sarah. Just before the voicemail kicks in, she picks up.

'Podge!! Podge, Podge, bloody Podge! Where have you *been*?'

'Sorry, did I wake you up?'

'Oh, don't worry about that, where the hell are you?'

'Listen, I'll explain later. Need to ask. Is the Afterparty happening today?'

'Well... no, because we didn't know what to do without you and Felix and we didn't think people would come back if they'd seen what happened and we weren't sure whether today's acts would show up or whether-'

'Okay, okay, I get it... but is the gear still there?'

'The gear... uh... yeah, last time I looked...'

'Okay, great. Listen. Call the Infonet people. We're coming back... we've got John Lennon.'

'You've... *how*?!'

'Never mind. Put a message out, say John Lennon's going to be playing his set... for real this time... at... let's say... 7pm?'

I look at Jane and John, they both nod.

'Fantastic. Oh, and Sarah... contact his band, will you?'

'The band, yep... got it...'

'Apart from George Harrison, I'll deal with him.'

'Uh, right,' she says. 'Oh... and how about Felix... is he still really angry?'

I inhale and look out of the window.

'Um... I'll tell you the whole story later. Thanks Sarah.'

'Of course!'

I hang up. Jane and John both turn to me and smile.

'What?'

'You,' Jane says.

'What about me?'

'You're born for this shit, man,' John grins.

'You mean I died for this shit.'

'Yeah,' John concedes. 'Yeah, I guess that's what I mean.'

Plus

2

The journey back to zone T109 is very long and involves no less than five hill-climbing and passing-through-tunnel experiences, though thankfully, these being the gloriously convenient Plus zones which I'll never complain about ever again, there is no getting out and pushing and no turning upside down. Even getting up the so called 'chute' between S and T is barely worse than any of the other transitions. Apart from stopping to consult her notes a couple of times, Jane knows the way pretty well. It is, however, remarkably boring – up a hill, down a hill, downtown, back up a hill again – and each time I'm reminded how desperately featureless the whole place is. Curses, there I go – complaining already. The only bit that could be even remotely described as picturesque is halfway across S154 when we drive around a hill-lined lake, at which point we stop so Jane and John can have an ice cream.

Aw. I hope Felix finds some ice cream where he is.

I fill the time with phone call after phone call, trying to make this impromptu Afterparty happen. Most of the acts scheduled to play today have already flounced off in high dudgeon, but it turns out Phil Lynott and The Monkees' Davy Jones are still knocking around so they agree to kick off the show at 5pm. I dodge various questions – why didn't John show up in the first place? Where have we been? And where the fuck is Felix? – partly because it'll take too long to go into, but mainly because John has an idea: an idea I must admit I'm not entirely comfortable with, but which I've grudgingly agreed to. It is John Lennon, after all, and as we traverse the final boundary between T104 and T109 he's endearingly excited. As am I – not to mention stomach-churningly nervous.

Jane, however, becomes less and less enthusiastic the closer we get. She's either completely silent or a little snappy, such as when I ask her to turn the radio up when 'Ace Of Spades' comes on. Finally, early afternoon, just as we're rolling down the hill into my home zone, she pulls over on the verge and loudly wrenches up the handbrake.

'Everything okay?' I ask.

'I don't wanna go,' she says, staring straight ahead.

'Eh?'

'I can't do it.'

'But you have to,' John replies.

'Sorry, I can't.'

'But you're the total hero, Janey,' he says. 'Without whom, and all that...'

'Look, you'll both get your moment of triumph. But I can't do it. Me? At a rock festival? Ha! Not likely.'

'You don't have to go out in the crowd, if that bothers you,' I tell her. 'You can stand backstage with–'

'No. You'll... you'll both have to get out here and take the Local. I'm sorry.'

John looks at her in a kindly way and gives her shoulder a little shake.

'You sure?'

'Uh-huh. Sorry.'

I'm perplexed, but obviously we can't force her. John gives her a kiss on the cheek and gets out of the car. I wait for a second, expecting her to turn round. She doesn't.

'Um, Jane,' I say gingerly, 'can I have your surname?'

'Why?'

'So I can call you?'

She at last turns to me, with a little awkward smile.

'You'll see me around,' she says. 'Don't worry.'

I shuffle out of the back and disembark. I'm standing on the roadside with John Lennon, and we both give little confused waves at Jane as she releases the handbrake and motors off. The little green van gets smaller and smaller as it trundles down the hill.

'You know the strange thing?' Lennon says, as a Local slides towards us.

'Mmm?'

'I actually don't remember her at all. I just didn't want to be rude.'

He jumps on the Local. I watch Jane's van reach the bottom of the hill, then it abruptly turns left and disappears from sight.

1

And so, on a rapidly populating Local, Lennon and I find ourselves approaching the Afterparty site. He's still wearing his *How I Won The War* army helmet, but he is unmistakably John Lennon, and soon the Local is just one big seething mass of people wanting to say hello and sign an autograph. John handles it with warmth and patience, but by the time we're approaching the festival's public entrance things are getting a little crazy and I have to physically remove a couple of fans from him. Finally we're dropped at the end of the leafy road leading to the West Gate and, accompanied by a few giggling hangers-on, we finish the journey on foot. In the distance I can see various hopeful, anxious faces: our massive German security guard Frank, a clutch of people from HQ passing round a bottle of champagne, George Harrison himself with the rest of the band, and finally the permanently anxious Sarah, smiling awkwardly and hopping from one foot to the other. She breaks with protocol and runs up the road to greet us, from which everyone seems to take their cue, and a happy armada of Afterparty folk comes streaming down the road, with hugs and whoops and questions galore, most of which I manage to deflect. Then we hear the noise of a car behind me and for a moment I wonder if Jane has had second thoughts, but I turn to see Walter, smiling broadly out the window of the black and burgundy Rolls Royce.

'You shoulda called me, Mr Podge!' he grins. 'I got Phil Lynott and Davy Jones in here.'

Far from being a disorganised mess, I must admit things are ticking along just fine. The gear is in place, the engineers are ready, the crowd is swelling, even the TV cameras are back for a second stab at the live broadcast, which I acknowledge to myself with a rush of nerves. Curse John Lennon with his big ideas. Backstage is its usual buzzing atmosphere, everyone beavering away with an unusually industrious swing, which I realise must owe a lot to relief. If I've been feeling that the Afterparty is something I can't do without, I guess they all have been too. I dodge the many enquiries about Felix, fudging it with a general statement about him 'needing a rest after our ordeal'. This works well enough for almost everyone, but midway through watching Davy Jones knock out a blistering 'Daydream Believer', I spot a tall, beautiful but worried-looking lady making her way up the steps to the side-of-stage area. I remember what Felix said to me about Suzi. It's the oddest thing: I'm about to comfort an artificial entity, but somehow it doesn't feel unnatural. Suzi approaches me, sobbing gently, and falls into my arms. I'm not sure what I'm more flummoxed by: that a Rendering is so upset about something, or that she, somehow, already knows what's happened.

'I'm sorry, Suzi,' is all I can think to say.

I hold her for a moment or two, and for the second time today I just let myself relax and enjoy the human contact. And yes, I'm counting this as human contact. In the end, what difference does it really make that Suzi is a Rendering? Who is a Rendering, and who is real? What makes the Trav run? How does the Infonet radio know what you want to listen to? 'It's all an illusion,' Felix said, and I realise for the first time, the old bastard pretty much had this whole existence thing nailed. We're here, whether we like it or not. We can shape our illusions into pretty much anything we like. I loved Saffron, and she loved me. Nothing is ever going to change that. But where's the sense in depriving myself of any kind of happiness, solely for the memory of someone I loved?

Suzi finally lets go and draws away. She smiles a sad smile and I look into her eyes; the warmth there is as real as anything I've known. She touches my face, then turns around and wanders off, gently descending the steps again and padding softly across the grass. That's the last I see of her.

This experience leaves me a little dazed, but I have a job to do. The sky becomes a little darker, Phil Lynott is blasting out 'The Boys Are Back In Town' to the packed field, then finally Davy Jones ambles back on, and in true Afterparty style Lynott and Jones close the set with a supergroup version of 'I'm A Believer' infused with such kinetic energy that it's almost punk rock by the end, with some frantic pogoing down the front. Then the stage is cleared for the Lennon show and I can see the man himself, with his band, having a pep talk by the side of the stage. Amazingly enough – considering this show wasn't going to happen until a few hours ago – the crowd is even bigger than it was yesterday. The cameras whirl into place, the lights dip down, and John joins me, waiting next to the monitor desk.

'You ready then, boy?'

'No,' I smile.

'Go on,' he says, producing a couple of bottles of beer and handing me one. 'Spirit of Felix Romsey.'

'Spirit of Felix Romsey,' I repeat, clinking my bottle against his. 'Even though he's a bit of a dick.'

John laughs and rejoins his band. I sip the beer, which thankfully tastes as weak and disappointing as always. Maggie the monitor engineer gives me the signal, and I wander cautiously out onto the stage. The lights go up, the crowd give a medium-strength roar, understandably wondering who this nondescript oaf with a beer belly is. I spot a little red light appearing on the TV camera dead in front of me, I approach the microphone, and in a voice that starts a little feebly but thankfully grows in strength by the end of the third or fourth sentence, I start my short address.

'Good evening everyone. My name is Podge. You won't know me, but I'm... well, never mind who I am. As you know, yesterday evening, we had a bit of a... technical hitch.'

Laughter, thank goodness.

'I just wanted to let everyone know that, unfortunately, we were the victims of sabotage.'

Boo.

'Yeah, right... It seems that one of our... well, I suppose you'd call him a competitor... he decided to steal our headline act.'

Boo. Hiss.

'Well... I'm pleased to say... we got him back.'

Massive cheer, continuing for a good fifteen seconds, before I cut in. This is the important bit. Keep it simple, keep it general, keep it vague.

'We got him back, but at a price. We had to say goodbye to our dear friend, and the man who made this festival happen... Mr Felix Romsey.'

At first some of the crowd cheer and whoop automatically, but then there's a shocked gasp, and... well, silence.

'We had quite an adventure, I tell you, but after all that... Felix decided he had to... um... retire from the Afterparty.'

More gasping and a few cries of panic, particularly from backstage.

'But I want to assure everyone... that we're going to continue, just as before. The biggest festival around, and the only festival with a hundred-percent no-Rendering policy. And we will be here... bigger and better... for a very... long... time.'

A huge cheer, all of it coming from the crowd in front of me. Backstage, more stunned silence.

'Okay, well, thanks for listening... that's quite enough from me. Please will you now all go absolutely fucking nuts for Mr John Lennon.'

Everyone goes absolutely fucking nuts.

I turn around and walk offstage, meeting a grinning John on the way, from whom I receive a warm hug. I can see the confused faces gathered behind the monitor desk, so I decide, for the moment, to linger right here, just within the area of stage-light: an area into which very few of our staff would dare stray. I want to buy myself a few minutes before all the questions, and all the answers, which I'll need to keep just the right side of scary. I need a few moments to enjoy something I've been anticipating as long as anyone: perhaps since Felix and I confirmed Lennon's appearance a few months ago; perhaps since I first arrived here, and discovered (eventually) what the Afterparty was; perhaps since I started going to gigs as a teenager and realised there were several people I'd simply never get to see perform live; perhaps even since December 8, 1980, when I heard – on the radio, in the car on the way to school, if memory serves – that John Lennon had made his untimely exit from that world, and his first appearance in this one.

A reverent hush descends over the entire festival, broken only by drummer Ola Brunkert chiming a little bell three times, after which Lennon approaches the mic, strums a few loose chords and begins to sing. And it really is just like starting over.

It's the Lennon show everyone's been yearning for: a dizzying, wildly exhilarating barrage of passionately played hits, taking in solo highlights ('Whatever Gets You Thru the Night', 'Cold Turkey', 'Mind Games'), Beatles bangers ('Help', 'Revolution'), album classics ('Dear Prudence', 'Hey Bulldog', 'Everybody's Got Something to Hide Except Me and My Monkey'), and delicately beautiful acoustic moments ('Norwegian Wood', 'Julia', 'You've Got to Hide Your Love Away'), all delivered with humility and warmth for the enraptured, banner-waving crowd. George Harrison ambles on to sing 'While My Guitar Gently Weeps', and remains part of the band for the next few Beatles numbers, 'Lucy in the Sky with Diamonds', 'In My Life' – and even 'Hey Jude', dedicated, with a wink, to 'our old mucker'.

But the surprises aren't over.

During the chaotic outro of 'Hey Jude', when it seems like everyone in the entire Afterparty is screaming the coda's refrain at the top of their lungs, I turn to give Maggie at the monitor desk an excited wave, but she's staring straight ahead looking very serious about something indeed. She locks eyes with me and gives a little nod to her left. I glance to where she's nodding, and see a skinny guy with slicked-back strawberry-blonde hair standing next to her, wearing a black hooded jacket. This figure doesn't register with me at first, then just as I'm turning away, I notice the colour, or should I say colours, of his eyes and I almost wee myself.

As 'Hey Jude' finally finishes, the man edges out from behind Maggie's desk until he's standing right next to me. He smiles, and I smile back, although I doubt my smile looks particularly attractive as all my face muscles are slack with shock. We just stand there in silence for a few moments while Lennon and band prepare for the next song. I mean, can you blame me? What does one *say* to David Bowie?

Lennon introduces him to the crowd, and the place almost spontaneously combusts.

Bowie delicately wanders into the spotlight. It's quite an event for a debut public appearance – Felix usually advises some sort of intimate setting to kick things off – but Bowie confidently clasps the microphone while the band strike up the atmospheric intro, followed by the tight beat, of 'Fame'. Lennon and Bowie seamlessly trade the vocal stabs as if they've been doing it together for the last forty years; it's an unfeasibly perky, energetic version that has everyone in the whole place grooving their asses off. After this, Bowie, in a speaking voice much more faltering than his singing one, addresses the crowd.

'I don't know if you know this, but… someone told me this morning that today is Christmas Day.'

Christmas. It's a distant memory to most people, and date keeping being what it is around here, no one bothers much. Nonetheless, this piece of news receives another ecstatic cheer.

'Anyway, whether it's true or not, we're going to sing a Christmas song now.'

They burst into 'Happy Xmas (War Is Over)', at which point the giant baubles from yesterday's Kirsty MacColl singalong make a reappearance, and the party rages on.

I've remained in my place just in front of the monitor desk for the whole set thus far, filled with a sense of contentment that I doubt I've felt many times since my arrival, if at all. Having made it through the last ridiculous twenty-four hours, it feels beyond incredible to be finally doing what we should all have been doing all along, and as the beer in my hand gives me its weak but comforting little buzz, I start to think that everything really will be all right…

…and then the whole place stops.

The colossal sound vanishes. Musicians stop in mid-pose. The audience pauses in mid-dance. Bowie's hair freezes in mid-flop. A giant Christmas bauble, presently careering its way cheerfully across the happy heads of the crowd, halts in mid-air. And me: I'm once again completely petrified.

Trust the men in lab coats to ruin absolutely everything.

Footsteps approach from behind, and I sigh as deeply as I'm able.

'Why do you guys always approach from the back?'

'It suits us, Mr Jones,' comes the forebodingly gentle and sardonic voice. 'You never quite know where we've come from.'

'So, what now?' I demand angrily, refusing to pander to any of their shit this time. 'I was having the time of my death just then.'

'Sure you were, Adrian,' comes the American twang, the man himself veering into view, with all accompanying stiff hair, dandruff and dirty lab coat. 'But we just wanted to cut in real quick... to congratulate you.'

'On what, for fuck's sake?'

'There's no need to be so snappy, Mr Jones,' says the English-accented voice, as the bald head appears in my sightline. He strolls around the keyboards, apparently inspecting the make and model of synth. 'We realise you've had a hard day, so we won't be troubling you for long.'

'All we wanted to do' – and here the American gives me a thumbs-up followed by a sarcastic wink – 'is say thanks.'

'For what?' I spit.

'It didn't quite work out as we planned it,' drawls the Englishman, 'but the outcome is... satisfactory.'

'What plan? What outcome? You're just a pair of conniving, corrupt little crooks.'

'Come on, Adrian.'

'No, I'm serious. What did he offer you, huh? Drugs? Endless booze? Threesomes with those vacuous tarts?'

'Oh, tut-tut, Mr Jones. It's never that simple.'

'You're telling me.'

Bald man stalks around to the solidified figure of Dee Murray and examines his bass guitar.

'Running a system of zones like this, Mr Jones, is a very... tricky... task... Problems arise, people start having... *thoughts*... and then zones get completely out of hand... much like the charming destination you've just visited. It was all working perfectly well until people started getting these... *ideas*... All the more reason for us to make sure things are managed correctly... and sometimes... unforgivingly.'

He plucks one of Dee's bass strings, sending a deafening low note reverberating across the stage and around the field.

'I'm sure you appreciate that, Mr Jones? Sometimes bonds have to be formed, and sometimes...'

'They have to be broken,' completes the American, helping himself to one of Ola Brunkert's drumsticks. He performs a decidedly un-rock'n'roll underarm toss and sends the stick spinning crowd-wards.

'I've always wanted to do that,' he grins.

'So, what now?' I growl. 'You've robbed me of my boss and my best friend, and totally fucked up our festival.'

'Nonsense, Mr Jones,' replies the Englishman, grandly indicating the field of happy punters. 'This... ah... *musical recital*... will be stronger than ever after this little stunt, as I'm sure you'll discover...'

'But–'

'Although... and I trust you'll approve of this... we decided that "Adrian Joneses Afterparty" doesn't have quite the same ring to it. So in... ah... *loving* memory of your former employer, we've elected to keep its existing moniker...'

'And we'll be keeping an eye on John.'

'Oh, yes. Naturally... I myself remain unconvinced that his little... ah... *compositions*... will amount to anything much, but rest-assured...'

'We'll be watching closely,' says the American.

'But,' I splutter, 'I need to–'

'Goodbye, Mr Jones,' sighs the Englishman, wandering from my view.

'See ya,' leers the American, once again prodding me in the belly. 'Wouldn't wanna be ya.'

'You fucking...'

But before I can even finish the insult, the universe restarts, the band resumes rocking and the crowd carries on raving. I whirl around to see where The Men have gone but they're already nowhere to be seen.

My joyous mood thoroughly broken, I shuffle off the stage, feeling decidedly lightheaded, and make my way through the backstage throng. There are many greetings, pats on the back and urgent questions as I push past, but I manage to avert providing any answers by smiling warmly and indicating that I need to run and attend to something. Finally free of people, I trot down the steps and traipse morosely along for a few moments. A bit faint now, I sit on the lawn next to a tree, and finally I lie down, my hands running through the soft grass, my eyes looking up at the cloudless and starless sky. I remain there for a few minutes, listening to the current song ('Instant Karma') blasting out to the masses, who roar out the chorus with a passion as great as in any church. Then once again I'm shaken out of my reverie by the buzz and beep of a text message from my trouser pocket. I sigh, expecting some sort of mundane enquiry, but when I fish the phone out and glance at the screen I have to blink and look away a few times before I can believe who the message has come from.

The name consists of just two letters: 'SP'.

I take a deep breath and open up the message.

Similar to the texts Felix previously showed me, it consists of no more than four words, and a reference. I gasp with surprise at the magnitude of the meaning it holds for me, and at the scale of the earthly musical loss.

The message reads:

'George Michael' has arrived. Zone T136/House 12267.

'Felix, my old friend,' I whisper. 'It looks like we're back.'

Thanks

For providing their reading, supporting, listening, answering, editing, creating, translating, checking and tea-making skills, the author would like to thank the following: Rachel Rayner; Mike Sweetman (also for *Bucket!*); Katherine Mengardon; Nick Coates; Kwaku, Annabel, Xander and all at Unbound; Colin Midson; Nikesh Shukla; Hauke Steinhof; Guy, Fin and the Fink compadres; Jan, Olivia, Sumit, Alex and all at ATC; Chris Lopez; Dawn Kelly; Mark Ecob; Damian Samuels; and last but probably most, Crestina and Chiara – with love.

Patrons

Morten Bo Larsen
Nick Brown-Warr
Nicola Cavanna
Nicolas Clemesac
Cat Clymer
Adele Contreras
Chris Day
Karsten Dines Johansen
Marcella Dolan
Alexandra Florence Werner
Robert Giles
Deb Henderson
Ritch Keeling
Catie Lévêque
Lissy Lovett
Anne Masson
Lea & David Mueller
Helene Müller
Rico Neeter
Elizabeth Norris
Nikke Osterback
Julia Owen
Louisa Roach
Sasha Sasha Daniel
Leonardo Skrelja
Scott Smith
Jeremy Swingler
Jack Turner
Yolanda Ulger
Ali Vallette
Susanne Wadell
Gareth Watkins

Julie Weideli
Mandie Wraxall
Nigel Wraxall
Toets Zwitserlood